Random Acts of Greed

Holly Anna Paladin Mysteries, Book 4

By Christy Barritt

Published by River Heights Press

Cover design by The Killion Group

Complete Book List

Squeaky Clean Mysteries:

#1 Hazardous Duty

#2 Suspicious Minds

#2.5 It Came Upon a Midnight Crime

#3 Organized Grime

#4 Dirty Deeds

#5 The Scum of All Fears

#6 To Love, Honor, and Perish

#7 Mucky Streak

#8 Foul Play

#9 Broom and Gloom

#10 Dust and Obey

#11 Thrill Squeaker

#12 Cunning Attractions (coming soon)

Squeaky Clean Companion Novella:

While You Were Sweeping

The Sierra Files:

#1 Pounced

#2 Hunted

#2.5 Pranced (a Christmas novella)

#3 Rattled

The Gabby St. Claire Diaries (a Tween Mystery series):

#1 The Curtain Call Caper

#2 The Disappearing Dog Dilemma

#3 The Bungled Bike Burglaries

Holly Anna Paladin Mysteries:

#1 Random Acts of Murder
#2 Random Acts of Deceit
#3 Random Acts of Malice
#3.5 Random Acts of Scrooge
#4 Random Acts of Greed

Carolina Moon Series:
Home Before Dark
Gone By Dark
Wait Until Dark

Suburban Sleuth Mysteries:
#1 Death of the Couch Potato's Wife

Standalone Romantic-Suspense:
Keeping Guard
The Last Target
Race Against Time
Ricochet
Key Witness
Lifeline
High-Stakes Holiday Reunion
Desperate Measures
Hidden Agenda
Mountain Hideaway
Dark Harbor

Cape Thomas Mysteries:
Dubiosity
Disillusioned (coming soon)

Standalone Romantic Mystery:

The Good Girl

Suspense:
Imperfect

Nonfiction:
Changed: True Stories of Finding God through Christian Music
The Novel in Me: The Beginner's Guide to Writing and Publishing a Novel

Chapter 1

I'd just pulled my fourth batch of cookies from the oven. Ella Fitzgerald crooned on my Bluetooth speakers. Chase Dexter—my boyfriend—watched football with my brother in the living room, while my mom and sister solved every world problem over coffee at the kitchen table.

This was my perfect rainy Sunday afternoon.

All of my loved ones were here and safe and healthy. Though the January day was cold and rather bleak, there was enough warmth in this house to make it feel like summer.

I paused a moment, closed my eyes, and inhaled the scent of warm, gooey chocolate mixed with butter, sugar, and vanilla. Cookies were the cure for nearly every ailment. Thankfully, my life had been surprisingly absent of ailments over the past few weeks.

For real. Thank You, God.

Hands appeared at my waist, and my eyes popped open. I didn't have to turn to know it was Chase. I felt his towering presence behind me. I smelled his woodsy cologne. I recognized the heavy feel of his thick fingers.

"What are you doing?" His breath hit my ear as he pulled me close, wrapping me in his warmth.

"Enjoying the moment. Capturing the joy of the ordinary. Reflecting on how simple times make me happy. You?"

"I'm enjoying the moment also." He planted a soft kiss on my neck.

I wrapped my arms over his and leaned into him, relishing his embrace. I adored Chase, and being with him seemed like a dream come true. But I was wise to the ways of a man watching football.

"Let me guess: There's a commercial on?" I teased.

"Are you saying that's the only time I'll come over and give you attention?" His voice contained a playful lilt.

I shook my head, wishing that my family wasn't close by so I could turn and plant a big kiss on his lips. But public displays of affection weren't good manners, no matter how tempting. And I was Holly Anna Paladin, the queen of good manners and etiquette.

"It's good to see you enjoying yourself," I told Chase. "You deserve it after working so hard lately. I know your caseload has been overwhelming."

We hadn't been able to spend as much time together as I would have liked. But I couldn't fault him. He was doing his job. Being a detective in a large metro area was more than a career—it was practically a calling. I knew he'd been busy lately with some drug-related murders, a hit-and-run, and a domestic violence case, just to name a few.

"You're incredibly understanding, Holly. And that's just one more reason to love you." He rested his cheek against mine. "It's been a year, you know."

I nodded, flutters racing through my stomach at his nearness. I could feel his ever-so-slight scruff. Smell the manly scent of his cologne. Feel the ripple of his muscles.

Chase had stirred something inside me that I'd never felt before, not in any of my twenty-nine years.

Of course, I remembered that this month marked one year since we'd been dating. I'd even marked it on my calendar, along with a little red heart that I'd drawn by hand. "Hard to believe, huh? And what a year it's been."

To say we'd had ups and downs would be an understatement. While I didn't feel like our relationship had been inordinately rocky, to look at it on paper one might think that was the case. Chase and I had gotten together and nearly said "I do" when I thought I had only a few more months to live. We'd taken steps back when my medical diagnosis changed. Then I'd broken up with Chase at the demands of a psycho who threatened Chase's well-being if I didn't follow his orders. We'd again taken some steps back when Chase went all rogue in order to help his ex-wife.

But, despite all of that, deep down, we'd been happy.

"Every obstacle we overcome just works to make us stronger, right?" Chase said.

I turned to face him, desperately wanting to see his eyes. And I wanted him to see mine and know how sincere I was. "That's right. And that's what's important. It's not the storms we've weathered but how we've weathered them."

"So poetic. Too bad Ella can't take those words and write a song about them."

"Me and Ella Fitzgerald . . . we would have been a team." I gave him a quick kiss.

"Would you two cut it out over there?" my sister called over her cup of coffee. "Why don't you just put a ring on? Everyone knows it's coming."

A little of my delight disappeared at the mere mention of a ring. Chase and I had many long talks about this. There were deeper issues we had to conquer before we committed to forever with each other. I was ready, but Chase wasn't, and I respected that.

Most of the time.

Another part of me wondered just how long we were going to be in this state of limbo. Of being together yet feeling uncertain about the future. Of remaining stagnant, moving neither forward nor backward.

"Now that you're married, you think everyone should experience wedded bliss," I called back to Alex playfully. This was not the time or place to let other people see my fears and doubts and psychoanalyze them.

The truth was, the desire of my heart had always been to get married and have a family. I wanted nothing more than to feel sticky fingers wrapped around my own and go to PTA meetings and kiss boo-boos.

But I had to be patient. Everything happened in good time. Everything happened in *God's* time.

Thankfully, at that moment, the doorbell rang and saved me from taking this conversation any further. I didn't want a discussion with my family about my future with Chase. For some reason, my mom had started thinking recently that "noncommittal" could be interpreted as "going nowhere."

And my mom *loved* Chase.

She wanted nothing more than to see us together at the end of all this. But she'd apparently felt obligated to bestow her motherly wisdom on me recently and point out that our relationship seemed to have plateaued rather than grown lately. She'd confirmed what I already knew.

"Excuse me," I murmured as I stepped from Chase's arms and headed toward the front of the house.

I wondered who might be coming over. My best friend,

Jamie, was working on a newspaper article. Alex's husband, a doctor, was on call at the hospital. Everyone else who'd normally drop by unannounced was already here.

As I opened the door, a frigid wind swept inside. My knee-length dress and the apron over it did nothing to protect me from the cold blast. The January day even *looked* cold with its gray hues and dreary clouds.

I blinked at what I saw on the other side of the door.

Nothing.

Strange.

I definitely hadn't been hearing things. Someone had rung that doorbell. Other people in the house had heard it also.

Maybe it was one of the neighborhood kids pulling a prank. There was no crime in that—only if I burned my cookies as a result. Then it would be a crime against desserts.

"Holly?" Chase stepped behind me and peered out.

"No one's here." I started to close the door and ward away the cold. "Weird, huh?"

He gravitated closer and planted another quick kiss. "Very."

I grinned up at him, feeling another rush of attraction. Chase had been my first kiss. My first crush—although the crush occurred ten years before we actually dated. Our history was complicated. With his Thor-like good looks and compassionate heart, there was nothing not to love about him.

"You're trying to steal a moment alone with me." I laid a hand on his chest as he smiled down at me, flashing straight white teeth and sparkling blue eyes.

"Can you blame me?"

I grinned. "Not at all."

He tried to draw me toward him, but something nagged at the back of my mind. Something that said there was more to this doorbell-ringing incident. Something I was missing.

"Hold that thought." I raised a finger and did a polite curtsy back toward the door.

With tension forming between my shoulders, I stepped outside. Another whip of wind surrounded me and chilled me all the way down to my bones, making me feel sorry for anyone who had to be out in this weather today. The gusts alone were brutal. Add the mist of rain to it, and it was miserable.

"What are you doing?" Chase followed behind me.

Before I could answer, something caught my eye at the corner of the porch. It was a bundle of pastel-colored blankets. They hadn't been there before. No, my mom believed in everything being in place, and that included her yard and porch.

"Chase, look at this." I gravitated toward the bundle, my curiosity pinging like a sonar radar in the Graveyard of the Atlantic.

"What is it?"

Anticipation buzzed through me as I sensed something big was about to happen.

That wasn't just a pile of blankets.

As if to confirm my initial thought, the heap moved ever so slightly. It wasn't the wind that had moved it, either. The motion wasn't fluid, like a ripple. Instead, the movement appeared random.

Something was under that blanket.

Ignoring the cold, I knelt beside the bundle and pulled the first layer back.

I gasped at what lay beneath it.

An adorable face. Tiny hands that reached upward. Big, blue eyes.

A baby.

Someone had left a baby on my porch.

CHAPTER 2

I gathered the baby—a boy, I assumed from his blue outfit—into my arms, desperate to get him out of the cold. His body and the blankets around him were still warm, like he'd been somewhere heated until just recently. Thank goodness.

"Any idea who he is?" Chase peered over my shoulder, his voice taking on his no-nonsense cop tone.

"I have no idea." I hurried into the house, my eyes still focused on the squirming bundle of joy in my arms. "I've never seen him before."

Chase shut the door and followed behind me as I rushed across the room. I quickened my steps, certain to be careful, until I reached the warmth of the crackling fireplace. My family followed me.

In the safety and comfort of the living room, I pulled the baby away from my chest and took a good look. Chubby cheeks. Runny nose. Bright eyes. Caucasian. Probably six months old.

Perfect. He looked perfect.

"A baby . . ." My mom whispered the words as if I'd just found one of the most sacred things around.

I had.

As the baby's blue eyes observed each new face, his smile faded. He drew in a quick breath, and I waited for the wails to begin.

"It's okay, sweetheart." I gave his belly a little rub,

trying to sooth him.

The expression froze on his face. I held my breath, anticipating his cries when he realized his mom wasn't here. Instead, his mouth widened, and the corner curled. He reached for my hair, tugged it, and let out a giggle.

Everyone in the room seemed to release their breath and giggle too.

Footsteps sounded behind me. Chase. He must have gone back to the porch to look for anything suspicious. That seemed like Chase. Thorough. Analytical. Cautious.

"There was a note." He held up a white sheet of cardstock. "It must have fallen from the blankets when you picked him up."

I let the baby boy grab my fingers, and I turned toward Chase. My heartbeat quickened as I waited for him to read it. "What does it say?"

"Please take care of him, Ms. Holly," he read. "I need your help. Don't trust anyone."

I processed the words a moment, impulses of shock traveling through my brain. *Don't trust anyone.* What did that mean? Whatever it was, a new tension threaded through my back muscles. "There's no signature?"

Chase studied the note. "None. You said the baby doesn't look familiar?"

I looked into the infant's big, blue eyes again, searching my thoughts for even a hint of recognition. Finally, I shook my head. I couldn't remember ever seeing this baby before—and certainly I'd remember someone this adorable. "Not at all. Is the note handwritten?"

He nodded. "Black marker. Block letters. I'll save it in case there are fingerprints."

That was when I noticed he was holding it only by the

corner. That was Chase for you. Always a cop.

"Anything else out there?"

His expression remained grim. "The car seat carrier he was left in. I brought it inside."

What wasn't he telling me?

He pressed his lips together before sharing, "There was blood spatter on the bottom."

I sucked in a quick breath. Blood spatter? Just what had happened to this baby's loved ones? I couldn't even bear to think about it.

"You didn't see anyone outside?" I asked instead.

"No one suspicious. I looked, thinking the mother could have been waiting to see if we answered. If she did, she's long gone by now."

"She must have rung the doorbell and ran," I mused aloud. "She probably put him on that side of the porch to try and block the wind."

"We've got to report this, Holly." Chase said the words carefully, as if treading uncertain waters.

He knew that child welfare was my area. It was what I'd done for six years of my life as a social worker. I knew the basics here, but my heart was already jumping ahead of my logic. However, the blood on the carrier pushed aside any of my doubts.

"Of course. Someone asked me to take care of him, and I need to do what I can until this is resolved." I began bouncing the baby in my arms as his whimper turned into a cry. "Mom, call Doris with Children's Services and let her know what happened. After I talk to her, we can file a report with the police."

"Sounds like a plan." My mom rose and grabbed the phone. She had Doris's number in her cell phone from my old days of working with her.

I glanced again at the baby as he quieted for a moment. His blue eyes stared at me, as if trying to ascertain the answers to all of his questions. *Where's my mom? Who are you? When am I going home?*

Fear. I saw a moment of fear in the depths of his ocean blues.

I'm going to do my best to help you, Buddy. I tried to send him a silent message of reassurance but settled instead on kissing his head.

"We'll need to take him to the hospital to be checked out," I said, trying to think the process through. "We should call an ambulance."

"I'll take care of that." Chase rose and pulled out his cell phone.

"He's an adorable little boy." Alex reached for his hand, and the baby's fingers slipped around hers. "And he looks healthy."

"I think he likes you, Holly." My brother, Ralph, smiled as the baby grabbed my hair again and tried to eat it.

My smile quickly faded as the reality of the situation hit me again. This wasn't a fairytale, dream-come-true moment. This was serious. This baby's mother would most likely be pursued by authorities and charged with abandonment. If she was alive.

After all, there was blood.

The realization caused the color to drain from my face. Just what had this baby been through?

"Why would anyone leave someone as precious as you?" I whispered.

I'd seen it before. I wasn't a stranger to abandoned babies. When I'd worked for Children's Services, I'd seen some real parenting horror stories.

But for a mom to leave her baby on a stranger's—or a near stranger's, at least—doorstep instead of with a family member or friend showed desperation. And the note she'd left, urging me not to trust anyone, made my guard go up. What did that mean?

Whatever it was, it didn't settle well with me. I had the feeling this was only the beginning of a long, intriguing story.

***

"He looks like a healthy baby boy." The doctor pulled down his stethoscope and wrapped it around his neck. "I don't see any health problems. He appears to be well fed and well taken care of. I'm going to guess he's about six months old, based on my physical examination."

Relief filled me, and I scooped the baby up in my arms, holding him close to me as we stood in a little curtained-off room at the hospital. The doctor, a man in his late fifties with an Asian tint to his skin, had spent the last hour with me.

He was good with the baby, speaking in low, lilting tones and offering lots of smiles. I was grateful the man seemed compassionate.

I was also grateful that Chase had come with me, because numerous times since I'd arrived at the hospital I'd found myself holding my breath. I already disliked hospitals. They brought back too many bad memories. Adding an abandoned baby to the mix only upped the stakes.

What if something was wrong with the baby? What if he was sick or injured or had signs of abuse?

I'd seen none of those things, but I hadn't wanted to rule them out until I knew for sure.

Knowing he was healthy was an answer to prayer.

Funny . . . I'd only known this baby for two hours, and I already felt a bond with him. He was all alone in the world. He needed someone to love and protect him.

I was going to be that person.

"You two are free to take him home," the doctor said.

He thought Chase and I were married, I realized.

My cheeks warmed as visions of what it would be like to have a family with Chase filled my mind. I imagined a cute, little baby with Chase's eyes and smile. Maybe a couple of them. I hoped that would become a reality one day.

I pushed those thoughts aside but didn't bother to correct the doctor. Neither did Chase.

As I stepped from the curtained area, my former boss appeared down the end of the hallway. Doris Blankenship was in her fifties, with short, mousy brown hair and a constant scowl that had left wrinkles on her face. She was skeletal skinny and wore fitted skirts and tops that emphasized her malnourished look.

I'd always said pretty is as pretty does. Doris was neither pretty on the inside nor the outside. I questioned at times why she even did this job since she disliked people so much.

No, I didn't really care for the woman, nor did she care for me. I'd kind of hoped that I wouldn't ever have to work with her again. But here we were.

Doris's heels clicked at a fast clip as she made her way toward me. I could already see the stress pouring off of her in waves. Her shifty gaze quickly went to the baby before going back to me.

"You were approved," she announced, stopping in front of me. Her lips flinched downward in a frown. "I just talked to the judge about it."

"Wonderful."

"You just need to fill out some paperwork to make it official. We'll have to do another home inspection and have weekly follow-ups, to start with. Thankfully your certification is still valid—the home study, your physical exam, your interview. The only thing you don't have at this point is a designated room for the baby."

"I can make that happen," I told her.

"I figured you'd say that."

My heartbeat quickened with excitement. I was so glad I'd already taken the time to go through that process to be a foster parent. It had been extensive, but I'd done it in preparation for the future. However, I'd put a hold on any children being placed with me when I'd thought I had only months to live. That all tied in with my fear of hospitals, but that was a story for another day.

"That's great news," I said.

She glanced at Chase, her beady eyes narrowing. "The police will look for his real mom in the meantime. She'll be lucky to get custody back after a stunt like this."

If she's alive. I remembered the blood on his carrier. What if it was his mom's?

Chase squeezed my shoulder, knowing from our many conversations just how riled up this woman made me. The motion was his small way of reminding me to keep myself in check.

"My captain has already been made aware of the situation," he told her.

"I'll talk to your captain also, of course." Doris's gaze went back to me. "You sure you're okay with this?"

I nodded, probably a little too hard. "I'm definitely okay

with this. For some reason, someone wanted me to watch after him."

Why was that? Why had someone picked me? I didn't have time to worry about that now. Right now, I had to take care of this bouncing baby boy.

Doris stared at me a little longer before offering a curt nod. "Okay, then. Let's sign those papers."

Ten minutes later, it was official. I was going to foster this baby until we had some answers.

I pulled the blanket up higher around the baby as his eyes began to droop. My arms ached slightly. They weren't used to carrying eighteen pounds of baby. But I wasn't complaining.

After everyone went about their various tasks, Chase and I stood in the busy hallway, and it hit me. Now this was up to me. I had to figure out the next steps here.

If I'd been helping someone else in this situation, I would have known immediately what to tell them about how to proceed. But, for a moment, I felt bewildered and slightly off-balance at the task before me.

And I didn't like it. I usually thought of myself as more competent than this.

"Alex dropped off a car seat." Chase brushed a hair from my shoulder, his gaze soaking me in, studying me, trying to ascertain my emotional state.

I knew him well enough to know that.

"She wanted me to reassure you that it's still up to code and good to go," he finished.

I smiled. Alex knew me all too well. That was going to be my first question.

"I'm going to go install it, and then I'll pull up to pick you two up. Okay?"

I nodded, grateful Chase was with me. "Okay. Thank

you."

He kissed my forehead before sauntering away, getting a few second glances from the nurses stationed at the desk down the hall. I should be used to that. The former professional football player was the definition of a head-turner.

Instinctively, I brushed my lips against the baby's forehead. He was being so good and quiet right now. His eyes continued to droop, and I had a feeling he'd be asleep soon. The thought of him snoozing in my arms turned my spine to jelly.

Holding him felt right. Too right.

I shoved those thoughts aside, knowing they weren't helpful or healthy.

"It's been a hard day, hasn't it?" I murmured instead, staring down at his round face and chubby, Gerber-baby cheeks.

As if in response, he let out a yawn. I tugged the blanket up closer around him and slowly made my way down the hallway toward the exit.

I paused at the emergency room door, waiting for Chase to pull up since it was too cold to wait outside. He'd followed behind us in the ambulance, having the foresight to realize we would need a ride home.

"Hey, how's he doing?" a deep voice said behind me.

I looked up and spotted one of the paramedics who'd given the baby and me a ride to the hospital. He was probably my age, with dark, curly hair and crystal-blue eyes. His smile was charismatic and wide, and I had a feeling he was the life of the party with his never-met-a-stranger personality.

He'd sat with me in the back of the ambulance on the way here and kept an engaging conversation going the whole time. He had a way of putting people at ease, which probably made him great at his job as a paramedic.

I rocked the baby in my arms. "He's perfect."

The paramedic smiled and tried to catch a glimpse of the baby's face. "That's good to know. Do you know his name?"

His question stopped me. His name? I'd had so much on my mind that I hadn't really given his name a second thought. "No, I have no idea. I think I'll call him Sweet Pea."

The man's lips curled up, and light danced in his eyes. "Sweet Pea?"

I shrugged. "I don't want to confuse him, so maybe a pet name's better than naming him myself. Once the police figure out who the mom is, they'll look for next of kin. His stop here with me is just temporary."

And don't you forget it, Holly Anna Paladin.

He smiled. "Sounds smart. I'm Evan, by the way."

"Holly. Nice to meet you."

He leaned closer and stroked Sweet Pea's hand. "He's going to be a linebacker one day."

I glanced at Sweet Pea again. "You're right. Cincinnati Bengals, maybe?"

"I don't know—I think the Colts might be a better choice." Evan grinned again before stepping back and glancing at me. "No idea who his mom is?"

I shook my head. I'd been through it in my mind countless times in the past couple of hours. I was clueless. "I have no idea. But the police are working on it."

Evan touched my elbow. "Well, I think it's great you're taking care of him. We need more people like you in the world. I was a foster child myself, so I know how important it is."

Evan's words warmed me, for some reason. "Thank you."

A voice crackled over his radio, and he raised his hand in a wave goodbye. "I've got to get back to work. Best of luck, though!"

"Thanks again."

Just as Evan disappeared, I spotted Chase pulling up in his Jeep.

Now it was time for the real adventure to begin.

I looked down at Sweet Pea. "Here goes nothing, darling. Here goes nothing."

CHAPTER 3

"You look . . . exhausted." My best friend, Jamie Duke, stared at me the next morning with squinty eyes and a frown. "Like, I've never seen you this exhausted."

Only a moment earlier, I'd let her inside my house, and she'd followed me into the living room, where I promptly plopped down on the couch and grabbed my coffee. I was on my third cup, and I still couldn't feel any effects. Even Peggy Lee singing "I'm a Woman" in the background didn't cheer me up, nor did the early morning sunlight that streamed through the thick, wooden blinds on the windows.

"Remember to keep your voice down," I whispered. "We can't wake the baby. And I am tired. Taking care of an infant is demanding."

Although it was nine a.m., I'd just gotten Sweet Pea to sleep an hour ago. It had been a bad first night, but I couldn't blame Sweet Pea for it. He was simply being a baby—a baby who'd just been through a trauma and who was probably missing his mama and his bed and the familiar smells and sounds of home.

He snoozed right now in a Pack 'n Play in the library, which was close enough where I could hear him but far enough away that I could pull the curtains in the room closed and keep it quiet for him.

"So what happened?" Jamie gently sat on the couch

beside me, a half-full bottle of water in her hand. She looked bright-eyed and fresh with her ray-of-sunshine springy curls and mocha-colored skin. She'd recently taken up jogging, and it didn't matter the weather. She went every day, claiming the act of her exercising wasn't a pretty sight but it got the job done.

First, she'd lost nearly one hundred pounds, and now she wanted to firm up her muscles. I was proud of all her hard work, but I'd love her whatever size she was.

I took another sip of coffee. This would be my first time rehashing this with her. My mom had told her a version of events last night, but I wanted to run through everything with my BFF.

"Let's see," I started. "We got home last night. Everyone was great. My sister ran to Walmart and picked up a Pack 'n Play, bottles, clothes—anything I could possibly need. Sweet Pea—"

"That's his name?"

I shrugged. "That's what I'm calling him."

She nodded a little too slowly and skeptically. "Okay."

"Anyway, Sweet Pea didn't like the first two bottles, and we went through three different formulas—the hospital gave us several samples—until we found one he'd actually take. Except maybe he didn't really like it after all because he was up for most of the night with gas pains."

She frowned. "That's not fun."

I nodded as I remembered how desperate I felt to help him. There had been a point when I wasn't sure he'd ever stop crying, and I'd briefly considered taking him back to the hospital. Maybe the doctor had missed something. Thankfully, a few burps later, Sweet Pea had calmed down.

"I know," I told her. "I kept him in my room with me and sent everyone else either home or to bed. Adjusting to taking care of an infant with an audience all around me only added to the stress of the situation."

"I can imagine. He's finally asleep?"

I sighed and raised my coffee mug. "Finally. Now I know why new moms look so harried."

She studied me a moment with an upturned nose. "The bathrobe, tangled hair, circles under the eyes look isn't really you. I'm used to perfect hair, makeup, and coordinated dress, shoes, belt, etc."

"This is something I rarely say, but I don't even care at the moment. I just want coffee. Lots and lots of coffee." I usually cherished being proper and put together. Today, priorities had changed, and I was in survival mode.

"I take it you're not going into work?" She stared long and hard at my outfit one more time.

I shook my head. I worked for my brother. He'd recruited me when he'd been elected as a state senator, and I worked as a Constituent Aide. I'd hoped to make a greater impact in this position than I'd done as a social worker. The jury was still out on whether or not that had come to fruition, though.

I missed working hands-on with people and situations, and questioned my decision to give up my job with Children's Services. I mostly felt like I pushed papers now and fought a system where change came slowly and people could be bought.

"Ralph understood," I said. "I'll have to answer a few emails and return a couple of phone calls, but I'm staying here with Sweet Pea today. A caseworker is going to stop by for a home inspection sometime this week. My mom checked out everything this morning, and I think we're good."

A few minutes of silence passed. I didn't mind them. The quiet gave me a chance to collect my thoughts and try to pull myself together.

"That's so crazy that someone actually left a baby on your doorstep." Jamie shook her head, her eyes holding a faraway look as she probably tried to comprehend everything. This was not an everyday situation.

I'd replayed everything several times in my mind, trying to make sense of the turn of events. "I know, right? But last night, as I wasn't sleeping, I kept thinking about it. Someone is in trouble. There was blood. The note said, 'Don't trust anyone.' Why else would there be blood on his carrier?"

"Maybe it's a custody dispute that turned ugly."

I nodded. "Maybe."

She narrowed her eyes. "But you're thinking something else?"

I sucked on my bottom lip, pondering whether or not I should share my next thought. If there was anyone I could share it with, it was Jamie. "I need to figure out who his mom is."

She jerked her head back. "Retro Girl, maybe she doesn't want to be found. Maybe she has a good reason for all of this."

"Maybe she's dead. Whoever left Sweet Pea wrote, 'Help me.' That's practically a plea for me to get involved, Girl Genius."

Jamie and I had codenames we used when we were working undercover. It was just something silly we'd come up with, and using the names now helped to break some of the tension in the room.

The diva look captured my friend's face. "The person who left Sweet Pea probably meant 'help me by taking care of my baby.'"

"Maybe. I still think this person needs help other than that. That blood proves someone was hurt. Maybe it was Sweet

Pea's mom. His dad. I have no idea."

Jamie's eyebrows shot up. "Okay, well, hypothetically speaking, how do you plan on *helping*?"

I'd thought about this during my sleepless hours. "Whoever left Sweet Pea obviously knows me. He or she called me Ms. Holly and chose me for a reason."

Jamie shifted to face me better. She knew me all too well. Knew about my penchant for helping people. My soft spot for the hurting. My drive to find answers. Those traits may have gotten me in trouble more than once. And, more than once, Jamie may have been along for the ride.

"So what are you thinking?" she asked. "After all, this could be your story of finding Moses on the River Nile. It could all be a part of a plan."

I cleared my throat, reminding myself that this was all temporary. "After I get dressed, feed Sweet Pea, and get him ready, I'm going to head down to the youth center. I'm going to see if anyone there knows someone who had a baby in the past six months. I figured that was a good place to start."

She gave an affirmative nod. "I'll go with you."

"Thanks, Jamie." I knew I could always count on my BFF. Especially in matters of nosiness. She was a reporter, after all, and she loved investigating almost as much—if not more—than I did.

She raised her eyebrows, a sly smile on her face. "You know I wouldn't miss this kind of adventure for anything."

***

"You're sure you've got this?" I asked.

My mother gave me a pointed look as she rocked back and forth with Sweet Pea in her arms. "I raised three children. I think I'll be okay."

My mother had agreed to take care of Sweet Pea for me while I ran to the youth center. I already felt like I was leaving a little part of my heart behind. I wanted to bring the baby with me, but I knew that it was a better idea if I left him with my mom instead of exposing him to this cold weather.

Though the note left with him had warned, "Don't trust anyone," certainly that hadn't included my mother . . . right? I mean, she was my mom, and she was as trustworthy as they came. She was "Mom of the Year" material in every way.

I really didn't know exactly what that note meant, and that fact was one of many that had left me feeling unsettled.

I gave her one last glance of concern before stepping toward the front door. "Okay, I'll be back soon. Call me if you need anything."

"Yes, dear." Her tone was riddled with amusement.

I stepped outside to meet Jamie. I felt more put together after showering, fixing my hair, and adding some makeup—makeup that didn't quite cover up the circles under my eyes. Maybe I should consider them a badge of honor, however. I'd donned an olive-green dress, knee-high black boots, and my favorite wool coat. Chase would tell me this wasn't practical for the weather, but I was in love with dresses—especially the flattering kind that were popular in the fifties. I was seriously born in the wrong generation.

Jamie put away her cell phone as I approached her on the sidewalk. "I'm trying to get an interview for a story on an art show in a couple of weeks. You'd think they'd want the extra publicity, but I'd have an easier time getting up with POTUS." She shook her head.

My gaze traveled to a dark sedan that drove past.

A lot of cars drove past my house, which was located on

a relatively busy street. I wasn't sure why this one caught my eye. Maybe it was because it had cruised past slowly and the windows were tinted.

"That car went past a few minutes ago," Jamie muttered.

That was when it hit me. "You know what? Chase said he was going to have someone from the force patrol by the house every so often. It's probably an unmarked police car."

"Good point. That would explain it. No need to read too much into things, right?"

"Right. Contrary to popular belief as of late, danger does not lurk around every corner."

Jamie and I got to the youth center just before lunchtime. It was located in Price Hill, and I usually volunteered there a few times a week. Price Hill had once been a sought-after area of town, but it was now battered and old. The rich had moved out, and a lot of poor had moved in. I still thought it was charming, though. Certain places had unmatchable views of downtown Cincinnati.

The youth center was located in an old strip of shops right along the main street that cut through town. At one time it had been a restaurant, but it had been converted into several rooms including a kitchen, some offices, and a lounge area. Most of the place's regulars were in school right now, but I mostly wanted to speak with Abraham Willis, the center's director.

Abraham was a good guy who sacrificed a lot in terms of material comforts in order to live out his calling in life. He worked tirelessly here for relatively no pay, even taking on a second job in order to make ends meet. Whenever I could, I liked to do nice things for him and his wife, Hannah, and his son, Levi . . . things like anonymously giving him gift cards to restaurants and movie theaters—things they couldn't afford otherwise.

Abraham was in his thirties with a protruding midsection and dark hair. When I knocked at his door, I spotted him poring over some paperwork. He did a double take when he saw me. "Holly . . . I wasn't expecting to see you here today."

"I'm hoping you can help me with something." I sat down across from him while Jamie lingered in the doorway, texting someone about her work.

I went through the details with Abraham and then showed him a picture of Sweet Pea that I'd taken on my phone. "Six months old. Caucasian. Healthy. Any idea whom he might be?"

He took my phone and studied the picture before shaking his head. "I wish I could help you, Holly. I really do. But I can't think of anyone who fits this description. The only person I can remember who's had a baby within the past seven or eight months is Tasha—but she's Hispanic. This baby is blond-haired and blue-eyed."

I nodded, halfway disappointed but, at the same time, not surprised. "That's what I thought."

"If you want, I can ask around when everyone shows up after school. Maybe it's a friend of a friend."

"I'd appreciate that, but I really need you to keep the details on the down-low. Please don't let any of them know I'm taking care of the baby—not until we know what's going on."

"Of course."

"Thank you. There are just so many questions and uncertainties right now. Until I know more of this story, I have to remain cautious." I stood. "All of that said, I'm not sure I'll be making it in this week."

"That's understandable. I know the kids will miss you,

but having a baby is a big adjustment. Take all the time you need. I'll be praying for you."

"I appreciate that."

Jamie and I stepped outside, and I checked the time. I still had an hour and a half until the time I told my mom I would return to help her. Part of me wanted to rush home and check on Sweet Pea, but I knew I had to use this time wisely. He was in good hands with my mom—and an officer was patrolling the area.

"What now?" Jamie climbed into the passenger seat of my powder-blue 64 and a half Mustang.

I cranked the engine, and Frank Sinatra crooned through the speakers about being on the sunny side of the street. "I want to swing by the Children's Services office and see if Doris has discovered anything. Some conversations are best had face-to-face."

"Let's go then."

CHAPTER 4

Jamie and I arrived back at my house just when I'd told my mother I would. We'd discovered no leads at the Children's Services office. In fact, Doris looked just as perplexed as I felt. On top of being stressed, everyone in the office was also overworked with too many caseloads, too many tragedies, and not enough success stories. I knew because I'd been there and done that for six years.

Sometimes I missed the job. It was demanding and heartbreaking. But it was also rewarding and challenging and difference-making.

When we'd left Children's Services, Chase had called and said the police had no leads so far either, but they were investigating several possibilities. They had tried to get prints off the note that was left, but nothing had popped up in their system. That was good because it meant Sweet Pea's mother didn't have a criminal history but bad because it offered no clues.

I knew Chase had also canvased the neighborhood to see if any neighbors had seen anything. Apparently, no one had.

Next on their list was to check video footage from the area. There was a drugstore and gas station not far away. Cameras there could have picked up something.

I knew the reality was that finding answers would prove

difficult. Our best hope was that a childcare provider would call to report an unexplained absence. However, today was Monday, and it could take two or three days before someone got suspicious about not seeing Sweet Pea or his mother.

So, it looked like Baby Doe would remain Baby Doe for a while longer.

"I just put him down." Mom met Jamie and me at the door, drying her hands with a paper towel. She had an odd glow to her cheeks as she ushered us out of the cold. "I gave him a bottle, changed his diaper, and he went right to sleep."

"No problems?" I took a deep breath—the scent of orange, vanilla, and rosemary comforting to me. There truly was no place like home. The familiar scents always calmed me.

My mom shook her head. "No problems at all. He's a baby doll. I can't wait to be a grandma. I hope your sister will get on the ball. I'm ready for it."

Something about her words caused a strange hollowness to form in my gut, but I wasn't sure why. One thing I did know was that my mom had loved being a mom and that she was going to be a fantastic grandmother one day.

She glanced at her gold watch. "Now, I do need to run. I have that scholarship committee meeting. Will you two be okay?"

I nodded as I placed my purse on the foyer table. "We'll be fine."

"I'll keep her in line, Ms. Paladin," Jamie said.

My mom raised her eyebrows. "I sometimes wonder which of you keeps the other in line. It's one of the great mysteries of life."

Neither Jamie nor I denied it. We were both equal-opportunity offenders when it came to finding trouble lately.

Mom pulled on her coat. "I'm just a phone call away if

you need me."

After she left, I asked Jamie to give me a moment and then I sneaked upstairs to peek into my room. It was dark with the shades drawn. I crept over to the Pack 'n Play and peered inside. I had to see for myself that Sweet Pea was okay.

My heart rate calmed when I saw the sweet baby sleeping like a tiny angel. This little guy was so precious. I wanted desperately to do right by him in the brief time he would be under my care.

As his lips made a little suckling motion, I placed a hand on his belly and closed my eyes. "Dear Lord, watch over this boy. Keep him safe. Protect his mom. Give me wisdom."

I kissed my finger and then touched his forehead before quietly creeping out of the room. I made a mental note that I needed to clear out the guest bedroom and make it more kid-friendly in order to be in compliance with foster care rules. It should be easy enough to do—remove knickknacks, make room for the Pack 'n Play and a changing table. I'd try to do that tomorrow.

As I rushed down the stairs, I spotted Jamie in the living room at the front of the house. She'd pushed aside one of the heavy, designer drapes covering the window and peered outside with a frown.

"What's wrong?" I asked.

She shrugged. "Nothing, I guess. You'll be glad to know I saw the unmarked police sedan again. It looks like the police are keeping a good eye on this place."

"That's always good to know. You can never have too many people looking out for you."

She dropped the curtain and crossed her arms. "What now? I know you well enough to know you're not ready to let this drop."

I let out a long breath. The question had been simmering in the back of my mind since we left Children's Services. "I don't know where we go from here. We have no good leads, at this point. If my connection with Sweet Pea's mom wasn't through the youth center or Children's Services, then where?"

She tapped her lip in thought. "There was nothing left with him?"

"A couple of blankets, a car seat carrier, some diapers, and a note. I've looked through them, but I didn't see anything of record."

"May I?"

"Sure thing." I led her through the house to the living room, where I'd deposited most of the items. The police had taken the carrier, the note, and the blankets, but left the rest.

Jamie examined the clothes we'd found him in.

Nothing.

She examined the pacifier.

Nothing.

She picked up the diapers and started to put them back down when she paused. She opened each one. "One time, I couldn't find my driver's license. I'd stuck it back in my purse, but it got caught in one of the twins' diapers. Before I realized it, I'd already gone down to DMV to order a new one."

Just as she said that, a piece of paper fluttered out.

I plucked it up. "It looks like part of a business card. It's torn, but the second part says '—da's Fitness.' Ring any bells?"

"Not even a broken one."

"It can't hurt to do a little Internet search. It's amazing the things that can pop up."

I grabbed my electronic tablet from the kitchen hutch and entered the words into the search engine, along with

Cincinnati, Ohio.

Nothing came up.

I extended my search to Ohio, Indiana, and Kentucky and finally got a hit.

"There's a Rhonda's Fitness in Kentucky—just on the other side of the Ohio River," I said. "It's close enough that it could be a lead. Plus, the last three digits of the phone number match."

"I say we try it."

"Sounds good—but after Sweet Pea wakes up."

***

Sweet Pea slept another thirty minutes. While he slept, I'd returned some more emails, double-checked all of the safety requirements in preparation for my home inspection this week, and took phone calls from both Alex and Ralph.

When the baby woke up, I changed him before bundling him up, and then we set out.

A touch of nerves hit me as I loaded Sweet Pea into the back of my Mustang. Something about driving with a baby in my back seat added a whole 'nother level of stress to my travel. It wasn't like I hadn't done it before. I'd driven kids back and forth numerous times during custody disputes and foster family placements.

This time felt different somehow.

Jamie sat in the back with Sweet Pea, talking to him as I drove into Kentucky. She told him how much he'd love watching Elmo one day, explained why he should look forward to sunny park days and swinging contests, and warned of the dangers of ever eating sugar—one of her personal crusades.

I smiled as I listened. I was so glad God had brought

Jamie into my life while we were in college. To say we were thicker than thieves would be an understatement. We'd gotten each other through some of our toughest moments.

Twenty minutes later, I pulled into the parking lot of Rhonda's Fitness. On the outside, it appeared to be a privately owned gym that had opened in an old department store. Despite that, the place looked neat and tidy—on the outside, at least.

I popped Sweet Pea's seat into a stroller and pushed it toward the entrance. He looked up at me, and his lips curled.

Jamie peered over my shoulder. "He's got a great smile."

"Doesn't he?" I rubbed his tummy and, as I did, his tiny fingers curled around mine. My heart tumbled into a pit of warm and gooey endorphins.

The feeling was short-lived as a chilly breeze swept through and reminded me that I needed to get him out of the cold. I tugged his blanket up higher and hurried carefully through the parking lot.

Inside, the musty scent of sweat and body odor was a welcome change from the bristly cold outside. In the distance, cardio equipment and free weights were arranged in neat lines. TVs were strung in various places overhead. Behind us was a smoothie bar and a rock wall.

It was a fitness lover's dream world.

Based on the impatient look the woman at the reception desk gave me, she fully realized that Jamie and I weren't here to get a gym membership. Maybe my dress gave it away. Or was it the stroller?

The phone was shoved beneath her ear, and she tapped her keyboard, an air of desperation around her. Tapping was too nice of a word. She was practically assaulting it. "I don't think you understand. Tomorrow's too late. I need this fixed now!"

She muttered something else into the phone before hanging up and plastering on an annoyed smile. "Can I help you?"

The woman looked just as I would expect a gym employee to look: trim, healthy, and vibrant. She had glossy brown hair that was pulled back in a neat ponytail, and her skintight tank top showed off brilliantly sculpted biceps.

I loosened my scarf and told myself I needed to start exercising more. "I hope so. We're actually trying to track down a woman who belongs to this gym. But because of some unfortunate circumstances, we don't have her name."

The woman blinked at us, and the look on her face hinted that she might call security. Cover stories really weren't my thing—probably because they were awfully close to lying. Okay, they did involve lying, and lying was something I didn't condone.

She swirled some liquid in her grass-green water bottle before popping the top open. "Okay . . . I'm not sure what I can do to help. What does she look like?"

Jamie and I glanced at each other. We really should rehearse stuff like this more.

"We're not really sure," I said.

She took a long sip, and that was when I realized the bottle wasn't green, but her drink was. She and Jamie should get along just fine because Jamie loved to drink her meals almost as much as she liked to put apple cider vinegar in her water.

"Then what can you tell me?" The woman wiped her mouth with the back of her hand, which surprisingly didn't look repulsive.

"She has a six-month-old baby boy," I started.

"We have more than a thousand members here, and most of them, if they are moms, don't bring their babies. We don't offer childcare."

My hopes plummeted. "I see."

She narrowed her gaze. "Can I ask what this is pertaining to? Because we don't freely give out information about our clients here."

I glanced at baby Sweet Pea and remembered that note. *Trust no one.*

It was one thing for my family and Chase to know. Even Jamie and Abraham. I knew I could trust them.

But the fewer people who knew I had Sweet Pea, the better. At least until I had some answers.

However, I was terrible at making up cover stories. Terrible. Had I mentioned that yet?

"Here's the truth." Jamie leaned against the counter and lowered her voice. "We're with a nonprofit that likes to anonymously help people in need within the community. The Red Heart . . . Army. Maybe you've heard of us?"

The woman's eyes subtly traveled from left to right and then back again, as if trying to recall any familiarity.

I could sense her thoughts. Red Cross, American Heart Association, and Salvation Army, all rolled into one. What wouldn't sound familiar about that?

"I think so," the woman finally said.

"We received a nomination about a local woman in need of assistance," Jamie continued. "Unfortunately, we lost the printout with her name and contact information. We remember that she was a member here and that she has a six-month-old baby boy. We knew it was a long shot coming here, but we were hoping for the best. We hate to see an unmet need."

"That's all you remember?" The woman stared like she didn't believe us. Rightfully so.

A flutter of anxiety rippled through me. At that moment, I saw a flyer offering reduced gym rates to people who were in need. I remembered the woman's computer problems. An idea struck me.

"Coming to the gym is one of the only ways she rewards herself, even though she's struggling financially in so many other ways," I began. "Her friend who emailed us said this woman was really grateful for you guys and how you'd helped her out. Especially because of the baby weight. She really wanted to lose it. We're just so sorry that our computers crashed. It's been a real nightmare."

"I totally understand that." She scowled at her computer. "I'll tell you what. Leave me your contact information. I'll ask around with some of our trainers. Maybe something will turn up. Don't get your hopes up, but you never know."

I smiled. "That would be great. Thank you. This means a lot."

CHAPTER 5

"So, I'm doing an interesting article," Jamie said as we sat across from each other at a coffee house not far away from Rhonda's Fitness ten minutes later. She raised her cup of tea, sweetened with stevia as per her no sugar rule, and took a sip.

Her eyes sparkled and caught my curiosity. "Oh really? On what?"

"I'm sure you remember the triathlon accident that happened about almost a year ago. There was that car that ran a barrier and hit three cyclists."

I cringed at the thought. Of course, I remembered. It was horrible to hear about it and think about the impact it had on the athletes' lives.

I gripped my own cup of espresso, warming my hands, and glanced down at Sweet Pea, who had fallen asleep. Unfortunately, the only seats available in the coffee shop were close to the line that nearly went out the door. People were crowded near us, so we had to keep our voices low.

"You're doing an article on the accident?" I asked.

Jamie shrugged, the action causing her oversized wooden earrings to swing against her jaw. She'd gone to Jamaica on a mission trip not long ago and brought back all kinds of handcrafted goodies, including necklaces and earrings. Most were made from hand-carved wood, and the look somehow fit her.

"I just turned in an article on how those three cyclists are doing now," she continued. "They've had to deal with long hospital stays, physical therapy, being unable to work. One man lost a leg."

"It does sound interesting." But it still didn't explain the sparkle in her eyes.

As more customers crowded into the business, I scooted Sweet Pea closer to me. I hoped we didn't regret coming here. A coffee house seemed like a safe enough place. But there was risk everywhere, and we didn't even know what kind of risk we were facing, at this point.

Jamie nodded. "It really is interesting. In fact, other newspapers and news stations are covering their story since it's the one-year anniversary."

I forced myself to look back at her, fighting my sudden feelings of crowdphobia, which I wasn't actually sure was a word. "So . . ."

"Even though I write for a smaller newspaper, these guys agreed that I could do a story on them, especially since they're all from the west side of Cincinnati. It's been really incredible to hear their stories. Very inspiring." Her eyes still danced with excitement, and her hands flew across the table as she talked with enough animation to make Walt Disney proud.

I put down my coffee and leaned toward her. "I can imagine. But why are you smiling like that?"

Her index finger tapped against her mug as she stared off into the distance. "I don't know. One of them is kind of cute. We've been staying after the other guys leave and talking some."

Now it was making sense. A grin spread across from my face. "I see . . ."

She waved a hand in the air. "It's not like that. We're

just friends. But I really feel like this story could do good things for my career."

"That's great, Jamie." She worked really hard. I knew she wanted to work for the *Ledger*, and she hoped with enough experience at the smaller paper that she could eventually get a job there.

"Maybe you'll get to meet him one day," she continued. "You know, especially since the last guy I dated didn't work out all that well."

I had to lean closer because the lunchtime crowds seemed especially loud. "We all have those horror stories."

Jamie gave me a pointed look.

"Maybe not quite as bad as yours," I obliged.

At my acknowledgement of her especially horrible love-turned-horror story, she relaxed. "Exactly."

Without turning my head, I glanced at one of the men in line beside our table. His hands seemed to have taken on a mind of their own. His fingers clenched and unclenched.

My throat went dry at the sight.

Maybe he had a disability that made his hands ache, that made him keep moving his fingers. But something about the action made me uncomfortable, whether justified or not.

I stole a glance upward, trying not to be too obvious.

The man was probably in his early thirties. He had long, stringy brown hair despite being nearly bald on the top. His black shirt only made his complexion look paler.

And he was looking right at the baby carrier.

Was this man somehow connected with this whole mystery? Had he followed us here? Would he try to snatch Sweet Pea back?

"You haven't heard a word I said, have you?" Jamie's voice brought me back down to the moment.

"What was that?"

She shook her head. "What are you thinking about?"

With my eyes only, I motioned toward the man beside us. Unfortunately, the line wasn't moving fast, so he remained close. His hands still clenched and unclenched. The action instantly gave me visions of a man trying to work up his courage before snatching the baby carrier and running.

I scooted Sweet Pea even closer to me. I suddenly didn't care about my coffee. Or the crowds. Just the man beside us.

Jamie's eyes widened, and she nodded.

Without saying a word, we both knew what needed to happen. I grabbed my purse, lifted the baby carrier, and hurried out of the coffee house in five seconds flat. Jamie was right beside me the whole time.

As soon as we stepped outside, I looked back.

The man was still in line, and he wasn't even looking at us.

"Maybe I overreacted," I muttered.

"Better safe than sorry. He was acting suspicious."

I nodded, my heart rate slowing ever so slightly.

I walked more quickly than usual to my car, casting two more looks over my shoulder to make sure the man hadn't followed us. He hadn't.

I placed Sweet Pea in the car seat base and started to climb in when I noticed a flyer on my windshield. I quickly grabbed it, anxious to get out of the cold.

As I climbed into the driver's seat, something on the paper caught my eyes. This wasn't a flyer. It was a note. Hand scrawled.

It read, "Stop investigating. For everyone's sake."

***

"Do you think Sweet Pea's mom left it?" Jamie asked as she stared at the note behind the locked doors of my Mustang.

My hands quivered as I glanced around the area for a sign of any shady characters. I didn't see anyone except a mother with a toddler in tow and a senior adult with a walker. "That's my best guess. That would mean she's been following us."

"*Someone's* been following us."

My trembles traveled from my hands all the way to my bones as I sat in my car. "Let's say this was Sweet Pea's mother. Why doesn't she want to be found?"

"Same reason anyone doesn't want to be found. She's hiding something. Scared. Maybe she's running from the police."

I stared at the note again, remembering the blood on the car seat carrier. Jamie could have a point, but there was something else I needed to consider. "This isn't the same handwriting. The other one had big block letters."

"This one was probably written more quickly. Whoever wrote it was probably afraid we'd come out and catch him or her."

"Probably true. Then again, what if this was left by the person responsible for the blood? What if, for that matter, it was Sweet Pea's mother who died and the person responsible didn't want to take care of a baby?"

"We have plenty of what ifs, don't we?"

Jamie had a point. There was nothing else I could really do about this except hand it over to Chase. We needed more information before we could draw any conclusions.

I was just grateful that the media hadn't picked up on this yet. There were more abandoned infant cases than were reported. If Sweet Pea had been left in Walmart, it might be all over the news. But since he'd been left with me, I supposed it didn't seem newsworthy. If word about the blood on his car seat leaked, it would become front-page news.

I carefully placed the note in my purse, gave one last glance around the parking area, and put my car into Drive.

As I drove away, I tried to flesh out other possibilities. What if the mom was killed and the baby taken. Had he been given to me by the killer? Did that mean I knew the killer?

That thought was disturbing.

Maybe no one had died, I mused. Maybe the blood was all from an accident. I mentally sighed. What I needed was something concrete. Maybe clearing my head at home would be the best thing I could do.

When we got back to my house, I spotted someone walking from the front door toward the sidewalk. It took me a minute to recognize who it was. Evan. The paramedic who'd taken Sweet Pea to the hospital and who'd stopped by to talk in the waiting room.

I retrieved Sweet Pea's carrier from the back seat, looped my arm through the handle, and walked toward Evan. My curiosity rose with each step.

Why was he here? Had something happened? He was wearing his paramedic uniform, but I didn't see an ambulance anywhere.

He met me halfway across the lawn with a huge smile stretched across his face. "Hey there. I know it's not polite to stop by unannounced, but I just happened to be in the area." His gaze fell on Jamie, and his smile remained in place. "I'm Evan."

Jamie grinned. "Jamie. Nice to meet you."

"I just thought I'd check on the Sweet Pea." He peered

into the baby carrier. "He's asleep again?"

I glanced at the baby's closed eyes and deep breathing, willing my insides not to turn to goo every time I looked at him. Babies had always had that effect on me. "I guess our little trip wore him out."

He raised an eyebrow. "Trip?"

I shrugged. "We thought we had a lead on his mom's identity. It turned out to be nothing."

Surprise flashed in his gaze. "You're looking into this case yourself?"

Careful about who's aware of this information. "Looking into it would be putting it strongly. I mostly just want to make sure his mom is okay."

"She must know you," he continued. "She picked you on purpose."

"You're assuming it was even his mom who left him."

"You think it was someone else?"

I shrugged. "I'm trying not to jump to conclusions."

"That's probably smart."

"Either way, I'm concerned about his mother. No one has reported her missing yet, and it seems like someone should care. Someone should notice."

He shifted weight from one foot to another. "Hopefully, the police will discover something soon, right?"

Jamie elbowed me. "Knowing Holly, she'll figure it out first."

Evan's gaze fell on me, curiosity lingering there. His blue eyes danced, sparkling like the ocean on a tempest day. As half of his lip curled, it revealed a dimple in his cheek—one that had certainly made the ladies swoon before.

"Is that right?" he finally said.

I shrugged, unsure how to respond and not sure I

wanted to divulge all my history. I finally settled on, "I've been accused of being persistent."

"Not a bad trait to have." He reached into his pocket and, with flair, pulled something out and handed it to me. "This is the other reason I stopped by. I wanted to drop this off for you."

His head bobbled in a very George Clooney-esque way.

As I took it, I glanced at the words on the front. It was a gift card to a local baby store. My heart warmed with gratitude. "Thanks. That's very kind of you, Evan."

His foster parents had obviously taught him great manners. That was always a positive in my book.

He shrugged. "Like I said, I was a foster kid. I know about the challenges. If there's anything else I can do, please let me know."

"Do you always go above and beyond like this?" I asked before he could walk away.

His smile dimmed. "Life is too short to operate on cruise control, right?"

I nodded, totally agreeing with his mantra. It always inspired me when I saw people who took life by the horns instead of waiting passively. "I understand."

He flashed his trademarked, dimpled grin.

"See you around, Holly, Jamie." He nodded before continuing down the sidewalk.

Jamie let out a low whistle as he left. "He seems too good to be true. Handsome, kind, and thoughtful? I think he likes you."

I scoffed and started toward the front door. "Don't be silly. He saw me with Chase."

"He doesn't seem like the type to let something like . . . oh, I don't know . . . *being taken* stop him. That would require too much cruise control and not enough gumption."

I didn't believe that. She was reading too much into this. "It's like he said. He was a foster kid. He understands all of this more than most people. He also seems to have turned out remarkably well after everything he's been through. That's inspirational. Besides, I want to believe there are some people in this world who are simply good people and who want to help—with no ulterior motives in mind."

She grunted. "You're probably right."

I glanced at my friend as I unlocked the door, trying to get a read on her. "He does seem nice. Maybe *you* should get to know him."

She snorted this time. "Nice idea, but no thanks. I don't like being a leftover. That said, he is one fine specimen. Almost as fine as Wesley."

"Is he one of the triathletes?"

"You know it."

As soon as I stepped inside my house, I heard voices in the distance. My mom must be home. But whom was she speaking with?

I found her in the kitchen, sitting at the table with a police officer across from her. The man was probably in his fifties with a square face, graying hair, and a calm, easy demeanor. He was tall, thin—but not too thin—and he wore a patrol uniform.

The two of them seemed to be having more than a professional conversation. There were two coffee mugs between them, as well as cookies. Cookies that I'd made.

I stopped in my tracks. "Mom?"

She looked up at me, and her a-little-too-loud laugh came to a dramatic halt. "Holly, you're home. And just in time. This is Officer Truman. Officer, this is my daughter Holly."

Introductions went around.

"It's been hopping around here," my mom continued. "You just missed that paramedic. He said he'd come back later. Someone from church brought over some food for us earlier too." Mom pointed to a casserole dish on the kitchen counter.

"Some food? Why?" I set Sweet Pea on the floor and walked over to the oven where a white dish with little flowers on the edge sat covered in aluminum foil. Whatever was inside, it smelled savory and delish.

"They heard about the baby, of course."

I pulled my coat off, a weight of concern pressing against my shoulders. "How'd they hear about the baby?"

My mom waved her manicured hand in the air. "I may have mentioned it to Louisa, and you know how Louisa is. Now everyone at church has heard. Anyway, you've always been so good to people, bringing them food and cookies. They wanted to do the same to help us out. They've set up a meal train for the next two weeks."

"Wow . . . that's nice." Although it was in direct contrast to my plan to keep this quiet. Half of Cincinnati would soon know about the baby.

My gaze fell back on Officer Truman. He must have seen the questions in my gaze.

"I'm doing patrol by your house until we have some answers. I just thought I should introduce myself. If you need anything, I can be here in less than five minutes. Chase made sure of that himself."

I smiled at the mention of Chase. "We appreciate that."

"You're probably not in any danger, but we just want to be careful until more facts emerge."

"Of course." It was strange—one nameless baby showed up, and the entire community rallied behind us. It wasn't a bad thing. Not at all. In fact, it was rather refreshing to see so many people care. "Were you the one driving the unmarked car earlier?"

He stared at me a moment, as if he had no idea what I was saying. I hadn't seen any unusual cars parked outside, but a lot of people parked around the corner and off the main street.

"I saw the same car pass by several times today. A black sedan. A Crown Victoria, maybe?"

He shook his head, uncertainty in his gaze. "That wasn't me. I drive a patrol car."

CHAPTER 6

When Chase came by at six that evening, I was lying on the couch with Sweet Pea cuddled up beside me. We'd had quite the afternoon together, one filled with an overloaded diaper, a lot of gas, and me attempting to trim tiny, razor-sharp fingernails that had done a number on my arms.

I was worn out by the end of it all.

Like, more tired than I thought possible. I'd assumed I was made for stuff like this, but taking care of an infant was much more draining than I'd realized.

I sat up as Chase approached, securing Sweet Pea against the back of the couch and trying to blink away any sleep from my gaze. My mom had let him in before scurrying back to the attic so she could sort through things there. That was her number one on her priority list this winter.

As soon as I saw Chase was wearing a suit, I instantly went on alert.

I was missing something, but my tired, fatigued brain couldn't figure out what.

"Are you okay?" He stared down at me and blinked.

I must really look terrible because he was the third person who'd asked me that today. I nodded. "I'm fine. Just tired and adjusting."

"I should have called before I came, but I got busy with other things."

"Don't apologize. You look really nice." I patted the seat on the other side of me, away from Sweet Pea's sleeping figure.

What are you forgetting, Holly? Whatever it was, it was at the edge of my recall. I wasn't quite there yet, though.

"I guess you won't be joining me tonight at the awards banquet?" he asked.

That was when it hit me. *Tonight. The awards banquet. Chase being honored.*

Guilt washed through me. I'd totally and completely forgotten.

How could I have forgotten?

My hand went over my gaping mouth. "Chase, I'm so sorry. I—"

He held up his hand to stop me. "I should have reminded you, Holly. You're usually so on top of things that I figured you'd call and let me know if it wasn't going to work out. Maybe I was being optimistic. Maybe I was just so busy that I didn't have the proper time to call you. Either way, it's fine."

"No, I should have remembered. You asked me a month ago. I know this is important to you." Tears started to rush to my eyes. I hated letting people down. Hated it. "Let me see if my mom can watch Sweet Pea. I can be ready in ten minutes—"

He squeezed my leg. "Really, Holly. It's okay. I can attend a banquet alone."

"It's not just a banquet. It's *your* banquet. The one where you're being honored." I rubbed my forehead, wishing I could rewind time to about an hour earlier. "I'm a lousy girlfriend."

He nudged my chin back up. "No, you're not. You've had a lot on your mind."

I fell into his outstretched arms—but only for a minute. Then I reached for Sweet Pea, knowing I needed to secure him.

"Thank you."

He rubbed my back, even as I pulled away. "How's motherhood treating you?"

I glanced at Sweet Pea as he lay beside me on the couch, his lips moving in and out with every breath. "It's been totally exhausting. But I've already fallen in love with Sweet Pea. He's such an angel."

"Holly, you know—"

I raised a hand to stop him. "I know, I know. I can't get too attached. I haven't forgotten."

"I just don't want to see you heartbroken at the end of all this." He squeezed my knee.

"I appreciate your concern. I'm just trying to embrace this for all it's worth. This little guy needs all the love and attention he can get right now. But I also think a lot about his mama. I pray she's alive but I know that if she is, she's probably desperate and scared."

"Or she could be a drug addict who's on the run. The choice could be selfish. She could be a criminal, for that matter."

I shifted to face him more, careful to keep one hand on Sweet Pea. "No updates, I take it?"

"Not yet. We're still trying to figure out his mother's identity." He glanced at his watch. "Now, I have a few minutes until I need to leave. Tell me about your day."

So I did. I filled him in on going to the youth center and the gym, the man with the crazy hands, and arriving back home. I gave him the note that was left on my car, just in case he needed it for evidence, and explained to him what had happened.

"You should have called us," Chase said.

Half of the time my leads didn't pan out. The other half I

got a lecture from him about snooping, so one might understand my hesitation to share. "You're right. I probably should have. But nothing came of it."

"I'll look into this myself tomorrow, just to make sure." Chase stood. "I should be going."

I stood also, that familiar guilt still plaguing me. "I really am sorry about tonight. I wanted to be there."

He kissed my forehead. "You get some rest. I'll be okay."

But, after he left, I couldn't help but wonder if he was as okay with this as he said he was.

CHAPTER 7

An hour later, my mom and I had cleaned up from dinner after nibbling on some kind of casserole with a creamy chicken filling and crusty cracker topping. It was good, but my appetite wasn't very strong this evening. I had too much on my mind.

With everyone fed and happy, and the kitchen clean, Sweet Pea sat in a little bouncy seat and played with the colorful toys that hung over the front of it. My mom sat at the kitchen table with some boxes from the attic around her, and I did my normal stress reliever: I made some cookies, beating myself up still for forgetting Chase's event tonight.

"Holly, look at this," Mom said.

"What is it?" I glanced her way as I put a pan of cookies in the oven.

"It's a project you did in fifth grade. The teacher asked you to predict where you'd be in the future." My mom held up a poster with crayon-smeared words across it. "You had to imagine the next fifty years of your life. At fifteen, you saw yourself going on mission trips."

"Check." I had done several mission trips, starting way back in high school.

"At twenty, you wanted to be in college and be active in volunteering."

"Another check." No arguments from me.

"At twenty-five, you were going to be married with two

kids and a third on the way."

I frowned at her words. I was twenty-nine now. Nowhere close to having children. Definitely not married.

The thought caused a lump to form in my throat, but I didn't want her to see how much that fifth-grade prediction affected me. "Interesting."

"At thirty, you were going to have three children of your own and you were going to have adopted two more."

"You know what they say about the best laid plans . . ." I frowned.

"Isn't that the truth? Life doesn't always work out the way we'd like. You've just to got to roll with it."

I cast Sweet Pea one more glance, saw that he was still content, and then I sat down a little too hard across from my mom.

"What's wrong?" Mom's eyes narrowed, and she paused from her organizing.

"I just feel badly that I missed Chase's banquet tonight."

"What was he being honored for again?"

"His work in ending the police riots last year." The city had fallen into chaos after a police brutality case caused racial tensions. Just when the violence had gotten totally out of control, Chase risked his life to save one of the rioters from certain death. That one act had somewhat helped ease tensions in the area. It hadn't solved them, but it had started the process.

"Yes, yes. He does deserve the honor. But he understands that you couldn't be there. He's not the type who always needs a woman by his side."

"I'm not sure if that's good or bad."

My mom tilted her head. "What do you mean?"

I started to shake my head and try to weasel out of the

conversation that I'd initiated, but I stopped myself. "What if Chase never overcomes his past?"

Mom's lips pressed together compassionately. "He will."

"It's been . . . what? Three years? Three years since his brother was killed and Chase's life fell apart. I know these things take time to process and learn to live with. But there are certain things in life that we'll carry with us every day. There are things we have to learn to live with. We don't ever get over them. We just have to learn to accept them."

"Wise words, Holly. It's very true. Life isn't always a Hallmark movie, is it?"

I shook my head. "I'm trying to do this thing called life right. Trying to make the biggest splash with what time I've got. I just really hate wasting even a moment."

"Oh, sweetie. You really think Chase is a waste of time?"

I swallowed hard. "No, I didn't mean it like that. I don't know what I mean. I think lack of sleep is messing with my mind."

"Why don't you get some rest? I'll watch Sweet Pea for a couple of hours."

"Are you sure?" I wasn't used to depending on other people to help me function. I liked being independent. But I couldn't deny the fact that I was exhausted—after only a day. I thought I had more stamina than this.

"Yes, now go. Lie down. Relax. We'll be fine."

***

I stared down at Sweet Pea as I pushed him through my church building and my chest swelled with joy. He'd gotten so much attention today, everyone wanting to catch a glimpse of his adorable little face. I loved having a baby.

Movement beside me caught my attention and pulled me away from my idyllic thoughts.

It was a woman. She moved through the crowds like a panther.

Before I realized what was happening, she scooped her arms into the stroller and grabbed Sweet Pea. Despite the stream of people, no one noticed her or stopped her. So she ran.

I chased after her, desperate to get Sweet Pea back. How could I have let someone snatch him? How had she approached so quickly and without notice?

An alarm began sounding in the distance.

An alarm?

Was it a car alarm? Why else would there be an alarm in church?

I sat up straight in bed, sweat across my brow. It was just a dream, I realized. A dream.

Then why was the alarm still sounding?

The security system, I realized. We'd recently had a home security system installed at the house after a string of break-ins in the area. Well, after a string of break-ins—all at this house. But that was neither here nor there at the moment.

My heart leapt into my throat as the high-pitched beeps continued.

Someone was trying to get into my home.

I sprang out of bed.

I had to get Sweet Pea. Was this connected to his sudden appearance in my life?

That was my best guess.

I peered into his Pack 'n Play and saw that he was sleeping peacefully, oblivious to the noise. My instinct was to grab him, but I didn't want to wake him up unless it was absolutely necessary.

At this point, I wasn't sure.

My door opened and my mom peered into my room. Worry was written on the lines across her face.

"Are you okay?" she whispered.

I nodded. "Just fine. You?"

"The police are on the way. I think it would be wise for us to stay upstairs."

I rushed toward the window and peered outside. My room faced the backyard, but I couldn't see anything, only darkness.

Was someone out there?

Trust no one.

The words from the note resonated in my mind.

What did that mean?

With my mom standing near Sweet Pea, I rushed toward my nightstand and grabbed my cell phone. I dialed Chase's number. He answered on the first ring.

"What's wrong?"

"The alarm is going off on the house."

"Officer Truman should be there any minute. I'm on my way also. Stay where you are. Lock the door."

"Okay." My hands were trembling when I hung up the phone.

This was nothing. The wind. An accidental trigger of some sort.

I was sure there were other reasons for the alarm to go off, reasons that didn't include anything nefarious.

Then why did I feel so nervous?

Someone rapped on the door downstairs.

I turned to my mom, my blood pressure skyrocketing.

No way was I leaving Sweet Pea up here alone. But I needed to see if that was Officer Truman.

"Stay with him?" I asked my mom.

She nodded, remaining by his Pack 'n Play. "Of course."

"Lock the door behind me . . . just in case."

I prayed there was no just in case. But I had to use caution here.

I pulled on a robe and wiped my hands against the cottony material. Then I slowly turned the door handle and peered out into the hallway.

Darkness stared back.

I swallowed hard, praying no one was waiting on the other side of this door, just out of my line of sight.

After some of the things I'd been through lately, I'd realized that sometimes worst-case scenarios did happen. They terrified me. Though I tried to battle fear with faith, I had to admit that worst-case scenarios could terrify me. Paralyze me, for that matter.

I pushed myself forward. I had to do this. For Sweet Pea.

Sucking in another deep breath, I pulled the door open farther. By all appearances, the hallway was clear.

I took my first step out and jerked my head to the right.

No one was there.

Thank You, Jesus.

The pounding at the door downstairs continued.

That's right, Holly. You just have to make it down the stairs and to the front door. Easy peasy lemon squeezy. Right?

It didn't seem so easy at the moment. All I could picture was someone jumping out from behind one of the closed doors lining the corridor.

Dear Lord, help me.

I took my first step, moving at a snail's pace. That was when I realized speed could be my friend and that being slow would only make me more of a target.

I darted toward the stairs, flew down them, and finally reached the front door. I peaked out and saw two officers on the other side. My hands trembled as I tried to open it, making the task nearly impossible. Finally, I undid the latch and jerked the door open.

Officer Truman and another cop stood there. They didn't wait for me to ask them inside. They charged into the house, immediately on guard.

Officer Truman took my arm. "Are you hurt?"

I shook my head. "No, just shaken. Did you see anything outside?"

"No, everything appears in place. We're going to check the inside, though."

I nodded, trying to process everything.

"Stay here," he said.

I wasn't going to argue. I posted myself near the wall and counted down the seconds, continuing to pray that everything would be okay.

Lord, I just need Your wisdom. I'm kind of selfish and needy. I ask for Your wisdom all the time. I can't get enough of it. But so many things are coming at me, and the fact that I'm tired isn't helping me. Please be with me, Lord.

"Holly," someone muttered.

I opened my eyes and saw Chase at the door, dressed down in jeans and his favorite University of Cincinnati T-shirt and boots. Before I could say anything, he pulled me into his arms. His embrace immediately made my heart rate return to some semblance of normal. He'd always been my protector.

"Anything?" he asked.

I stepped back and shook my head. "Truman and another officer are checking things out. Last I heard, they hadn't found anything."

"The baby?"

"He's fine. He's upstairs with my mom."

At that moment, Truman pounded back down the stairs and approached Chase and me. "Everything appears okay upstairs. Your mom said she'll stay with the baby for a while so you can talk to us."

"Did you see anything?" Chase kept an arm curled around my waist as he addressed the officers.

Truman shook his head. "No, nothing."

The other officer joined him. The twenty-something's name badge read "Mclean," and he was a tall, gawky man with short, dark-brown hair, and an expressionless face. "There's no one here, but there's something I thought you might want to see."

We followed him to the back door. He pointed to one of the bay windows around our breakfast nook and shined his flashlight there. "It almost looks like pry marks," Mclean said.

Chase leaned closer. "You're right. And they look fresh. You don't know anything about this, do you, Holly?"

I shook my head. "No. No idea. To my knowledge, they were not here before."

"How often were you driving past?" he asked Truman.

The older officer looked into the distance and shrugged. "Every twenty minutes usually. But there was an altercation at the bar down the street. I was there as backup for about an hour."

"Right before this happened?"

He nodded. "Right before this happened. I came as soon as I got the call."

"Let's get a forensic team out there to see if there's any evidence," Chase said.

"Yes, sir." Truman stepped away and pulled out his radio.

As he did, Chase pulled me back into the house and out of the cold. I braced myself for whatever conversation might happen, unsure why I felt so much tension. But I did.

Chase led me to a corner and lowered his voice. "Did anything else happen that you need to tell me about?"

He was using his detective tone with me, and I didn't really appreciate it. "Did anything else happen? What do you mean?"

He sighed. "I know you like to look into things on your own. Is there anything I should know that you didn't mention earlier?"

I shook my head, trying to shove down my frustration. Did he really think I'd bypassed his award banquet in order to look for more answers? "No, I've told you everything. You think someone was trying to grab Sweet Pea?"

His hands went to his hips as he looked off into the distance. "That's my best guess."

"Why? If it's a family member, shouldn't this person just fight for custody? Why do things under the cover of darkness?" I tried to think it through. I'd assumed Sweet Pea was an innocent bystander who'd had the unfortunate opportunity to be present at a crime scene where blood spatter was left on his carrier. Maybe I needed to look outside that theory.

Why would someone try to snatch the baby?

Black market baby sales? That seemed extreme.

Heir to a fortune? That also seemed unlikely.

Could the boy's biological father want him back? Again, why wouldn't he just come forward and claim relation? That seemed a lot simpler than being sneaky.

Unless he was involved in a crime.

What other reason would someone want to grab a baby?

The answer hit me like a slap in the face. As leverage.

Could someone be using this baby as a way to wield power over someone else? Was that why someone—the baby's mom, most likely—had dropped him here for safekeeping?

I didn't know the answer. But the theory scared me and kicked my sense of justice into overdrive.

CHAPTER 8

An hour later, Officers Truman and Mclean had left, along with the forensic team. My mom had fallen asleep in my bed, and Sweet Pea still dozed in the Pack 'n Play, unaware that anything had happened.

Unfortunately, I was wide awake. Awake enough that I'd thrown on some black leggings with little, pink umbrellas on them—a gift from Jamie at Christmas—and my favorite pink T-shirt. Chase had made some coffee, and we sat beside each other on the couch downstairs.

A glance at the clock beneath the TV told me it was 4:30 a.m.

"Let's start over. I feel like I haven't seen you in days." Chase stroked my arm. "How are you holding up?"

I shrugged and hugged my cup of coffee with my fingers. "I'm doing fine. At least, I was until tonight."

"The crime scene techs got a print off the windowsill. We'll run it and see what turns up. Maybe this isn't related at all to the baby."

"I'm just thankful we have the alarm system we do. Thanks for encouraging that." *Encouraging* would be putting it mildly. Chase had strongly suggested it and practically set up the security company to come and install it. He'd also taught me some self-defense moves and bought me pepper spray.

"The way trouble keeps popping in and out of your life, it was the only logical choice." He smiled.

I put my coffee down and rested my hand on his chest, remembering my earlier guilt. "How was your banquet?"

He nodded. "It was nice. No big deal, really—"

"Of course, it was a big deal."

He shrugged nonchalantly. It wasn't false humility, either. The hard knocks of life had humbled him and changed his priorities.

"It's an award," he said. "You can't take it with you one day."

"That's true. But it's still an honor—an honor that you deserved. I'm sorry I couldn't be there." My voice cracked.

He pushed a hair behind my ear, his eyes penetrating mine. "It's okay, Holly."

"It doesn't feel okay."

"It's just a glimpse into what life would be like with kids."

I smiled at the thought. "Yeah, I guess it is. It's like a test run."

His smile dimmed before he said, "Sure."

I suppressed a frown. We weren't on the same page, were we? He saw that as a negative, while I saw it as a positive. "I wasn't trying to make you uncomfortable."

He shifted. "Who said I was uncomfortable?"

"It's written all over your face."

He rubbed his thumb over my jaw, his gaze at once sad, regretful, and something else I couldn't read. "I just hope I can give you what you want—what you deserve—one day, Holly."

A knot lodged in my throat. He made it sound doubtful, and that made warning lights begin flashing in my mind.

I glanced down at where my hand rested on his chest,

trying to slow down my thoughts before they reached Jump-to-Conclusionville. "You're uncertain, huh?"

"You know we've had these talks," he started, his voice husky. "You know I love you, right, Holly? I'm just . . . well, not at the forever stage. I want to be, because you're everything I could want in a forever kind of relationship. There's just something . . . I don't know. Holding me back?"

"Maybe that something is . . . me?" I suggested.

"You're too good for me. I'm lucky to have you." He stroked my cheek. "Maybe we should talk more about this at a different time. It's late, and we're both tired and . . . I'm not sure we'll accomplish anything that we haven't already talked about."

I nodded, my throat still tight. In one way, he was right. We had been over this. I suppose all of that was just Chase's way of saying that nothing had changed since we'd last spoken. He wasn't ready to settle down. Didn't think he was ready. Thought he still had issues.

I didn't know why that thought left me uneasy. I mean, I should be happy he at least knew this in advance. It was better that way, right? Better to know that before diving into a lifelong commitment.

"Of course. You're right." My hand slipped down into my lap.

He raised my chin, which I hadn't realized I'd lowered. "You know I care about you, right?"

I forced myself to nod and pull back my emotions as the room went still around us. "Of course."

"You make me want to be a better man, Holly."

Something about his words caused my heart to soften. No one could deny that we were good together. We had the whole ying-yang thing down pat.

The truth was that Chase made me a better person also. He was my rock. My first kiss. The man I wanted to marry.

His eyes went to my lips.

My throat tightened at the smoky look in his eyes.

His hand went to my hair, and he stroked my locks back. I found myself leaning toward him, almost as if a magnet was pulling me.

His lips met mine, and no part of me wanted to stop it. I reached my arms up and wrapped them around his neck, closing the space between us.

Being with him like this still took my breath away and made my insides turn to jelly.

We pulled away, and my lips burned. I touched them. Felt my cheeks flush. Listened to the erratic pounding of my heart.

There was something about the late-night hour. About the dim room around us. The elusion of privacy.

It made me feel more vulnerable than I wanted. Than I should. Than I could afford.

Our faces still touched. Our arms remained around each other. I could feel his heartbeat, his deep breaths.

The tension in the air seized me, made me not want to move.

I wanted to kiss him more. I could tell he wanted to kiss me more.

But, if we did, I knew it wouldn't be a good thing. There was too much temptation. Too much room for error.

Neither of us moved, though.

He kissed my neck, and I fought a groan.

I needed to get up. To put distance between us. Why wasn't I?

"Chase." My voice sounded scratchy and wrought with

emotion.

He kissed my neck again. "Hmm?"

I forced my hands to his shoulders. "Chase."

He paused and brought his head up. His gaze was filled with heat and longing that threw me off guard.

He'd lived a different life than I had. He'd been married. Before he'd been married, he hadn't exactly been a good boy. In other words: he was experienced.

I was not. And I didn't plan on becoming that way until I was married.

I looked up and saw the look in his eyes. My resolve began to melt. Just one more kiss couldn't hurt . . .

His lips met mine again, this time hungrier. His hands went to my hips and he pulled me closer. The kiss deepened. Swept me away even more. Made all of my senses feel haywire.

Chase's fingers brushed at the edge of my shirt, causing my heart to race. My thoughts went places they didn't usually go.

Places they *shouldn't* go.

Stop, Holly!

Just then, a noise made me freeze. Chase must have heard it also because he slowed.

It was a cry.

Sweet Pea was awake.

I leaned back, feeling breathless and off-balance.

And thankful.

Thankful for Sweet Pea.

Because for a moment—and just a moment—I'd gotten carried away. I knew better.

"I've . . . I've got to go," I mumbled.

Before he could stop me, I hurried upstairs.

***

I'd managed to get Baby Sweet Pea back to sleep, and he'd remained asleep until nine a.m. That was the good news. The bad news was that I had some kind of mom brain going on, even though I hadn't actually given birth.

Whenever I thought about my kiss with Chase last night . . . my cheeks flushed with heat. What had I been thinking? I usually prided myself on being in control.

Chase had been gone when I came downstairs this morning. He'd left a note that read, "Call me if you need me."

We were definitely going to have to talk and put some boundaries in place. I didn't want to put myself in that position again. I'd been in a place—spiritually, physically, and mentally—where I could have done something I would have deeply regretted.

Sweet Pea smiled at me from the high chair as I fed him another bite of smushed apples from a jar. His sweet smile pulled me from my mangled thoughts. My heart warmed at the sight of his toothless grin. The doctor said I could try feeding him some rice cereal and apples, though his primary nourishment would be from formula.

This boy was just so precious.

I couldn't imagine a mom being so desperate that she'd give him up, even temporarily. If that was what had happened. There was so much we didn't know still.

"Good morning," my mom called, practically floating downstairs. Mom always floated. It was just the way she moved—with grace and style and elegance.

"Good morning."

She paused at Baby Sweet Pea long enough to stroke his cheek and offer a smile. "Good morning to you too, little one. I didn't hear anything out of you last night, even during all the craziness."

"He slept pretty well." I stifled a yawn. "Especially considering."

"But you didn't? Even after the police left?"

My cheeks flamed. "Not really. I kept waiting for him to wake up. And then I started thinking about his mom and wondering about all the possibilities."

"I see. Being a mom isn't an easy job." She grinned and tapped the tip of his nose.

"Maybe I should have thanked you more."

She flashed another grin before straightening and grabbing a coffee mug. "Would you like some?"

"I'd love a refill." I'd already had three cups.

Normally I'd wake up, fix a homemade breakfast of some sort—nothing premade or processed—and then I'd read my Bible and get dressed.

Today I'd be lucky to get out of my pajamas.

I was just adjusting, I told myself. This wasn't a permanent reflection of me. I could still pull myself together. I only needed some time.

"Plans for today?" Mom sat across from me and watched as I gave Sweet Pea his last bite of food.

He stared at me, as if silently begging for more. Or was he fussing at me because I made everything homemade for myself while feeding him stuff from a jar?

"You're right. I should be making this homemade. I'll do better next week. I just need a little more time." I wiped his mouth with a burp cloth and leaned back to drink some more coffee.

"Oh, Holly," my mom scoffed. "You're so funny."

"What was funny about that?"

"Cut yourself some slack sometimes, dear. You survived on baby food from a jar just fine." She let out another chuckle before taking a sip of her coffee. "So . . . plans for today?"

I thought about it a moment before saying, "I'm not really sure. I guess I'll just be taking care of Sweet Pea and answering some emails from work. I've already told Abraham I won't be making it into the youth center." Just for good measure, I threw in, "Maybe I'll make some baby food . . . You?"

"I have another scholarship committee meeting. I'm also preparing to list a house on the other side of town. It's an old fixer-upper that just needs some TLC. You should see it."

I should see it? For a brief instant, I imagined myself in my own house. With a baby. Like Sweet Pea. That I'd adopted.

The problem was I didn't see Chase in the picture. Not because I didn't want him there, but because I wasn't sure he would be ready for a scenario like that.

The thought settled hard on my chest.

What was going on with me? One minute I felt madly in love with him, and the next I was doubting the foundation of our relationship. I wasn't sure if I should attribute this to the natural ups and downs of a relationship or to something more.

"All right—go take a shower," Mom said. "I have thirty minutes until I have to leave, and you need to make yourself presentable."

"Even if I'm not going anywhere?" Those words didn't even sound like me. I thrived on looking put together.

"Yes, even if you're just working at home. Now go." She shooed me toward the steps.

Maybe a shower and wearing a new dress would help clear my thoughts.

A girl could only hope.

CHAPTER 9

Two hours later, Sweet Pea was snoozing in my arms when my cell phone rang. I didn't recognize the number, but I answered anyway—mostly because I was afraid the ringing would wake up the baby.

Thankfully, it didn't.

"Is this Holly?" a female asked.

"Speaking. Who is this?"

"My name is Missy. I work at Rhonda's Fitness. I heard you're looking for someone."

I pushed myself up straighter on the too-soft couch. "That's right. A woman with a baby boy."

"I think I know who you're looking for. I was helping someone with some personal training. She mentioned she had a baby. I think he's the right age. And she didn't show up for our appointment yesterday."

"Do you know her name or anything else about her?" Shoving my phone between my shoulder and ear, I grabbed a notebook from the table beside me and fished a pen out of the drawer.

"Her name's Katie Edwards. She's around twenty-five or twenty-six, I'd guess. She works at a pharmaceutical company. I don't think she likes her job that much, but it pays the bills."

My heart raced with excitement. Katie Edwards. Should

I know that name? The woman—if this was the right person—obviously seemed to know me. She had used my name on the note when she'd left Sweet Pea.

"That sounds right," I said, remembering our cover story. "Anything else you can recall?"

"Not really. She came in on Friday and seemed fine. She was talking about going out with her boyfriend that Saturday and getting a sitter for her baby. Nothing out of the ordinary."

Interesting. Had something changed between then and now? That was my best guess. "This has been very helpful. Thank you. If you think of anything else, please let me know."

As soon as I hung up, I called Chase, ignoring my natural instinct to begin searching for Katie on my own. Chase answered on the first ring.

"Hey, Holly." His voice sounded low, intimate, and apologetic.

"I think I have a lead." I ignored the need to talk about last night and explained to him the conversation I'd just had.

"Katie Edwards, you said? I'll see what I can find out. You don't recognize the name?"

I searched my memories another moment. "Part of me thinks it might be vaguely familiar. But maybe it's because it's such a typical name. I'm not sure. If I remember anything, I'll let you know."

"Sounds good."

I hung up and stared at Sweet Pea another moment. He snoozed quietly in my arms, his chest steadily rising and falling.

"What is your name, Sweet Pea?" I murmured. I knew I should put him down. Some would say I was spoiling him. But I couldn't help but think that he needed all the love in the world right now. It wasn't possible to love a baby too much. At least, that was my opinion.

I rubbed his chubby, little hand. “Do you miss your mama? I bet she misses you.”

I prayed she was still alive.

Why me? I asked myself again. Why had Katie Edwards—or someone else—decided to leave this baby with me, of all people?

Even though I told myself that I was going to let Chase handle it, I pulled up the Internet browser on my tablet and typed in “Katie Edwards Cincinnati.” Various social media sites popped up, and my heart quickened for a moment.

I held my breath as I pressed a button to check out the first social media profile.

A picture of a petite woman with a chin-length dark-brown bob filled the screen. I studied her picture a moment.

Did I know her?

I didn’t instantly recognize her, which left me feeling puzzled. I’d hoped I might find a connection and, with that connection, answers.

She did look vaguely familiar, but I couldn’t place her. Had she been associated with one of my social-work cases? Maybe not as a parent, but as a sibling or extended family?

Possibly.

She didn’t look like the type of inner-city youth I worked with at the youth center. This woman looked like she enjoyed a good party. She was wearing a tight black dress and holding a beer while people danced in a club-like scene in the background. Her makeup looked neat; her haircut was fresh; the club itself more like the type where rich college kids partied.

If the woman from Rhonda’s Fitness was correct, Katie was possibly three or four years younger than I was. That would probably rule out us going to school together.

So who was this Katie woman?

After another moment of hesitation, I scrolled down.

Sure enough, this Katie worked for Endless Pharmaceuticals. She was twenty-six years old.

My breath caught.

And there was a picture of her with a baby boy.

My baby boy. Sweet Pea.

Her last entry was on Saturday evening, the day before Sweet Pea had shown up on my doorstep. She had checked in at Club 21, a mecca of young-adult nightlife in the area.

I leaned back a moment, trying to process that.

Had something happened at the club that evening that sent her running and hiding? If not at the club, then what had happened between the time she left the venue on Saturday evening and Sunday afternoon when she brought Sweet Pea by? And that led me to my next thought.

Who was the baby's father?

I scrolled a little further but didn't see the baby named, which was only smart in social media. Katie looked like a happy mama, based on all the pictures she posted.

I scrolled back even further and found a picture of Katie in the hospital. A man was beside her. He was youngish—maybe closer to my age than hers. It was hard to tell. Something about him just looked a little more mature than Katie, though. He wasn't tagged in the photos, however, and identifying him by picture only would prove to be difficult.

There was one other person consistently tagged in her photos—a woman named Samantha Wilson.

I clicked the link, which took me to her profile.

I quickly scanned it and saw that she worked at Sugar Plum Bakery in an area of town called Clifton.

I was suddenly having a craving for a cupcake. And I wanted one. Like, right now.

***

Jamie met me thirty minutes later. I loved having a BFF with a flexible job and hours. Especially in situations like this. Actually, we'd had a lot of situations like this lately.

Sweet Pea was awake. I'd changed him and packed up a bag. I had a few reservations about taking him with me, especially when I remembered the note's warning: "Trust no one."

But taking him with me wasn't a sure indication that I was trusting anyone. I was, however, making other people aware of his location, and that had the potential to be equally as dangerous.

Please don't let me regret this, I silently prayed.

I had called Chase and let him know what I discovered, and he'd promised to look into it ASAP.

When Jamie and I stepped outside with Sweet Pea in tow, Officer Truman pulled to a stop in front of the house. I walked toward his patrol car as he rolled the window down.

"Morning," he called.

"Good morning." I came to a stop beside him.

"Any more problems since last night?"

I shook my head. "Not that I know of."

"Have you seen that sedan anymore?"

I shook my head again. "I haven't. Of course, this is the first time I've left my house since I saw you last."

"I've been keeping my eyes open for it, but haven't seen anything suspicious."

"Thanks. We appreciate it."

His gaze went to Sweet Pea. "How's the little guy doing?"

I looked down at him and smiled. "He's doing well."

"He reminds me of my son when he was young." A sad smile played across his lips.

"You're a dad?"

Officer Truman shrugged. "I was. I lost him over in Afghanistan."

"I'm so sorry." I couldn't imagine how hard that would be.

He seemed to pull himself out of his melancholy, looking embarrassed for oversharing. "It's been almost two decades. Two hard decades. I'm former military, and he wanted to follow in my footsteps. Navy."

"I know that made you proud."

"It was hard on my wife and me. We split shortly after, and I got out of the military." He offered a tight nod. "I decided to become a cop, even though most of the guys in academy with me were young enough to be my sons. I've done this ever since. Never really wanted to be a supervisor or detective. I just enjoy working patrol."

"It's good to do what you enjoy."

"It's not an easy line of work. Life isn't easy, for that matter. But my hope isn't in this world. That's the good news. I know I'll see my son again someday."

He must be a believer. With that thought, I looked at him more closely. "You go to my church, don't you?"

He raised his eyebrows. "Community?"

"That's the one."

He nodded and studied me a moment. "I sure do. I thought you looked familiar."

"I usually go on Saturdays."

"And I go whenever my work schedule allows. Sometimes Saturdays, other times on Sundays." He smiled, the action lighting his face. "Good to know there's that connection. That said, I can let you know that I've been praying for you. I can imagine how taxing a situation like this would be."

"I appreciate it." As a cold breeze swept over the lawn, I nodded toward my car. "Well, I should go. We're going to grab some lunch."

Jamie leaned closer as we walked toward my car. "He seems nice. Losing a son in battle. I can't imagine that."

"It sounds like his son's death destroyed his relationship with his wife also. Tragedy can ruin relationships pretty easily."

"Relationships are pretty fragile sometimes anyway, aren't they?" Jamie said.

I tucked Sweet Pea into the back seat, delighted when he offered another smile. "Yes, they are. Unfortunately, little one, you'll learn that too one day when you're older. Or maybe you'll learn it when you're way too young. If so, I'm so sorry. I wish children could be spared from all that pain."

I kissed his forehead before closing the door and climbing into the front seat. Jamie climbed in beside Sweet Pea and pulled on her seat belt before we took off down the road.

"Holly, is that the sedan that keeps driving past your house?" Jamie pointed straight ahead.

A dark vehicle about the same size and make of the one we'd seen yesterday zoomed ahead of us. However, the car was pretty typical. I couldn't be 100 percent sure it was the right one.

"Maybe," I said.

"We should follow it."

"We should have totally learned our lesson last time," I said. We'd gotten ourselves in trouble when we stuck our noses into business that wasn't our own. Though everything had worked out, I'd almost gotten killed in the process. Our lives had been on the line more than once. And it all started with following people who, in turn, followed us.

I nibbled on my bottom lip as I followed at a safe clip behind the vehicle. Either the driver didn't notice me—because I was so sly? Doubtful—or they were just a normal citizen out doing their normal tasks. This could all be for nothing, but maybe we'd know what the answer to that was here soon.

"They don't appear to be circling around to go past the house again," I muttered.

"No, but maybe the driver knows we're following and doesn't want to raise our suspicions."

I shrugged. "Maybe."

I didn't like this. It was one thing if Jamie and I put ourselves in danger, but it was a whole different story if I did anything to put Sweet Pea into danger. I had to carefully consider each of my actions. If this situation gave the slightest hint that it would turn ugly, I would abort the mission.

I continued to weave through the streets, trying to stay a careful distance behind the sedan. There was nothing remarkable about the vehicle. The license plate was standard issue. There were no bumper stickers or stuffed animals in the windows or snarky decals.

Nothing.

And, of course, the windows were tinted. I couldn't tell how many people were inside or if it was a man or woman driving.

Finally, the sedan pulled into the parking lot of a nearby corner drugstore.

"Wait and see who gets out!" Jamie said.

"I know. But I can't exactly pull in behind the car. That's a little too obvious." I glanced around before my gaze stopped on a bank across the street. I jerked the wheel and pulled into the parking lot. I found a shadowed parking space and put my car into Park. Then I watched, my heart thumping in my chest as I waited to see who would emerge from the vehicle.

A moment later, a blonde stepped out. She had long, straight hair, was dressed nicely in black slacks and a pastel top, and she wore heels. She was in her early thirties, if I had to guess.

I waited for her to look back. To show some sign that she knew she was being followed or that she'd been made.

She didn't glance back even once. Instead, like a woman with a mission, she charged inside the drugstore.

"I don't think she was our woman," I muttered.

"I agree. She must have just been driving a car that looked the same."

"I guess so. Now, let's get to the Sugar Plum Bakery."

CHAPTER 10

The Sugar Plum Bakery was located about ten minutes away in an area near the University of Cincinnati, where I'd just happened to attend college. It was decorated with everything sparkly and sweet, including pink chairs, glitter-top tables, and enticing hand-painted pictures of fruit on the walls.

But it was the aroma that got to me. Sugar and spice and everything nice.

My stomach grumbled.

What made it even better were all the signs promising customers that there were gluten-free options, that all ingredients were locally sourced when possible, and that every treat was handmade.

Nice.

As I stepped farther inside, I pulled the shade down lower over Sweet Pea's carrier. I didn't want anyone getting a glimpse of him unless absolutely necessary. If I was operating under the assumption that Katie was alive, then why did she leave her baby with me instead of her best friend? And if I was operating under the assumption that something had happened to Katie, then her best friend could be a prime suspect.

I had to be careful. Caution was my friend in this case.

I scanned the people working behind the counter, and my gaze came to a stop on Samantha. I recognized her curly blonde hair and pert expression from her social media page. She looked just like her pictures.

The place was busy. Jamie and I had arrived just as every businessperson within walking distance could stop by for lunch. It wasn't the best time to initiate a conversation, but I was going to try anyway.

Jamie took Sweet Pea and sat at a corner booth with him. Meanwhile, I licked my lips nervously as I stood in line.

"Can I help you?" An employee behind the register stared at me. She wore wings, just like a fairy, and I wondered how she felt about it. It took a special woman to wear that kind of outfit and not feel resentful or silly.

"I'd like two of your gluten-free scones—cranberry and orange, please."

"Sure thing."

I paid for the goodies, and Samantha handed me my order tucked into a paper doily over a glass case.

"Are you Samantha?" I fingered the scones in my hands as their scent drifted up to me and made my stomach growl.

Coffee. I should have gotten coffee to go with them.

My coffee cravings had quadrupled in the past couple of days.

She stopped midway, tongs raised, and looked twice at me. "I am. Do I know you?"

"Not really. Well, kind of. I don't know." *Convincing, Holly. Very convincing.*

She gave me a look and turned to her next customer, handing him a cupcake.

I was losing her and fast. "I have a few questions about Katie Edwards."

That got her attention. She paused from retrieving some maple-glazed cookies, and her gaze fixated on mine.

"What do you know about Katie?"

I shrugged. "Not much. I was hoping you could tell me something."

An unreadable emotion flickered in her gaze. "I have a break in ten minutes. Can you wait?"

"Of course."

Ten minutes later, just as promised, Samantha slid into the booth beside me. The baby carrier was snuggled in the booth next to Jamie and turned away from Samantha, successfully concealing Sweet Pea's face. Thankfully.

"Do you know where Katie is?" She got right to the point, and her gaze volleyed back and forth from me to Jamie.

"We were hoping you could tell us." I wiped the last of my scone from the table and placed the crumbs on a napkin.

She continued to glance back and forth from me to Jamie, her gaze assessing and measured. "How do you know Katie?"

Just then, Sweet Pea let out a little laugh. Samantha's face changed from suspicious to . . . something else. Alarm shot through me. Would she figure us out? Was this all a big mistake?

"You know Katie from that mommy and me group, don't you?" Samantha nodded, as if proud of herself for figuring it out. "She told me she'd just started taking Jonah there."

I nodded, a little too quickly probably. "Yes, of course. I realize we don't know her that well, which might make this seem a little strange."

"We're worried about her," Jamie said. "We haven't been able to get in touch with her, and we were supposed to have a baby play date."

Samantha frowned. "I haven't been able to get in touch with her either. I've been trying since Sunday."

I shifted, trying to remember my imaginary role as a fellow play-date mother who barely knew her. "Is that unlike Katie? She just comes across as being so responsible."

"Extremely. She's all about Jonah. People don't just disappear with their babies."

Jonah. That was Sweet Pea's name. And I loved it.

"I haven't been able to get up with Gage either," Samantha continued.

Gage? Who was Gage? Maybe he was the guy in that social media picture.

"We've never met Gage, though we've heard about him," I said. "What do you know about him?"

Samantha shrugged and glanced back at the long line of customers waiting to be served. "I don't know. They'd been dating for like, five years. He's Jonah's daddy. I kept telling Katie to leave him, that Gage isn't the marrying type."

"What do you mean?" I asked.

She shrugged dramatically. "You know how some guys are just like that? They'll lead a woman on for years but have no intentions of settling down. That's Gage. He's too married to his job and has 'women issues' after getting his heart broken once. Poor baby."

Something about her words caused my heart to constrict. I ignored it, not having time to analyze the emotion now. I had to stay focused.

"You said you haven't talked to him either?" Jamie rocked the baby carrier back and forth as Sweet Pea—Jonah—began to chatter more loudly.

"That's right. I tried to call him. It's unusual that he doesn't answer his phone. He *always* answers his phone." Samantha rolled her eyes.

"Why's that?" I asked, curious as to why it would induce

an eye roll.

"He's a reporter."

I glanced at Jamie, my blood spiking. Was he someone Jamie knew?

"For which newspaper?" Jamie suddenly didn't look so relaxed.

"*Cincinnati Ledger*. He lives and breathes it. He even gets death threats."

"Why?" I asked. Jamie was a reporter, but she didn't get death threats. Well, not usually. "Katie never mentioned death threats. Of course, we were just starting to get to know her."

"Gage likes his privacy. He won't even do social media, and he doesn't like for Katie to post things online about him. Anyway, he writes controversial pieces that no one else wants to touch. As a result, he's an easy target. He was getting so many hateful comments that he deleted his social media accounts. Said his life has been simpler since then."

"Understandably." I was tempted at times to do the same. I liked things simple. I enjoyed face-to-face conversations. Authenticity. Real life hugs instead of emoticons.

I leaned closer, desperately wanting more information. "Samantha, is there anyone who was angry with Katie? I know that sounds weird. But I have a bad feeling that she's in trouble."

Samantha thought about it a moment before letting out a long breath. "There was some woman at the gym whom she'd been having arguments with. It was about really stupid stuff, but the woman seemed to hold a grudge and have some anger issues."

It wasn't a lead that I'd expected, but I'd take whatever I could get. "What was she holding a grudge about?"

"It started over a treadmill. Weird, right? But then she

kept coming at Katie about stupid stuff. Parking spaces. Not cleaning the equipment after using it. Staring at her in the locker room."

"I guess it really bugged Katie?" Jamie said.

Samantha shrugged. "Who knows? I mean, you never know when people are going to turn psycho."

The mean gym lady could be a lead, but I had a feeling I should keep looking. "Was there anyone else?"

Samantha tapped the table a moment. "Her ex-boyfriend, Heathcliff Caswell, was a hothead also. Katie has been dating Gage for five years, like I said. But Heathcliff was her high school boyfriend. When she and Gage called it quits for a couple of months, Heathcliff tried to sweep back into her life. Katie quickly ended it, but he was having trouble letting go."

"You mean, he was obsessed?" Jamie continued to rock Jonah back and forth as his chatter turned into a cry.

"Possibly." Samantha shrugged. "I really have no idea. But, if you hear from her, will you let me know? I'm really worried. Especially about Jonah."

"Of course," I said.

"Listen, I've got to get back to work. You promise you'll keep me updated?" Samantha stood, but her eagle-like gaze remained on us.

I nodded. "We will."

With that, she walked away.

***

"Jonah, huh?" Jamie said as we climbed into the car. "Nice name."

"I agree. Although I was pretty fond of Sweet Pea." As I said his name, I tickled his belly and was rewarded with a smile.

I closed the door and climbed into the driver's seat.

"What now?" Jamie asked.

"I should call Chase."

"And then? Because I know there's a then."

I thought through everything we'd just learned. What we should do next was a great question. Samantha had given us some leads, but which was worth pursing? Which one would lead me to answers about where the blood on Jonah's baby carrier had come from?

"I don't think a woman at the gym who's catty is reason enough to hurt someone," I started. "I'm not sure the ex-boyfriend is a great angle either."

"Unless he thinks this baby is his," Jamie said.

She had a point. "True. Maybe we should look into him. And we should try to find Gage also. He works for the newspaper. You think you could track him down?"

Jamie shrugged. "I can definitely try. The thing is, we probably shouldn't bring Jonah with us to any of these places. What if one of those people are the very ones searching for him?"

I frowned. I'd thought of that also. Investigating with a baby was a lot more complicated than I'd thought. Jonah's safety was a priority.

"We've got to figure out what happened between the time she went clubbing on Saturday until she dropped off the baby on Sunday," I mused. "It had to be something big, something that made her desperate or put her in danger."

"I say we start with her current boyfriend and baby's daddy," Jamie said. "He seems like the most logical choice."

"I agree. In the meantime, I think I'm going to take a drive past Katie's house. I want to see where she lives. Maybe it will trigger something—some kind of connection."

"Sounds good. While you drive, I'll get on the phone and see what I can find out. Honestly, I'm really surprised this boyfriend of hers hasn't contacted the police himself to report her missing. Maybe their relationship wasn't as strong as it appeared."

"Maybe." I reached for my phone but paused. I'd just downgraded my phone to a device only boasting the basics—telephone services, text messaging, and a camera. I'd found myself getting too distracted with social media and longed to be more present wherever I was. I still wasn't used to not having a search engine at my fingertips.

"Uh . . . could you look up her address?" I asked.

"See, girl. I told you that you were going to miss that phone. But I respect your choice." She plucked around on her screen for a moment and then told me the address. I knew exactly where to go.

The car had heated up efficiently so I took off down the road. Jamie talked to two different people on the phone, asking plenty of questions. While she did, I tried to call Chase, but his phone went to voicemail.

"Guess what, Girlfriend? Girl Genius is at it again." Jamie did her little Z-shaped finger snap that I called The Diva as she lowered her phone.

"What did Girl Genius discover this time?"

"No one has seen good old Gage this week."

My heart leapt into my throat. Had he hurt Katie, dropped off the baby, and then run?

Katie's house wasn't terribly far away. It was in an area known as Westwood. We finally pulled onto her street, which was filled with skinny houses painted anything from gray to turquoise to bright pink.

But as I drew closer to her address, my foot hit the

brakes.

Police cars were scattered farther down. An ambulance. A fire truck, even.

My heart raced. What had happened here?

I got as close as I could before putting my car in Park. My thoughts rushed well ahead of me.

"Jamie, would you—"

"I'll stay here with Jonah. You go," she said. "There's a bottle and formula in here, right?"

"Of course. And he should be getting hungry soon. If you need me, shoot me a text and I'll come right back."

"Got it, Retro Girl."

I ran from the car and stopped by crime-scene tape that had been strung around the perimeter of Katie's house.

Dear Lord, what's going on? Be with those involved. Be with Jonah.

My gaze darted around as I desperately searched for answers.

Something bad had happened here. Something devastatingly bad.

Was Chase here?

My gaze went to the street, and I spotted his police-issued sedan.

He was. He must be inside.

An officer stood guard near the police line, and I knew there was no hope of getting to the other side.

Just then, a familiar figure stepped out of the house. He looked up and spotted me.

Evan.

He strode my way, grim lines on his face.

"I'm not even going to ask what you're doing here," he started. Gone was his life-of-the-party persona, and, in its place, was grief. "I guess what your friend Jamie said was right. You're pretty good at tracking down answers."

"What happened, Evan?"

His gaze locked on mine. "We discovered a dead body."

"A dead body? Whose?" I closed my eyes, squeezing out images of smiling Katie from her social media profiles. Poor Jonah. He was too young to lose his mom.

"I can't tell you."

"Please, Evan." I didn't want to sound desperate, but I was. I needed to know.

He looked around, almost as if to see if anyone was listening, and then sighed. Finally, he stepped closer and lowered his voice. "You have to keep this between us. The dead body has been identified as Gage Bowers. We believe he was the boyfriend of Katie Edwards. Based on everything we've seen here, we suspect Katie may have been behind it."

CHAPTER 11

I closed my eyes as my emotions clashed inside. Thank goodness it wasn't Katie. But, on the other hand, Gage . . . who might be Jonah's father. The poor baby. He would never know his daddy.

"What happened?" I asked.

He glanced over his shoulder again before responding. "He was shot. Based on rigor mortis, we suspected it probably happened sometime this weekend, even though that's not official yet."

"Any sign of Katie?"

He shook his head. "She's long gone. There could be a good reason for that."

Just then, I spotted Chase stepping outside. He saw me right away and stormed my way. His greeting toward Evan was less than warm. It bordered on hostile.

Strange.

"I've got it from here," Chase snapped. "Thanks."

Evan raised his chin, his shoulders drawing upward, before stepping away. "I'll see you around, Holly."

Normally, I might ask Chase about the reaction, but I had other things on my mind. As I remembered our steamy kiss from last night, my checks flushed again. My values were more in line with people raised in the 1950s than my millennial counterparts.

"What's going on?" I asked instead.

"I'm assuming you know that this is Katie Edwards' place. Based on all of the pictures inside, she's the mom of the baby you're caring for. We're still trying to piece together what happened between those walls."

I swallowed hard. "Gage . . ."

Chase's eyes darkened. "He's dead. Murdered. I've got to be honest here, Holly. It looks like Katie could be behind it."

"Why would you think that?"

"There are footprints in the blood. They match her shoe size. The weapon was also left. There are prints on it that we'll run, of course."

"So you think she shot Gage and dropped Jonah off with me so she could go into hiding?"

"Jonah?"

I shrugged. "I may or may not have figured out his name."

He gave me a lingering look before saying, "We're testing the blood that was found on the baby carrier against the blood in the house since it appears that the car seat was set in blood at some point. It's the most logical conclusion, but we're still investigating every possibility."

I nodded, feeling like I couldn't breathe. "I understand."

He glanced beyond me to where my car was parked. "You shouldn't be here, Holly."

"I had no idea this was what I'd see. I was just going to drive past."

"Where's the baby?"

"With Jamie in the car."

He nodded. "I need to get back inside. Be careful, okay?"

"Always."

He took a step away but paused. "Are we . . . okay? After last night?"

I shoved a hair behind my ear and nodded. "Yeah, we just got a little too swept away in the moment."

"We can talk about it more later. But . . . I'm sorry about that."

"No one ever said that remaining pure was easy." I offered an unconvincing smile.

"I can't deny that. I'll call you later, okay?"

I remained at the police line, watching everything play out. I imagined the body of Gage sprawled on the floor. I pictured the blood. The stench of death. I'd only been around it a couple of times, but the memories would never leave me.

Then my mind went beyond the present. It went back to Sunday, when all of this had gone down.

I imagined Katie in the house. Seeing her boyfriend's dead body. Grabbing Jonah and running.

Had she pulled the trigger first? Was she behind this? Or was she a victim also? Could this have been a domestic violence situation?

But there was one thing I didn't understand. If Katie was the one behind this, why had her note said: Trust no one? If she was the dangerous one then it just didn't make sense.

A crowd had gathered around the crime scene. I assumed it was mostly neighbors who'd come out to see what the commotion was about. But one woman caught my eye.

She stood out from everyone else, but I couldn't put my finger on why.

She looked nervous, I realized.

It was the way her gaze kept darting around. Plus, she wasn't dressed like someone who'd just wandered out of her home and stumbled up on this scene. No, she was dressed in business casual. She wore a heavy winter coat and her purse was slung over her shoulder.

I observed her light-brown hair. It was glossy and came down below her shoulders. She was probably in her early forties, if I had to guess.

Tears rimmed her eyes.

Who was she? How did she know Katie or Gage?

I wanted to go talk to her, but before I could Evan and Chase passed each other on the pathway leading to the porch. Based on the look each gave the other, there was no love lost between them.

What was going on? Certainly this wasn't about me. Evan had only been friendly, nothing more.

When I glanced back at the woman, she was gone.

***

I got back to the car to check on Jonah and Jamie. She sat in the back seat with Jonah in her arms and a bottle in her hand. I fought the need to take the baby from her and cuddle him, to tell him everything was okay.

Of course, he couldn't understand any of this. He'd have to deal with the effects later in his life.

The poor baby. I wished I could take all of the heartache from him and spare him the pain he'd face in the future. If only life worked that way . . .

"What's going on?" she asked as Jonah finished his bottle. She propped him up on her shoulder and began patting his back, waiting for a burp. She had two little brothers and was a pro at this.

I explained everything to her, and her eyes widened

with each new detail.

"I can't believe he's . . ." She glanced down at Jonah before mouthing the word "dead." In response, Jonah let out a soft burp.

"I know. I really hope Katie isn't behind it." My heart ached at the thought of it. It would be a travesty for Jonah to lose both his parents: one to death and another to life behind bars.

I surveyed the area one more time for a sign of the woman who'd caught my attention at the police line, but I didn't see her. Maybe it was nothing. But the way she'd acted had made me wonder.

"So, what's next?" Jamie asked, patting Jonah's back again.

I mentally reviewed everything, and my thoughts came to a stop at one thing. "I need to go back to the Sugar Plum Bakery and talk to Samantha one more time."

Jonah let out another burp. "I'll slip Sweet Pea back in his car seat, and we'll be good to go."

I drove across town, parked on the street, and then hopped out of the car and rushed inside the Sugar Plum Bakery. Samantha narrowed her eyes when she spotted me coming back again. The crowds had slowed as the lunch hour rush dwindled, so she approached me.

"What's wrong?"

I hadn't thought ahead enough to know how to phrase this.

Lord, give me the right words.

I shifted my weight as I stood in front of her, and the scents of everything sweet and soothing floated around me. I felt like my announcement might put a stain on this place and all of its goodness. "Samantha, I just heard something I knew you'd want to know."

Her face nearly looked paralyzed with suspense. "What?"

I licked my lips. "Gage is dead."

Her eyes widened, and she reached for the counter beside her. I grabbed her elbow before she collapsed on the fairy-dusted floor below. With my other hand, I grabbed a sparkle-bottomed chair and pushed it beneath her.

"Sit down. Please," I urged.

She slumped into the chair without argument and stared ahead with dull, perplexed eyes. "I don't understand."

"I just went to Katie's house. The police were there."

"Oh no." She buried her face in her hands.

I stared at her, trying to carefully watch her reaction as I asked my next question. "Were Gage and Katie having any problems?"

She raised her head, and her eyes widened again. "Gage and Katie? No. No, problems. No *real* problems, at least."

"You mentioned that he wasn't the type to commit. Did that cause a lot of tension?"

Her eyes flickered back and forth before she finally shook her head. "I don't know. Maybe. Some. I mean, every couple has disagreements."

"Of course."

She sucked in a deep breath and looked up at me as if realization had struck. "You're asking because you think Katie killed him, don't you?"

I used every ounce of my self-control to keep my expression neutral. "I didn't say that."

"Why else would you ask?"

"I'm just looking for answers, Samantha." I kept my voice calm and even.

Her eyes narrowed as she studied me, her back straightening some. "Why are you so interested in this? You hardly know her."

"It's true. But I know Jonah. I want to help, Samantha. I don't want to cause trouble."

She snorted. "You expect me to believe there are really people out there that just," she made air quotes, "'want to help'? I gave up believing in that a long time ago."

I clasped my hands together and lowered my voice. "I understand that this is a lot to take in. I can tell you this. My boyfriend is a detective. When I spoke with you, my gut told me something was wrong. That's the only reason I'm pursuing this."

She shook her head, her thoughts obviously going all over the place as her gaze skittered around and her breaths came more quickly. "I can't believe he's dead."

"You said he loved his job. Did he love being a dad as much?"

She shrugged again and let out a soft sigh. "I don't know. Not enough to marry Katie. The pregnancy wasn't exactly planned. He may have even accused Katie at one point of getting pregnant on purpose to manipulate him into marrying her."

"That would be hard to swallow."

"She didn't do it. She wasn't desperate."

"But I take it she wanted to get married?"

"Of course, she did. Being a single mom is hard. Her job didn't pay a lot. She doesn't have any family in the area to help out. Gage worked all the time."

"Did he help support her? I mean, they weren't living together, right?"

"No, he liked having his own space. I don't know. I guess Gage wasn't my favorite person, but Katie was hung up on him.

I never think it works out well when that happens."

I considered her words a moment but couldn't grasp exactly what she was saying. "When what happens?"

"When the girl likes the guy more than the guy likes the girl. Call me old-fashioned, but I think the guy should be the one doing the pursuing. Gage even cheated on Katie once, though he never owned up to it."

"Why would you say that?"

"I saw him with my own two eyes. I went out to eat at this restaurant that's below this hotel downtown—Hotel Plaid, that new trendy one. Who did I see step off the elevator? None other than Gage himself. And he was with a woman. They were whispering and talking real intimate like."

"Did he see you?"

Her face suddenly became animated as she wobbled it back and forth with enough attitude to challenge Queen Diva Jamie. "You better believe he did. I made sure of it. I marched right up to him and demanded answers."

I pictured that playing out and fought a smile. Cheaters deserved to be confronted, and Samantha was a good friend for not letting it slide. "How did he react?"

"He was shocked, of course. He stuttered and went pale and acted like he didn't know what to say. Finally, he insisted that it was a long story and he couldn't explain it. Typical. Guys are jerks."

I refused to add to her man hate. A few guys might give men a bad name, but they all didn't deserve that title. "But Gage didn't deny cheating on her?"

"He said it wasn't what it looked like. Isn't that what every cheater says?"

Perhaps it was. I couldn't deny it. But there was a chance he was telling the truth also.

"One more question: who took care of Jonah while Katie worked?"

She let out a long sigh. "I don't know her last name. Some woman that Katie found online through GregsList. Her first name was Sarah, and she sounded nice enough. That's all I know."

"Thanks, Samantha."

She touched my arm before I stood up. "Now I'm more worried about Katie than ever."

"I'm going to find her."

I only hoped the police didn't arrest her when that happened.

CHAPTER 12

"So I did some more research on Gage Bowers," Jamie announced as soon as I reached the car. "He has quite a history as a reporter. I mean, for real. He's covered some great stories. The man has nerves of steel."

"What do you mean?" I pulled my seatbelt on, curious to hear what she had to say and also anxious to share what I'd learned.

I tried to steal a glance at Jonah in the rearview mirror, but I couldn't see him. He must be asleep again. It was the only way to explain the quietness in the car. Now more than ever, I felt the desperate need to love on him and let him know everything would be okay.

Jamie stared at her screen, scrolling through something that I couldn't see. "I mean, there's no topic this guy is afraid to cover. He's done an exposé about the mayor's spending habits on the taxpayers' dime. He confronted a man who owned a car dealership for selling lemons and turning back the odometers. He went undercover at a factory to expose the working conditions there. He's kind of my hero."

"Your hero?" My eyebrows shot up in surprise.

She nodded. "That's how I want to be. Fearless. Unafraid to take on the bad guys, no matter the cost. To be an agent of change and stop corruption."

I hated to break the news to her, but . . . "He may have been fearless when it came to his job, but he was a coward when it came to love. Samantha thinks he cheated on Katie. Not only that, but he apparently wouldn't commit. He wasn't crazy about being a dad either."

Jamie frowned and glanced over at Jonah. "So maybe he wasn't always awesome. That's a shame. Did Samantha think Katie might have gone all scorned lover on him and killed him?"

"No, and she seemed sincere in her assessment. But who knows what lengths a person might go to if pushed hard enough. We need to figure out more information about Katie. Until we know more about her, we won't have any answers."

"How are we going to do that?"

"I say we pay a visit to Club 21. It's the last place we know Katie was seen."

Jamie shot me a concerned look. "With little baby Jonah? Are we taking him with us?"

I thought about it a moment and then glanced at my watch. It was two o'clock. The club wasn't even open for nightlife yet. "Let's go back to my house. I want to change him and let him play for a while. But I want to go to the club before it opens tonight."

"Sounds like a plan to me."

***

"As the saying goes, here goes nothing." I straightened my black dress, glad I'd chosen a classy one with a modest v-neck and a flowing skirt down to my knees.

I'd still stand out like a sore thumb at Club 21, but, I reminded myself, I wasn't going clubbing. No one else should even be here yet. Dress codes should be the least of my worries.

Despite those thoughts, I had some reservations about bringing Jonah with us. Was I putting him in danger? Were there any angles I hadn't thought through? Any scenarios where this was a bad idea?

You're going to be a terrible mom one day.

I shook my head, refusing to cling to that thought. If I thought Jonah would be in danger here, I wouldn't have brought him.

"Let's go do this." Jamie raised her hand in a fist bump.

We tapped knuckles before I picked up Jonah's carrier, and we stepped into the dimly lit club.

I was right—there wasn't anyone here yet. I'd heard this was the happening place in the evenings, with bouncers manning the outside doors and a line to get in that stretched for more than a block. I'd never been the clubbing type myself.

When my eyes adjusted to the darkness, I spotted a bartender across the room. I stepped farther into the building and noticed the overwhelming scent of sweat and body odor hit me. Someone had tried to cover it up by spraying air freshener, which only made me want to puke even more.

"We're not open yet, ladies," the bartender called.

I expected to see him wiping down the counters—I'd watched a lot of movies, I supposed. Instead he was playing beer pong by himself. The man looked a little scary for my taste, even though he could be perfectly nice. He had a huge blond beard and hair with a sharp part on the side. His well-muscled arms were covered with tattoos, and when he talked each word was said with a grunt.

"We're not here as customers," I started. "We have a few questions for you."

He stared at the baby carrier in my hands, bounced one more ping-pong ball against the counter, and turned long enough to watch it land in one of the shot glasses. “Shoot.”

“Do you recognize this woman?” Jamie held up a picture of Katie on her phone.

He didn’t even look at the picture. Instead, he looked back and forth from Jamie to me. “You the cops?”

I shook my head no. “No. Just two people who are concerned.”

“I’m the cop,” a voice said behind us.

I turned and saw Chase standing there. He cast a scowl my way before flashing his badge at the bartender and walking closer.

“Detective Chase Dexter. I was hoping to ask you a few questions.” He cast me one last glance, edging in front of me.

“Of course.”

“Was this woman in here on Saturday?” He held up a photo of Katie.

The bartender glanced at it. “Yes, she was.”

“What do you remember about her?”

The bartender shrugged and picked up a rag. “Can’t forget her. She and this guy got into a shouting match.”

“This guy?” Chase held up another photo, this time of Gage.

“No, not him. This guy had dark hair. He was taller. Lanker. No idea what his name was.”

I set Jonah’s carrier down on a stool beside me as my arm muscles strained under the weight of holding it. He looked up at me and smiled.

He was such a good baby. He deserved some answers.

“What were they yelling about?” Chase asked.

The bartender shrugged, looking nonplussed by the entire situation. “Not really sure, but it looked heated. She ended up storming out of here. We had the guy escorted out about ten minutes later."

"You have no idea who he was?" Chase continued.

The bartender shook his head. "No idea. Never seen him before. Don't care if I ever see him again. This is supposed to be a feel-good place, not couples' therapy."

"Can I borrow your phone?" I asked Jamie, really missing my old one.

She jerked her eyebrows upward before handing it to me. I found Katie's profile there and did a search under her friends for anyone named Heathcliff. A picture popped up.

I blinked when I saw it. With a name like Heathcliff, I'd imagined someone who was a part of society's upper crust. This guy looked like a punk. Like trouble. Like the kind of guy who'd make me cringe if I met him in a dark alley.

"Was this the guy?" I held up Jamie's phone.

The bartender paused from his work for long enough to nod. "That's him."

Chase cast another look my way before nodding toward the bartender and sliding a card across the counter. "If you remember anything else, will you give me a call?"

"Sure thing."

Then Chase turned to me. "Can I have a word?"

"Sure thing," I echoed the bartender's sentiments as I braced myself for the chastising I was sure would come.

***

"What are you doing here?" Chase asked as soon as we stepped onto the sidewalk.

I nestled near the building, trying to avoid the breeze. "Just asking questions."

"With Jonah with you?" He nodded down toward the

baby.

My defenses rose, and my spine tightened. "It's not club hours yet. There was nothing dangerous about being there at this time of day."

"It's not smart." His jaw flexed as he stared down at me.

I tilted my head up, all thoughts of being polite disappearing. "You think I should stay inside indefinitely and make a little prison out of my house?"

His eyes narrowed but his shoulders loosened ever so visibly. "That's not what I said."

Jamie pointed behind her, a dramatically awkward expression on her face. "How about if I take Jonah and walk back toward the car?"

I didn't say anything, just handed her the keys from my purse. It was better if no one heard the rest of this conversation because I was sure it wouldn't be pretty.

"You shouldn't be out here, Holly." Chase lowered his voice as Jamie's footsteps faded in the distance. "Leave the investigation to the police. Did you forget that there's already one person dead? We don't know who's responsible or what role the baby plays in all of this. You're setting yourself up as a target."

My jaw hardened this time. "Don't be a jerk, Chase."

His eyebrows flinched upward, as if my words surprised him. The surprise quickly turned to frustration then empathy. "I'm not being a jerk. I just worry about you. I try to keep you safe. I do, but I feel like you're working against me sometimes."

"I'm just trying to figure out this catawampus case!"

"Catawampus?"

"Yeah, you know . . . not arranged correctly."

"I know what it means, Holly."

"I was just asking questions." Weariness crept into my

tone. We weren't married. We might not ever be. I was free to be my own person and make my own choices.

"Asking questions can get you into trouble. I thought you would have realized that by now."

Fire flashed through me. "And I thought you would have realized that asking questions is just a part of who I am. It's what I do. I refuse to sit back and be a wallflower. I refuse to let life take me wherever the current is running. I feel like my calling in life is to speak for the voiceless. I thought you knew that about me."

We stared off at each other, and my heart pounded against my ribcage as I waited for what he would say next. He didn't look happy—at all. His hands were on his hips; his eyes were narrowed; and his lips pulled into a grim line.

But I refused to apologize or back down.

Finally, he let out a long sigh and slumped his shoulders. He raked a hand through his hair, looking away for a moment. "I don't want to fight with you. I'm sorry, Holly. I just won't forgive myself if anything happens to you."

My heart softened some. I didn't want to fight with Chase either. "I'm a big girl, Chase. I like the fact that you protect me, but I'm not your responsibility. I'm prepared to deal with the decisions I make."

He stepped closer, and his hands went to my waist. His eyes looked smoky, and his voice cracked as he said, "I just don't want to lose you like I lost Hayden."

His brother had been killed, and the anger over what had happened gripped Chase more than he wanted to let on. It didn't come out in violent ways, but it was always there, simmering in the back of his mind. It occupied his thoughts. Could turn his life upside down at any minute. Might control him, if he let it.

I squeezed his arm as pain flashed in his gaze. I hated to see him hurting, especially since he was the guy who was always there for people, who was always there for me. "I know, Chase."

He ran a hand over his face and stepped back. "Let's not do this anymore, Holly."

My heart panged. Do what? Date? Was he breaking up?

I placed a hand over my stomach as bile churned there. "What do you mean?"

"Let's not fight."

In an instant, my stress flushed through me. *Fight*. I could handle that better than breaking up. Much better. Even if I was having doubts and even if there was friction between us, I wasn't ready to call it quits. "I like that idea."

He pulled me into a hug, right there on the busy sidewalk. I nestled in his overpowering arms, not even caring if it was improper to show such PDA. I couldn't stand it when my relationships were out of balance. It always left me feeling unsettled and uneasy.

"You're definitely someone I want on my side and not working against me," he murmured in my ear.

I smiled. "I want to be on your side also. I don't like it when we fight."

When he released me, I stepped back. My heart still pounded as adrenaline surged through me after all that had happened. Almost hesitantly, Chase seemed to drop his hand. He scanned the area—probably for any sign of trouble—before looking back at me.

"Now, who was the guy in the picture back there?" he asked.

"Heathcliff Caswell—Katie Edwards' ex-boyfriend."

A mixture of amusement and exhaustion flickered in his

gaze. "I'm not even going to ask how you know that."

I shrugged, really not wanting to get into it anyway. "It's probably better that way."

"I'm going to question him and see what he knows. We've had no success in locating Katie yet. I thought you'd want to know that her fingerprints were found on the gun."

The words made me pause, made my thoughts race. Had Katie done it? There had to be other viable theories like . . . "Could have been left from when she handled it earlier."

"They were bloody fingerprints, indicating she handled it—finger on the trigger—after touching his blood."

"Whose gun?"

"It wasn't registered to her. It was actually stolen."

"Stolen?"

He nodded.

Where had Katie gotten a stolen gun? There was obviously a lot more to this story than I could comprehend. "Did any of the neighbors hear anything?"

"There was a silencer on the gun," Chase said. "No one heard a thing. It doesn't help that there are train tracks nearby."

A silencer? In my mind, only someone experienced would know about those. Katie didn't seem like the type. "I doubt Katie would know how to use a silencer."

"We really don't know anything about Katie, Holly. She could know a lot more about weapons than we think."

My throat clenched. I wasn't sure why I felt the need to defend her. I didn't even know her. But I knew Jonah, and I supposed that was why. "If you're sure she's guilty, why question everyone else?"

"We're not sure she's guilty. Besides, we need to find her—guilty or not. Maybe this Heathcliff guy has some answers for us."

I raised my hands in surrender. "I'll let you question him—and just you. Being a temporary mom and part-time detective has been exhausting, and all I want right now is to go home and have some dinner."

"It sounds like a good plan."

"And while you're questioning people, there was a lady at the gym Katie was having problems with. You may want to talk to her also. Rhonda's Fitness over in Kentucky."

He let out an airy chuckle. "You are one determined lady."

"I try to make that work in my favor as much as possible." I paused. "I guess dinner at my house tonight is out?"

He frowned. "Tonight is out, unfortunately. I'm sorry, Holly."

I shrugged, not wanting to make him feel bad. He shouldn't feel bad. He was doing his job—and it was a noble job at that. "Figure out the answers for Jonah, Chase. He deserves them."

***

"Well, that was awkward," Jamie announced when I climbed into the car.

I twisted my key in the ignition, the fire in my blood simmering. "Sorry."

"You want to talk about it?"

I put the car in Drive, ready to get back to my place and unwind. Though I'd defended myself to Chase, a touch of guilt crept in. Was I being irresponsible? What if my actions had put Baby Jonah in danger? I couldn't live with myself if something happened to him that I could have prevented.

"There's nothing to really talk about," I finally said.

"Well, you know I'm here if you need me."

"I know, Jamie. Thank you. Right now, I just want to go home and process everything. Maybe this was all a mistake."

She didn't say anything as I cruised back down the road toward my house. Jonah cooed in the back seat, breaking me from my somberness. Maybe Chase was right. The best thing I could do was stay home and take care of Jonah until we had some answers. I needed to build a little nest around him to keep him safe and sheltered. But would even that work? After all, someone had tried to break into my home.

"Is this a bad time to give you an update?" Jamie asked.

Part of me screamed yes! But the other part of me wanted to know what she'd learned. Listening could do no harm, right? "Let's hear it."

"I did a little search on this Heathcliff guy, and this is what I found out. He's thirty. He works for the railroad. He's originally from Cincinnati. Not to sound all judgy-judgy, but he looks like a punk. It's the way he's dressed—jeans sagging well below his waist, the I've-got-no-fashion-sense white tank top, the defiant expression. I'm sure you can imagine."

Yes, I certainly could. How we presented ourselves, whether we liked it or not, was exceedingly important when making first impressions. People didn't like to acknowledge it—and it wasn't always right—but stereotypes became stereotypes for a reason.

"Did you get on his social media account?" I asked.

"Girl, you know I did. Thankfully, he hasn't set his profile to private, so I could access quite a bit. He did check in at Club 21 on Saturday evening. He posted this late Saturday night: Some women just string you along in an effort to get their way. They ain't worth it. Now or ever. Good riddance. Wordy dird. Wordy dird. Wordy dird. Wordy dird."

Translation: bleep, bleep bleep.

My heart stammered in my chest. That didn't sound good.

Good riddance? Was he saying goodbye to Gage? To Katie? To both of them?

The mystery surrounding Jonah's mom continued to grow, and, at every turn, I seemed to have more questions and fewer answers.

"Holly, check that out." Jamie pointed in the distance.

I looked up and saw that same sedan from earlier behind us.

My muscles tensed as I realized we were being followed.

CHAPTER 13

"Why do people like following us so much?" I mumbled as I wove in and out of rush-hour traffic.

"That's a great question." Jamie glanced behind us again, her earrings bobbing at the sudden motion.

I pulled my gaze back to the road in front of me. "Can you see the driver?"

"No, the windows are too dark. The good news is that the driver isn't being aggressive."

"That is good news." My hands tightened on the wheel. What should I do? Try to lose them? Try to turn the tables and follow them instead, in one of those the-hunted-becomes-the-hunter type of ways?

I'd rather just be baking cookies.

But was that the truth? You couldn't prove it by my actions as of late.

"Can you see the license plate?" I asked, trying to get as much information as possible. I glanced in the rearview mirror for long enough to see Jamie craning her neck.

"I can't make it out. Maybe slow down some."

I hesitated before easing my foot off the accelerator. Chase's reprimand echoed in my head. Jonah. I had to think about Jonah.

If it was just Jamie and me out here, I wouldn't think

twice about following every lead. But how did I do that while being responsible?

With that thought, I pressed the accelerator again.

"You're speeding up?" Jamie asked.

"I can't let whoever that is get too close," I said. "Not if it puts Jonah in danger."

"Follow your gut. Like I said, the driver isn't being aggressive right now, but we don't want to do anything to change that."

My heart slowed slightly. I just needed to get to safety. Or lose them. I needed to lose them safely.

Was it Katie following us? After all, she'd most likely left that note that day at the coffeehouse. Or what if it was Heathcliff, if he was desperate to get back the baby whom he thought was his flesh and blood. Maybe he knew a judge would never award him custody. I was making assumptions here, but he could very likely have a criminal history.

With those thoughts, I turned onto a side street. The move was risky because this area was more secluded. But it would also expose the driver following me. I hoped it might dissuade this person from continuing any farther.

The tension threaded in my neck pulled tighter as I glanced in the rearview mirror.

Would the driver follow? Or had my plan worked?

The air left my lungs when I realized the car had continued straight.

Thank goodness, they hadn't followed us.

We were safe. For now.

How did I ensure it stayed that way?

***

The next morning was the home inspection.

I'd been pleasantly surprised to find that Ralph had purchased a crib. He'd set it up in the spare bedroom when I was gone yesterday. He'd also bought a little green dinosaur rattle that Jonah was now obsessed with. It was just the right size to hold in his hand and stare at, try to gum, and hit himself in the face with.

I hadn't been sure which social worker would be assigned to my case, but I was happy to see Bethany Ellis show up. I'd worked with her a few times, and I thought she was kind and fair, two traits that were essential in social work. The woman was young—probably twenty-four—and she had a slim build, light-brown hair to her shoulders, and glasses.

She'd walked through the house and examined every little nook and cranny—and that was only after she'd loved on Jonah for a little while.

Finally, she paused at the front door. "Well, everything looks good."

Relief washed through me. "Great. I'm not sure why I was so nervous."

"I'm sure everyone is a little nervous. It's the people who aren't nervous who make me suspicious." She offered a gentle smile. "I have to admit, I didn't know you lived with your mom still. It's a bit of an unusual situation for a foster mom."

It was true. My mom had to go through the whole approval process with me. Sometimes I wondered if I would have been approved if I hadn't been a social worker. The situation wasn't exactly traditional.

"I'll move out eventually. I was about to when my father passed away, and it made me sad to think about my mom being in this big house all by herself."

Bethany nodded and tilted her head. "I understand. You

have the rest of your life to be on your own, right?"

"That's right." Sometimes I did have dreams about owning my own home. I pictured how I would decorate it and what I would plant in my garden and hosting parties.

My mother wasn't as fragile as I thought she was. I knew that. But if I could do anything to ease her grief, I wanted to do that.

I paused near the door with Jonah on my hip. I didn't want to ask my next question, mostly because I was afraid of the answer. But I knew I couldn't remain in the dark, that it wouldn't be healthy.

"Now that you know the name of Jonah's mother, will you be looking for extended family for guardianship?" As soon as I asked the question, I wanted to snatch it back. Time seemed to stand still as I waited for her answer.

"As I'm sure you know, placement with the family is usually our first choice. However, we're working off the assumption that the baby's mother wanted you to watch him—provided she's the one who actually left him. It's really too early to know how all of this will play out."

She glanced at Jonah and smiled. "You do look good with a baby on your hip, by the way."

I felt my cheeks heat. "Thanks."

Her smile faded when her gaze met mine again. "But you do remember our mantra to get attached but not too attached?"

I swallowed hard and pulled Jonah a little closer. "Of course. I've said that many times."

And never, ever realized just how truly difficult it would be.

***

After Bethany left, I walked back into the kitchen to meet my mom.

"Well, that went well," she started, taking a sip of her tea.

"Did you hear that we discovered who Jonah's mom is?"

She nodded. "I did hear something about it. Tell me about her."

I shrugged and sat down, pulling my hair away from Jonah's mouth. He studied me, and I had to force myself to look away from his baby blues. "I don't know much. Her name is Katie Edwards."

"You didn't recognize her?"

I shook my head. "No, not really. I mean, she seems vaguely familiar but . . ."

"What does she look like?"

I handed Jonah to my mom, grabbed the tablet from the table, and found Katie Edwards' picture via social media. I showed it to Mom, and she studied the photo a moment.

"You know who she reminds me of?"

"No idea."

"Katie Mallard from youth group when you were growing up."

"Katie Mallard?" I nearly snorted at the absurdity of her statement. Until I looked more closely at the picture. I supposed there were similarities. But . . . "They have different last names. And this Katie isn't married."

"But has she ever been married?"

That was a great question. I didn't know the answer, and I hadn't thought to ask.

"The Katie from high school youth group has a slightly different nose. Lighter hair. And she was heavier."

"So she had a nose job, dyed her hair, and lost weight. It wouldn't be that unusual."

I looked at the picture again and tried to picture the changes. Could my mom be right? I couldn't say she was, but I couldn't say she wasn't either.

"It just wouldn't make sense, Mom," I muttered.

"What do you mean?"

"That Katie hated me. Don't you remember all the nasty things she used to say? Holly Anna the Pollyanna? Ms. Perfect. Ms. Hoity Toity. Ms. Prim and—"

Mom raised her hand. "I get it. And I do remember she gave you a hard time. She was . . . kind of troubled, right?"

I tried to remember all the details. "That's right. Her dad was out of the picture. Her mom was a drug addict. She started coming to church with Karla Maples—who was also slightly troubled." By troubled I just meant they had a hard home life and dealt with many of the difficulties that came with that, sometimes in less than positive ways.

I'd tried to reach out and befriend both Katie and Karla, but they'd had no interest in being my friend. In fact, I thought they liked antagonizing me. They always whispered when I was around, scoffed at things I said during group discussions, and made sure there was no room for me at our church's lunch table at an area-wide youth event.

I'd tried my best to ignore the duo, and I had some great friends in youth group, which had made it easier.

But Katie had acted like she hated me. Hated me.

If this was the same Katie—and with every minute that passed I became more certain of that fact—why had she chosen me to take care of her baby? Or was the social worker right—what if someone else had left Jonah?

The front door opened and someone yelled, "Hey,

everyone!"

I recognized Alex's voice. Besides, only a handful of people came in without invitation.

She appeared in the kitchen a few seconds later, tall and well put together. That was my sister, Alex, for you. An overachiever to the max, just like the rest of my family.

Except my dad.

I was more like my dad, and I missed him every day since he'd died.

Alex dropped some mail on the table and turned all of her attention on Jonah. While Mom filled her in, I ruffled through the letters. I stopped by one addressed to me. I slid my nail beneath the fold and popped it open.

When I saw what was inside, I frowned.

"What is it?" my mom asked.

I shook my head. "It's . . . it's nothing. Just an invitation to another baby shower."

"You love stuff like that!"

I nodded, my heart surprisingly burdened. "I do. I really do. And I'm happy for Harper and her husband. They're going to be great parents."

"Then why do you look so melancholy?" Alex asked, stealing a raspberry cheesecake cookie and sitting down.

"I guess all of this," I motioned toward Jonah and the invitation, "is stirring some buried feelings inside me."

"You're realizing your biological clock is ticking? Just think: I'm ten years older. Can you imagine how I feel?" Alex gave me a pointed look.

"I can only imagine." And that made me wonder if Alex and William were trying to have a baby. The thought was strange to me only because assistant district attorney Alex and her surgeon husband had always been so career oriented. I'd just assumed that neither wanted any children.

And then there was Ralph. His first wife had died tragically in a car accident after only six months of marriage. He hadn't really dated anyone since.

My mom might be waiting a long time before she actually became a grandma.

"Oh, Holly." My mom held Jonah up and scrunched her nose. "I smell a dirty diaper. It looks like Jonah left a present for you. Welcome to motherhood!"

CHAPTER 14

The weather turned out to be surprisingly balmy today. Even though it was January, the day crept up into the fifties as a mini-warm front pushed into the area. Forecasters said it would only be temporary and the weather would be cold again tomorrow.

I wasn't complaining.

I needed to clear my head, so I loaded Jonah into the stroller and decided to take a walk. I headed toward a park not terribly far away, figuring I might as well enjoy this weather. Most children would be in school during this hour.

Jonah smiled at me as I pushed him, and my heart melted a little more. It was going to be hard when he wasn't with me anymore. Though he'd only been under my care since Sunday, I was finally feeling more comfortable and adjusted to caring for a baby. He'd slept all night yesterday, and life was beginning to feel halfway normal.

I reached the park—a little hillside area with a few swings, a slide, and an open field for kids to play flag football—and I sat on a bench in the sunshine, which made me feel about ten degrees warmer. I gently eased the stroller back and forth, trying to keep Jonah happy while telling him stories about playing here myself as a child.

About how my dad would bring me here and see how high he could push me on the swing, which would then freak out my mother. I remembered having a family reunion at a sheltered picnic area here one year where we'd had watermelon eating contests and laughed until our sides hurt. It had been one of the few times I could remember my mother letting down her hair. She was usually prim, proper, and reserved.

Jonah listened to every word I said, even responding with little gurgles and grunts. "You're just the most handsome little man ever," I whispered, brushing his cheek. He grabbed my hand in response and tried to bring it into his mouth.

Something was changing in me. It seemed weird, and I didn't know what it was. But, whatever it was, it was there, nagging at my subconscious.

Maybe it was because I was approaching thirty. Maybe something internal was telling me it was time for my next phase in life. Time for me to grow up. To make—and achieve—some new life goals. To stop living like I was right out of college.

The thoughts seemed so foreign. For the past couple of years, I'd had no doubt that I was supposed to stay at home with my mom so we could grieve together. I'd taken each phase of life as it came—including giving up my career in social work to work for my brother.

But now I wanted a place of my own, a family, trips to Disney together, and backyard barbecues.

Maybe I'd been in denial. Maybe I'd try to insist to myself that I was okay with where I'd been. But Jonah had awakened something in me.

Before I could mourn my lost dreams anymore, someone sat down on the bench beside me. The woman must have come up behind me, because I hadn't even seen her approaching. As I scooted over to give her room, I did a double take.

I'd seen this woman somewhere before, I realized.

Around the neighborhood? No.

Then where?

At the crime scene yesterday.

At Katie's house.

She was the woman standing at the police tape, the one who'd caught my eye because of her nervous glances.

My muscles tightened when I realized her presence here was no accident. She nervously twisted her hands in her lap, sat up straight, and stared ahead. The air between us seemed to change.

Was she dangerous?

I scooted the stroller to the other side of me and lifted up a quick prayer for safety.

Dear Lord, watch over us.

Was it too late for me to run? To call for help?

"I need your help," the woman whispered, still staring straight ahead.

My fingers tightened around the handle of the stroller. "Do I know you?"

She pressed her lips together, each of her actions stoic and almost robotic. "I saw you yesterday. At the crime scene. You were talking with the detective like you knew him."

My uneasiness grew deeper, fiercer. "How'd you know I was here?"

She shrugged, her hands still twisting nervously in her lap. "I followed you. I didn't have any other choice. I knew I wouldn't be able to get in touch otherwise."

The tension continued to grow in me. She'd been following me? How had I not noticed that? And why were all these people following me lately?

"Are you the one in the sedan?" The sedan that had been everywhere. In front of my house. At Club 21. Who knew where else?

"In the sedan?" She shook her head. "I drive a red compact. As soon as I figured out where you lived, I stopped following you because I didn't want to creep you out."

Too late!

"What's your name?"

"You can call me Violet."

Violent Violet. It rhymed. But that wasn't a sign, I reminded myself. Just a coincidence. Assumptions weren't good manners, but in an emergency situation, all those rules went out the window.

"What do you need my help with, Violet?" My throat clenched until I could hardly breathe. I honestly hadn't thought coming to the park would be dangerous. In fact, I thought the fresh air would be good for me, for Jonah.

I scanned the street, looking for Officer Truman's car. Of course, I didn't see it.

The woman's gaze darted around, some of her porcelain-doll-like façade cracking. "My brother died a month ago. It was . . . authorities said it was a suicide."

"How horrible. I'm sorry."

"Thank you. His name was Bo. He worked in advertising and loved rock climbing."

I waited for her to continue. She still stared straight ahead, and that was when I wondered if she was battling grief or fear? Or maybe both?

"Bo was diagnosed with cancer two years ago. He had some horrible surgeries, some dreadful treatments, and a grueling recovery. He was eventually cancer free. But afterward he was different. The experience changed him."

I could understand that. When the doctor had told me I had a year to live, something had clicked inside me also. I wasn't the same person today as I was twelve months ago.

"I see," I told her.

"I thought at first that it was just the whole experience of nearly dying that was making him act differently. But then, it went beyond that. He was secretive. Behaving strangely. I think he got caught up in something. I think he got in over his head."

"Like what?" I continued rocking the stroller back and forth, hoping Jonah stayed happy until I finished this conversation. Violet had hooked me and reeled me in.

Her expression tightened. "I don't know. I really don't. Maybe drugs. Maybe weapons. Whatever it was, it was illegal. He'd been struggling with money after his treatments. The bills were astronomical. Then suddenly, he seemed to have more money than he knew what to do with."

"But he killed himself?" I clarified. "After getting a second chance at life?"

Violet swallowed hard. "That's what authorities said. But I just don't believe it."

"So how are you connected with Gage?"

"I found Gage's contact information in my brother's phone. I went to him to see how they knew each other."

"What did Gage say?"

"He said he was looking into a story idea involving my brother, but he couldn't tell anyone what he'd discovered so far. He needed to have all of his evidence lined up before he could go public."

All of his evidence lined up? What did that mean?

"He didn't give any hints?"

She shook her head. "None. But when I mentioned that Bo had come into money and that he may have gotten it illegally, it was like there was a spark of recognition in his eyes."

Very interesting. "What were you doing at Gage's

girlfriend's house that day?"

"I wanted to check and see if he'd discovered anything about my brother. Katie thought Gage was cheating on her with me."

Realization dawned on me. "You're the one her best friend saw him with at the hotel downtown?"

The woman jerked her head ever-so-slightly toward me, as if surprised. "Yes, I am. I work there. He met me on a lunch break. Anyway, Katie confronted me. I tracked her down to apologize a few days earlier, so I knew where she lived." Violet shook her head. "I just don't feel like I can move forward until I have answers."

Neither did Chase, and it had been three years. Death of a loved one wasn't meant to be simply gotten over. It took a long time to process, even longer if they'd died violently.

"Why did you find me, Violet?"

"You know the cops. Maybe you can get me answers."

"About your brother's death?"

She shrugged. "About his death. About Gage's death. They're connected. I know they are."

"I don't have much to go on. The police are doing everything they can to find answers."

She turned toward me fully, her gaze latched onto mine. "There was something marked on Bo's calendar for this Thursday night. He wrote 5th and Vine."

"Why do you think that's connected?"

"I don't know for sure. He usually put things on his phone, so the fact he marked it on his calendar . . . maybe he was trying to conceal it? I'm not sure. I was hoping you could pass that information along to the police."

"It would mean more coming from you. Why not tell them yourself?"

"Because I don't want to end up dead like Gage."

CHAPTER 15

Officer Truman was inside the house talking to my mom when I arrived back. They sat at the breakfast table, sipping coffee and nibbling on cookies—*again*. Their conversation seemed light-hearted and warm. Or, at least it had until I walked in. Then they both sat up straight and acted like they'd been caught doing something wrong.

I hardly had time to care, simply because my mind still lingered on the conversation I'd just had. As soon as Violet had told me what she wanted, she'd run off before I could ask more questions. I might have chased her except it didn't seem safe considering I had Jonah with me.

It was so strange. I was still trying to piece everything together, but nothing seemed to fit. Not yet, at least.

"Holly, how was your walk?" My mom smoothed her black skirt and matching jacket.

"Good," I decided not to tell her about Violet. There was no need of pulling her into this circus. She worried about me enough without adding recaps of twisted conversations with strangers to her list.

She touched her earring and exchanged a smile with Officer Truman.

Something about the action caused me to pause. The smile . . . it was almost hidden. Familiar. Secretive.

I glanced back and forth between the two of them. Certainly my mom wasn't thinking about dating again . . . right? My dad had been dead only two years. You didn't get over the love of your life in two years.

"I just stopped by to check on you all." Officer Truman stood, like he was wrapping up his time here.

"Well, isn't that sweet of you."

He nodded at my mom, almost seeming hesitant to leave. "Please, let me know if you need anything. Anything at all."

Mom's cheeks filled with color. "We appreciate that. You have a good day. And be safe."

As Truman started toward the door, I decided to walk him out, halfway surprised that my mom didn't jump up and fight me for the job.

Truman paused at the door, his kind eyes observing me for a minute. "So your mom tells me you're dating Chase?"

I nodded, surprised that the conversation had taken this turn. Perhaps he was just trying to initiate a conversation, though. "That's right. We've got one year under our belt."

His eyes crinkled at the sides. "It takes a special girl to date a cop. Especially a homicide detective."

His words caught me by surprise. "Why's that?"

He let out a low breath and shrugged, as if trying to backtrack some. "I'm sure you've heard about the divorce rate among cops. It's high. Among homicide detectives? It's even higher."

I swallowed hard. It seemed like I had heard that before, but I hadn't given it much thought. It hadn't seemed important at the time. "I see," I finally said.

He seemed to realize what he was saying and stopped himself. His grin slipped and he waved a hand in the air. "I don't know why I'm telling you this. Ignore me. Anything is possible with God."

Just then, there was a knock at the door. Relief filled me that I'd be able to get out of this conversation. I didn't know where else to go with it. First of all, Chase and I weren't married. Second, I didn't plan on ever getting divorced. I was sure most people didn't. But I was one pretty stubborn girl when it came to stuff like that.

I opened the door and saw none other than Chase himself. "Chase. I wasn't expecting to see you."

He kissed my cheek. "I had a few minutes."

He and Truman exchanged a few words before Truman scooted out the door.

Chase followed me into the kitchen. After a few minutes of small talk with my mom, he said, "Could I speak with you a minute, Holly?"

"Of course."

"I'm going to pull some more boxes down from the attic. You guys can have all the time you need." Mom scurried out of the room, and I turned to Chase.

"Can I get you some coffee?" There I went, falling into polite mode. When all else failed, be courteous. That seemed to be my MO. Mary Poppins and I had a lot in common.

"No, I'm fine, Holly. I have an update on the case. I figured you would want to know about it."

I lowered myself at the table, thrilled that he'd even thought to share anything with me. "Okay . . ."

Chase sat across from me, looking surprisingly stiff and professional. "First of all, the fingerprint left on the windowpane outside your house has a match."

I braced myself for what he'd say next. "Who?"

"Nick Nixon."

I blinked, trying to recognize the name.

"We suspect he's responsible for several break-ins in the area. He left prints at one other home that was broken into, but we couldn't track him down. Not until this morning, that is."

"Did he confess to being here?" I asked.

Chase shook his head. "He hasn't owned up to anything. But we're still working on him. I hoped it would at least put your mind at ease. We don't believe this was connected with Sweet Pea."

I glanced down at Jonah, relief filling me. "Thank you. That does make me feel better."

"I also checked on the woman at the gym who had some conflicts with Katie. She was a nasty person. However, she had an alibi for the weekend that checked out. She was visiting a friend in Florida."

"Good to know."

"And finally, I also spoke with one of Katie's coworkers today. Apparently, Katie recently came into some money. She bought herself a new wardrobe. Talked about getting a new car. Started buying her coworker drinks when they went out after work."

I raised an eyebrow. "Is that right? No idea where that money came from?"

And how did this tie in with Violet's brother, Bo? He'd also come into some money. I'd think about that more later.

Chase shook his head. "No, she never told anyone. We're looking into her financials."

I wanted to tell him what I'd learned, but I'd wait until he finished.

"There is one more thing."

"You've been a very busy detective."

He ran a hand over his face. "Yes, I have been. I tracked

down Heathcliff and talked to him about the fight he and Katie had on Saturday night. He said he's still in love with her and was trying to convince her to break up with Gage and date him again. Said her relationship with Gage was going nowhere."

"She heard that from several sources, apparently." Should Katie have listened? Would things have turned out differently if she had?

"She drank a little too much, which only escalated everything."

"It usually does." Sometimes people letting their inhibitions go was not a good thing.

Chase shifted. "Heathcliff has a record."

"What kind?"

"Black market weapons dealing. He's not a good guy, Holly. You should stay away from him."

Weapons? That was what Violet thought her brother might be caught up in.

"There was one other thing: Heathcliff mentioned that Katie was upset with Gage."

Now that sounded promising in a solve-this-case kind of way. "Did he know why?"

"He was working a lot. Obsessed with a story he was doing. We're asking at the newspaper office right now to see if they know what that story was on." Chase shifted again, his gaze heavy on mine. "I knew you'd want to know, and I have clearance to share that information since you're taking care of Jonah."

"Did you look into the name Katie Mallard, by chance?"

I'd called Chase this morning with that update.

"Yes, Katie Mallard is Katie Edwards. She was briefly married right out of high school. It only lasted about six months, but that explains her name change."

"Any word from any of Katie's relatives?" My lungs froze as I waited for his response.

"Her dad is out of the picture, and her mom died four years ago. We haven't found any other relatives. It looks like you're going to be taking care of him for a while."

A secret squeal of delight echoed from somewhere inside me. I was enjoying my time with Jonah, and I knew it was going to be hard to let him go. My heart would break if I had to release him to someone who seemed unloving.

I leaned closer, excited and nervous to share what I'd learned. "I have something I need to share with you—and I discovered it all by accident, you'll be happy to know."

His eyes narrowed. "Okay . . ."

I explained the conversation with the woman in the park to him, and he listened attentively.

"Maybe I do need some coffee," he said as I finished.

I stood and poured him a cup, giving him time to process. He took a few sips before he said anything.

"You have a theory?" he finally asked.

I shrugged. "I wish I did. I've been thinking about it since the park. Bo—the guy who died—must have been into something pretty bad. If this lady was right, he and Gage were killed over it."

"Scary thought."

"What if Heathcliff was a part of this, Chase? You said he has a criminal history? Maybe he was stealing and selling guns, and Katie went into it with him. Violet said Gage had a flash of recognition in his eyes when she told him about her brother. Maybe he realized it was all more closely tied than—closer to home—than he'd realized."

"Gage could have threatened to go to the police, he and Katie could have argued about it, and a fight could have ensued." Chase rubbed his chin. "Maybe that's when she pulled the trigger."

"It sounds like a possibility. Heathcliff could have even been there. Maybe that's why the note said 'trust no one.' Maybe Katie wanted to be sure if Heathcliff came around, claiming any biological rights to Jonah, that he would be kept far away."

"It's worth looking into."

I let out a sigh, trying to think all of this through, but coming up blank. "Any leads on Katie?"

"No, not yet." He leaned closer. "So, are we okay?"

I still needed to process my feelings on that. "I guess we're okay. Are you okay?"

He nodded slowly. "I know our conversation yesterday wasn't the most pleasant."

"It wasn't. But we have to be able to speak honestly with each other. That's important."

"I agree." He frowned. "I just feel like things are strained."

I shrugged. "Throwing a new baby into the picture probably isn't helping anything. I'm sleep-deprived and emotional. You're overworked and stressed. Put all that together and . . ."

"Yeah, I get that." He stared across the table at me a second before snapping out of it. "I guess I should get back to work."

"Yeah, thanks for stopping by and for giving me an update." I stood to walk him to the door.

As he opened the front door, I peered outside behind him but didn't spot his car—neither his police-issued sedan nor his Jeep. "Where'd you park?"

He nodded toward the street. "Right there."

I stared at a truck parked there. "But you don't have a truck."

He grinned like a kid on Christmas morning. "I do now."

I sucked on my bottom lip, certain I wasn't understanding correctly. "What do you mean?"

"I saw an advertisement on GregsList. I stopped by to check it out before work this morning, and figured it was a deal I couldn't pass up. You know my Jeep has been in the shop more lately than I've actually been able to drive it."

GregsList was an online classified site where people could post items for sale. I stared at the truck. It was black. High off the ground. A two-seater. You wouldn't get any baby seats inside it.

My gut churned, desperately unsettled. But why? Was I being an overly sensitive, overreacting girlfriend? I wasn't sure. Until I knew for sure, I decided to keep quiet. "It looks . . . nice."

"Thanks. I was hoping you'd like it."

We stood in front of each other there, like we'd done a million times before. My heart fluttered, just as it had done a million times before.

But when he leaned toward me, it felt like time stopped around me. His lips met mine sweetly, softly. Then he stepped away, his gaze heavy yet filled with emotions I couldn't read.

I couldn't help but think something between us was changing.

CHAPTER 16

"He actually bought a truck?" Jamie stuck a piece of celery in her mouth and crunched down.

She'd stopped by a few minutes after Chase left, on her way home from doing an interview. I held Jonah at the kitchen table, every five seconds or so making a silly face that would light up his expression with a smile. In between those moments, we talked and Jamie ate her veggies. Ella crooned in the background, singing about "Every Time We Say Goodbye."

I was being a good girl, staying home, staying safe, and picking at a lemon cake someone from church had brought by.

I remembered Jamie's question about Chase's truck and turned my gaze away from Jonah. "Am I overreacting? Because I don't want to be one of those women who are needy and controlling. That's what I'm struggling with right now."

"I don't think you're needy or controlling, Holly. I get what you're concerned about."

I leaned back in my chair. "I mean, that's a big purchase. And it's not one of those I-want-to-be-a-family-man types of purchases. It's a two-seater. No room for anyone else. I just feel like if we're supposed to be together in the future that he'd at least mention something to me about buying a new vehicle."

"I'm sensing trouble in paradise."

I shrugged. "I don't know. I am awfully tired lately. We

haven't been seeing each other as much because of work and other life circumstances. I think it's all just getting to me."

"I get that."

"And Jonah is stirring up feelings that I haven't wanted to acknowledge."

She touched her stomach. "I know what you're saying, Girlfriend. You mean that your uterus is crying it out?"

"My uterus is . . . crying out?" Was that what she said?

She nodded, like it was a perfectly normal expression. "You know, your biological clock is ticking." She made a little ticking-time-bomb sound.

I reluctantly nodded because I would have never worded it that way. "Yes, I suppose."

She patted the top of my hand and waved a piece of celery at me. "I'll pray for you . . . and your uterus."

"Thanks, Jamie. My uterus can use all the prayers it can get." I stifled a giggle but quickly sobered. "You know, I've learned that it's much easier to give other people relationship advice than it is to apply that to my own life."

"We're not objective about our own problems. I think you told me that once."

My mind wandered, reviewing today. As I did, I rubbed Jonah's cheek and he offered a toothless grin. The sight of it made all my problems feel like they could melt away.

"In other news, I've been wondering if my mom is interested in Officer Truman," I said.

Jamie's eyes widened, matching the wide "O" of her lips. "Your mom? I didn't think she had any interest in starting a new relationship or doing the boyfriend/girlfriend thing."

That thought was so foreign to me . . . and slightly disturbing. My mom couldn't date. It was just too weird. "I didn't either. Maybe she doesn't. There was just something about the look in her eyes, though, that made me wonder."

Jamie abandoned her celery and leaned toward me. All of her attention was on me in a typical BFF-turned-shrink mode. "How would you feel about that?"

The question caused all kinds of complexities to twist inside me. "I'm not sure. I mean, I want my mom to be happy. But the thought of her being with someone other than my dad . . . it's hard to swallow."

I felt like I'd be betraying my dad by supporting something like that. After all, the two of them belonged together. They'd had a happy life and were married for almost forty years. They'd still be together if cancer hadn't stolen my dad away too early.

Jamie picked up another piece of celery. "Your mom is still relatively young. What is she? Fifty-nine?"

I nodded. She was almost sixty, and she looked great with her perfectly coiffed blonde hair and trim figure. I only hoped I'd age half as well as she did.

"She still has a lot of years left," Jamie continued, waving her celery in the air. "I know it might be hard to hear that she'd be interested in someone, but I also know you want her to be happy . . . Maybe this is a good thing. If she moves on, maybe you can too."

I couldn't deny that. More than anything I wanted my family and the people I cared about to be happy, healthy, and content. It would just be an adjustment when the day came and my mom actually did have another man in her life.

My cell phone beeped, and I glanced at the screen.

"Speaking of my mom." I put the phone to my ear. "Everything okay?"

"Holly, I forgot to bring some comps on this house with me, and I'm supposed to have a meeting with the owner. Would you be a doll and bring them by? I guess you and I both are a little scatterbrained lately since we have a baby around."

"Sure thing."

She rattled off the address, and I put Jonah into the car seat.

Before I made it to the door, my phone beeped again. This time, it was Chase. Why would he be calling again?

"I wanted to let you know that we just found a body in the Ohio River. It's a woman, probably in her twenties. We haven't been able to identify her yet."

My heart pounded in my ears. Could this be Jonah's mom? Was she dead? Just like Gage?

***

"This is a cute little house." I turned around in the entryway.

Even though it was a bungalow, it had magnificent wood floors and an open design that every host on HGTV would go crazy over. With some fresh paint and new furniture, it could make someone very happy. If someone opened the window for a few hours, the scent of an enclosed space would disappear.

"Isn't it cute?" My mom looked around also. "It's going to be perfect for a young couple who's just getting ready to start a family."

Her words caused my heart to pang. She was right. I could totally picture it.

The neighborhood itself was blue-collar with lots of other little bungalows. The yards were decent, at least for this area. It was about ten minutes away from my mom's place and ten minutes from downtown. A glance out the back window showed a stunning view of Cincinnati's skyscrapers.

"I don't think I'll have any problems selling this," my mom said, her face glowing a little more than usual. "Thanks for bringing those comps by. Where's Jonah?"

"He's in the car with Jamie. No need to haul him out since I'd be here only a few minutes. By the way, is that really what other houses in this neighborhood are going for?" I'd taken a sneak peak at the asking price when I grabbed her papers.

She nodded. "Surprisingly low, right? I mean, sure, it's a small house, but it's also affordable. It's refreshing."

I knew this area wasn't exactly sought after by many people. The crime rate surrounding this street was considered high, but this street itself looked like the people who lived here actually cared.

At once, I remembered the dead body, and sorrow filled me, along with guilt that I was going along with life like nothing had happened. What if it was Katie? If so, Jonah's life would forever be changed. He wouldn't get to experience a warm home environment with his mom.

He deserved that chance.

"Okay, well I know you need to meet with the owners, so I'll let you get to work." I put my hand on the doorknob. "Let me know if you need anything else."

"Of course, dear."

Jamie convinced me to stop by her favorite pizza place for dinner, and she grabbed a newspaper on the way in. "Check this out. Front page."

I scanned the cover story. It was on the three triathletes who'd been injured last year. And right there was Jamie Duke's byline.

"That's awesome, Jamie," I said.

I took the newspaper with me to the booth. I slid

Jonah's carrier into the seat against the wall and then read the article. She'd done a wonderful job explaining how the three men had gotten into bicycle racing later in life, how they'd met through a training program, and had become best friends. They talked about how the experience of disciplining themselves for the race had also helped them to overcome the challenges after their accident.

When I finished, I nodded. "That's a really good article, Jamie. I'm so proud of you."

She practically beamed from the other side of the booth. "Thank you."

I stared at the picture on the front. There were three men. Each were in their thirties or forties, if I had to guess. Lightning tattoos graced their necks.

"Which one is Wesley?"

Jamie pointed to the man in the middle, her grin widening. The man had a bright smile that shone through his gaze.

"He's handsome. Any updates?"

Jamie's grin faded a little. "I don't know. He's out of town doing a race with Anthony—this guy—" She pointed to the man in the middle. "This weekend. Mark—this one—is out of town at a family wedding."

"I meant, any updates on you and Wesley?"

She let out a sigh and fanned the menu over her face. I knew she didn't even need to look at the menu because she always got the same thing every time she came here to eat. Something else was making her flush.

"I like him," she finally said. "I'm not sure if he likes me."

"He would be crazy if he didn't."

The menu hit the table with a slap. "You're such a good

friend. Thank you. I don't want to be the one who pursues him, but I want to let him know that I'm interested. We text back and forth quite a bit."

"Just give it time, right? See what happens."

Jonah let out a squeal, and I rocked his carrier back and forth, determined to keep him happy.

"You're really good with kids, you know," Jamie said.

My cheeks flushed. I knew I was good with kids. I loved kids. But hearing the affirmation heartened me. "Thank you."

The waitress came and took our order. Then Jamie pulled out her electronic tablet. "While you were inside with your mom at that house she's selling, I made some progress that I wanted to fill you in on."

"Okay . . ." I tried to guess what she had to say, but I had no clue.

"So, I went onto GregsList—do you have any idea of how much stuff you can find there?"

"A lot. Chase apparently found his truck there."

She nodded. "You want baby stuff? There's a ton." Her fingers scrolled across the screen. "Here's a baby stroller for sale. There's a slide. A high chair. Here's some juice even."

"Some juice?" Speaking of juice, I took a sip of my water.

Jamie nodded. "Five hundred cases of juice boxes. Bought in bulk." Her voice changed as she read word for word. *"I've got loads of it for sale. Come get yours for cheap, Friend."*

"Weird. I don't think I'd buy food or drink from a classified site."

"It's a site that a man like Crazy Hands might use." Her eyes widened and she flexed her fingers with a psycho look in her eyes.

I made a face, trying to put the man out of my head.

"Go on."

She turned back to her tablet. "Okay, here's another one that must have gotten in the wrong category." She changed her voice again into ad-reading Jamie. *"You'll hit the jackpot with this little monkey. She's like TNT but you'll love having her around.* It's a little Yorkshire terrier."

"There are weird people out there. Unsafe people out there. You have to be careful when you go to buy anything. You've heard the news stories about people who've been robbed, beaten, or worse. Anyway, were you going somewhere with this?"

"Oh, right, right. I went on to look for babysitters with the first name of Sarah."

Just like Samantha had said. Katie had found a sitter on the site, and Sarah was her first name. "Any luck?"

"Well, I found four people named Sarah. I called each of them, inquiring about how many children they watched, etc. None of them are our person, unfortunately."

My hopes fell. "It was worth a try."

She raised a finger. "Here's the good news. There are other babysitters listed, but they don't go by their first names. They might call themselves Happy Times Babysitting or whatever. I'm trying to locate which ones are relatively close to Katie's house. Once we find out who her sitter was, we might be able to find out some more answers."

"You're brilliant."

She shrugged with mock humility. "I try. I'll call more when I have the chance."

She took a sip of her water and then leaned closer. "What did you think of that house?"

I smiled when I thought about it. "It has a lot of potential."

"You ever think about moving out?"

Her question caused a knot to form in my throat. "I'm not sure. Something is shifting in me, and I keep feeling like it's time to make some kind of life change. I don't know what that is."

"It's not getting a new best friend, right?"

I patted her hand. "No, of course not."

Just then, the pizza appeared. In response, my stomach grumbled. Right on time.

But the thought of finding Katie never strayed far from my mind. What if she was dead? What if the same person who'd killed Gage had killed her also?

And there was one other question I couldn't ignore: Who was going to die next?

CHAPTER 17

I was trying to occupy myself by making homemade baby food while Jonah took a nap. It was a bit hit–and-miss, since I'd never done anything like this before, but I was determined to see it through to completion.

I tried a sample of apple and carrot and made a face.

This stuff tasted terrible. Just terrible. How could anyone eat this stuff?

When my doorbell rang, I welcomed the interruption. I wiped my hands on a kitchen towel, smoothed my apron, and went to answer it.

A man wearing a suit stood on the other side, which instantly put me on alert. I'd never seen him before. His affable smile put me a little more at ease.

"Holly Paladin?"

I nodded, keeping the door open only a crack. "Yes?"

"I'm Jim Dawson with Children's Services."

I studied him a moment but didn't recognize him. The man was fortyish with light-brown hair in a buzz cut. He was tall and thick, and his inexpensive suit made him appear authentic—social workers *were* vastly underpaid.

But still . . . "I've never seen you before."

"I was working in Elder Protection with Kent Williamson until about three months ago. Then I moved over to the

Children's Services Division with Doris."

I recognized those names, which made me feel a little better. "Okay . . ."

"Bethany Ellis sent me over here because she's on another case right now. We have good news. We've located the child's aunt. She lives up near Cleveland, and she's on her way down to take custody of Jonah."

My heart leapt into my throat, nearly choking me. Mentally, I'd already begun reeling, trying desperately to find solid ground to hold onto. "I thought there weren't any other relatives?"

"It took us a while to locate her. Doris didn't call and let you know?"

I'd just looked on my phone and hadn't seen any missed calls. "No, she didn't."

He frowned and shifted his briefcase from one hand to another. "I'm sorry about that. I know she had a workshop to go to. Maybe she was going to call you afterward."

This was the time of year when there were lots of local and state conferences on social work. Doris very well could be at one of those.

I eyed Jim again, trying to comprehend all of this, yet, at the same time, not wanting to. "So why are you here?"

"I know this is difficult Ms. Paladin, but I'm here to take Jonah to the office and hand over custody to the aunt."

Something inside of me threw on the brakes. Was it because I'd become too attached and didn't want to give Jonah up? Was that the reason for my caution?

Or was it something else?

"Please, Ms. Paladin. Can I come in? Let's not make this harder than it has to be."

I eyeballed the man still. Sure, he knew some names

and departments. He could have gotten them online, though.

Trust no one.

Did that include social workers?

"As a former social worker yourself, you know this was a possible—and likely—outcome," Jim continued, some of his empathy waning and replaced with impatience.

You knew you were going to have to give him up, Holly. You knew it would be hard. This is what you signed up for.

Jim waited for my response.

"One minute," I finally said. I just needed some confirmation. Or maybe I needed a moment to process, to buy some time. "I need to do one thing first."

I was going to call Doris and verify this, I decided. Then I would feel better about the situation. Any respectable social worker would understand that—should even respect it.

I started to shut the door but something blocked it.

My blood pressure spiked as facts collided in my head.

Jim. Jim had blocked it.

CHAPTER 18

I threw my weight into the door.

But the man was larger and stronger than I was. I caught a glimpse of his face. His eyes had gone from kind to malicious. His frame had once seemed large, but now he seemed like a brute.

He shoved the door again. I flew back, my body slamming into the wall. My head instantly throbbed.

I ignored the pain and pushed on the door again, knowing good and well that I was fighting for more than one life right now. I had to do everything in my power to keep that baby safe.

The man smashed into the door again, sending me spiraling backward into the hard plaster for a second time. My head hit the wall again with a sickening crunch.

I tried to catch my breath—the air had left my lungs. As I did, the man pushed inside and closed the door.

He was in my house, I realized. No one outside could see what was going on.

No!

Panic welled inside me. I needed a plan. Physically, I was no match against this man.

"You should have just given him to me." Jim's—if that was his real name—eyes suddenly looked dark and shady. His nostrils flared as he hulked in front of me.

What was he going to do? And how could I stop him? My head ached too hard for me to think clearly.

The man reached for me, grabbed me by my throat, and lifted me off my feet.

My air pipe clenched under the pressure. I couldn't breathe.

I clawed at the man's hands, desperate for him to let me go.

It didn't work.

I kicked my legs. Jerked my shoulders back. Tried to scream.

Nothing worked.

"Where's the baby?" he growled as he leered in my face.

I tugged at his fingers, unable to answer. Not that I would, even if I could. But I needed air.

He finally released his grip and lowered me back to my feet.

I doubled over, heaving in deep breaths and trying to calm myself.

Before I could, he pushed me against the wall again, his body pressing into mine until cold fear spread through my veins.

"Time's up. Where is he?"

"In there." I pointed to the living room, trying to buy myself more time. "Taking a nap in the Pack 'n Play."

He sneered before grabbing my arm and pulling me with him toward the living room. My muscles and senses heightened with adrenaline because I knew what was going to happen. I might be buying time but only a little. When this man discovered I hadn't told the truth, he was going to beat me. Maybe kill me.

Then he was going to find Jonah upstairs. Literally, over my dead body.

Tears pushed at my eyes.

Dear Lord, help!

"Where is he?" the man demanded, squeezing my arm until my fingers tingled.

I pointed to the Pack 'n Play, my hand trembling uncontrollably as I did so. "I told you. There."

He shoved me into the couch and stomped across the room. I held my breath as I watched. He got to the empty Pack 'n Play and grunted. When he turned back toward me, his eyes were full of fire and rage.

Adrenaline surged in me. I glanced around, looking for something—anything!—to protect myself with. I grabbed a ceramic lamp from the end table and swung it at the man as he lunged toward me.

He raised his arm and cut me off mid-stroke. The lamp flew out of my hand and crashed on the wood floor.

Based on the fire in his eyes, I'd ticked him off even more.

But I had to keep fighting. I couldn't let him get Jonah.

I grabbed a spray bottle from the table. It was my mom's orange, vanilla, rosemary essential-oil spray. Before the man could realize what I was doing, I sprayed it in his face.

He yelped with pain and rubbed his eyes.

I scrambled away and grabbed my phone. I hit Chase's number just before something crashed into my head.

Then everything went dark.

CHAPTER 19

"Holly? Holly? Can you hear me?"

The voice echoed in the distance, sounded like it was coming from the end of a long, hollow tunnel.

Where was I? And why did my head hurt so much? Did my limbs feel heavy? Did my tongue feel like sandpaper? I tried to make sense of things, but everything spun around me. I couldn't shake the darkness, the hollowness, the fear.

The voice came again. "Holly, I need you to wake up."

I knew that voice. I'd heard it many times before.

It was Chase.

I desperately wanted to talk to him, to feel his arms around me. But somehow I couldn't reach him. It was like trying to swim through plasma.

Where was he? Where was I?

And please, Lord, make this pain stop.

The numbing ache wouldn't go away. It made me want to bury myself in the darkness again.

A groan came from somewhere. Somewhere close.

Me. Had that been me?

Open your eyes, Holly.

I tried to pry them apart using sheer willpower, but they didn't cooperate.

"She's coming to!" the familiar voice shouted. *Chase* shouted.

I sensed movement around me. Some of the tunnel sound disappeared. The voices, the movement . . . it was close. Around me. Practically on top of me.

Something else—some other detail—begged for my attention. It nagged at the back of my mind. Pleaded with me to take notice.

It was a sense of urgency. Of panic. Of despair.

Jonah.

As soon as his name entered my mind, I felt like a bolt of electricity shot through me. I pushed myself up, and my eyes shot open. My thoughts scrambled inside me.

I had to help Jonah. Now.

In a flash, everything came back to me. The intruder posing as a Children's Services caseworker. The fight. Everything going black.

Jonah.

"It's okay. Lie back down," Chase urged, his hands gripping my arms as he knelt on the floor beside me. "You're going to be okay."

My eyes hit each of the paramedics around me until falling on Chase again. Worry creased his eyes. Shards of glass surrounded me. Blood trickled on my hands.

"Where's . . . Jonah?" My words were barely intelligible to my own ears, but Chase understood. I saw it in his eyes.

I also saw the sorrow there.

"Do you remember what happened?" he asked.

One of the EMTs took my pulse and another shined a light in my eyes. I glanced beyond them and saw other first responders swarming the house. I saw a broken vase. Splinters of an old table. A lamp lying on the floor.

Details flooded back to me, each one making me flinch with fear.

As I began to speak, an oxygen mask was strapped over my face. I pushed it away. "A man. Claimed to be a caseworker. Said he came to get Jonah."

"You realized he was a fake and fought him, didn't you?" Chase asked.

"Yes." A sick feeling gurgled in my gut. "Jonah . . ."

"He's not here, Holly." His words sounded grim and full of sorrow.

Another groan escaped, and everything spun around me again.

How could I have let this happen?

Before I knew it, everything went black again.

***

When I woke up next time, I was in the hospital. Chase was still with me, and that concerned expression—one I was all too familiar with—stained his gaze.

He leaned toward me when I opened my eyes, and it was obvious he'd been sitting there for a while.

My gratefulness was quickly pushed away by another emotion—worry. Chase must have seen it because he squeezed my hand.

"Any word on Jonah?"

He shook his head, deep lines on his forehead. "Not yet, Holly. We have everyone looking for him."

That ache—the one that was quickly becoming familiar—throbbed in my chest. A guttural cry rose down deep.

"Why . . .?" It was the only question my lips could form.

"My guess?" His lips pulled down in a frown, and I could tell he was measuring his words. "Leverage."

My heart lurched again. People should never be

leverage. Especially not babies.

"It was a man at my door." Had I shared any of those details? I couldn't remember.

"I know."

"I just hope Jonah's okay," I whispered.

"I know this sounds strange, but the good news is that this man took the baby. If he'd wanted to hurt him, he could have done that without taking him."

His words brought little comfort. But he was right. Whoever this man was, he wanted Jonah alive.

"Are you okay?" Chase peered at me a moment before running his thumb down the edge of my face.

I was crying, I realized. And he'd wiped away my tears.

How was I? I wasn't even sure.

"I don't know what I am at this point," I finally said. "I'm beside myself. I don't know how I could have let this happen."

It was all my fault. I was supposed to be his protector, and I'd failed.

"Listen to me—you didn't let anything happen, Holly."

I swung my head back and forth, which made my brain spin. I closed my eyes until my world righted again. Reality hit me again, even harder this time.

"No, you were right, Chase. I should have never taken Jonah out of the house. Maybe the bad guys would never have realized I had him. Maybe he'd be safe right now." The thought caused a physical ache to form in my heart. An ache of regret, of desperation to change things, to make life right again.

"The chances are that these people would have found him anywhere. Holly, you were almost killed trying to protect him."

Another guttural sob escaped, and Chase pulled me into his strong arms. I buried myself there, wishing I could find comfort but knowing I didn't deserve it.

"I should have done more," I whispered, my voice raspy as tears poured down my cheeks. "This is all my fault."

"Holly—"

I shook my head. I wasn't looking for someone to tell me I was innocent or someone to make me feel better. I just needed to confess my sins and pay whatever price I deserved. "You tried to warn me."

Chase turned my face until I met his eyes. "The one person who's to blame is the person who snatched him from you. Understand?"

I didn't say anything. I couldn't. Because I knew the truth. I'd failed.

Before Chase could try to placate me anymore, the doctor walked into the room. It was just as well because there was nothing else to say.

***

After I'd talked to the doctor and he'd told me about my concussion, as well as some minor scrapes and bruises, he said I could go home in the afternoon. I'd already been here through the night, and a midmorning sun shone in the sky outside my window. Right now, they wanted to keep me for observation.

I'd sent Chase away, insisting he needed to go find Jonah instead of babysitting me. If anyone could do it, it was Chase.

Another detective had stopped by and taken my official statement. Detective Reynolds was from the Special Investigations, and he'd be specifically handling Jonah's abduction. Chase wasn't officially working the case, but I knew he'd help out. There was also a good chance the FBI would be called in to help.

My mom and Ralph had shown up to check on me in the meantime and had ended up staying an hour. They'd tried to keep me occupied and take my mind off what had happened. It was no use. Jonah was the only person on my mind.

Was he scared? Was the man who'd snatched him taking good care of him? Where was he now?

Did the man realize that Jonah liked to eat every few hours? Or realize what kind of formula he liked? He got gassy if he drank the wrong one.

I knew Jonah had only been under my care for a few days, but we'd just gotten into our routine. I was finally learning what he liked and what he didn't.

Now he was gone.

More tears pushed to my eyes.

Someone knocked at my door. I fully expected to see Alex, but, to my surprise, it was Evan. He had yellow daisies in his hand.

"Come in," I called, pushing myself up in bed.

He strode into the room and handed me a bouquet of flowers. "For you."

I couldn't help but smile as I took them. "Thank you. This was kind."

"You're welcome."

I eyed him for a moment, trying to remember if I'd seen him earlier. The man was definitely handsome and affable. He was obviously assigned the area where I lived because I'd seen him numerous times over the past few days.

"Were you at my house after . . . ?" I couldn't finish my sentence.

His expression sobered. "I was."

"So you know what happened?" My throat burned with

more intensity with every word.

He nodded. “I do. I’m sorry, Holly. I can’t imagine how you must feel.”

I sucked in a long, shaky breath and tried to compose myself. I really wanted to get out of here. I’d sent everyone else away so I could console myself privately. But Evan was here out of the kindness of his heart, and I couldn’t repay that with rudeness.

“Why do you keep showing up?” I asked. Sure, our paths had crossed a few times. We had a couple of things in common—mainly the fact that we both liked to help others. But it was unusual that he’d gone out of his way like this.

His eyes twinkled and he offered a shallow shrug. “Because you’re lucky.”

My smile dipped. “You know I’m taken, right?” I just had to set the record straight. I realized this could be an awkward conversation, but it needed to be said to clear the air.

Those sparkling eyes locked on mine. “I don’t see a ring on your finger.”

“I’m not that girl, Evan.” I had to put my foot down.

He glanced over his shoulder as if to make sure we were alone. “I hate to see you waiting for a guy like that.”

A rock formed in my gut. Was he talking about Chase? He had to be. I pushed myself up higher, not letting his comment go. “What do you mean ‘a guy like that’?”

“He’s the type that likes to conquer. He likes the thrill of the hunt. He likes winning, and then moving on.”

My heart suddenly leapt into my throat, probably because a small part of me wondered about the truth of his statement. I didn’t want to show Evan that, though. “You don’t know that.”

He let out a cynical laugh. “Of course, I do. That’s why

he pours himself into work so much. He wants to win, to be the top dog."

Don't let him see your doubt, I told myself. I raised my chin. "Maybe professionally that's true, but that doesn't mean it's the case relationally. People are more complex than that."

He glanced over his shoulder again. For someone who seemed so brave, he was being awfully secretive. "I wasn't going to show you this. But you should know."

He pulled out his cell phone and brought up a picture of Chase leaning toward a woman in the dark nighttime hours. He wore jeans and a thick jacket. City lights sparkled in the background, and the woman looked over her shoulder suspiciously.

I looked more closely.

That was the blonde woman. The one who'd been following me. The one I'd seen go into the drugstore.

My heart stammered again, some of my façade crumbling.

I licked my lips. "Why are you showing me this?"

He shrugged. "It looks a little intimate, doesn't it? Middle of the night. They're doing the lean."

I refused to look again to see if he was right. "They could just be whispering."

"I'll let you make your own decisions."

"Why'd you take this picture anyway?"

He shrugged. "I saw it as I was passing a drugstore the other night. It struck me as odd."

"So you took a picture?" *That* seemed odd.

"I don't want to see him treating you poorly. It's not right."

"I see." I licked my lips, unsure what to say.

Evan narrowed his eyes and studied my face. "You're

going to pretend you didn't see it, aren't you?"

I didn't have an answer for that. I was on too much medication. I was tired. I was in shock. "I don't know what I'm going to do next."

He frowned. "You might hate me now, but at least I did what I thought was right. I can sleep better tonight knowing that."

With a wave, he walked away.

My mind raced when he was gone. I couldn't go down this rabbit trail again. I'd been there before. Been at the point where I'd questioned Chase and his actions.

Either I trusted him or I didn't.

He was involved with police work. That meant that, on occasion, he was going to do things that were secretive. Things I didn't understand. Things that he couldn't tell me about.

I could accept that.

I was going to choose to trust him, I decided. To have faith that his actions had an honorable purpose. To believe that he loved me like he said.

I couldn't let anything make me waver from that.

Because that was one emotional firestorm I never wanted to go through again.

CHAPTER 20

"What was that about?" Jamie's gaze followed Evan out the door. "Last I heard, paramedics don't do rounds in the hospital."

Of course, she'd shown up right as Evan left.

If there was one thing I could say, it was that I should feel loved. I'd had an endless string of visitors and people who cared about me come through the hospital.

Count your blessings.

I would. Plenty of people out there would love to be in my shoes in that regard. I had people in my life. People who were there for me when I needed them.

But my mind still reeled from the Chase bombshell. What was going on? How much did Chase know that he wasn't telling me? That he *couldn't* tell me?

Trust and let it go, Holly.

That was what I needed to do. After all, I had bigger concerns at the moment—like Jonah.

Some of the initial trauma was wearing off, and a touch of shock had set in, making me feel slightly numb. But my thoughts always came back to one person . . . Jonah.

Dear Lord, be with him.

My heart ached, a physical pain that made me lurch, that could consume me if I let it.

Where was that precious baby now? Was he scared?

What if he was hungry? The questions circled around again and again.

Jamie came to stand beside my bed. She stared at me, a mix of curiosity and concern on her face.

I nibbled on my lip a moment. I didn't even know where to start or what to say. Drama. Everywhere I went there seemed to be drama. All I desired in my life was peace.

So I did what any confused woman would do. I poured everything out to my best friend. Everything.

Halfway through, she pulled up a chair and sat. She leaned back as I finished and wobbled her head back and forth as if her brain was now on overload. "Wow. That's . . . that's a lot. Like *a lot* a lot."

I nodded. "I know."

She let out a long, thoughtful breath. "Well, first of all, I know the police are doing everything they can to find Jonah. I have no doubt that you would have given up your life to protect him. You could have easily been killed."

Why didn't he kill me? I wondered silently. *Why did he keep me alive?*

"Second, I really had no doubt that Evan was interested in you. Why else would he have shown up with a gift card at your house and flowers at the hospital? I give him props for being bold."

Yes, he'd definitely been bold.

"Finally, I'm proud of you for deciding to trust Chase, even after everything Evan said. I know that's not always easy."

My throat burned as I considered how to respond. Jamie made me sound a lot better than I actually was. My thoughts were far from linear. "I can't do that rollercoaster ride of being uncertain anymore. I feel like our relationship has been like that ever since it began, and I'm tired of it."

She tilted her head in surprise. "What's that mean?"

I sighed, deciding I didn't have the mental energy to go there right now. I needed to sleep first. I needed to find Jonah. Then I'd worry about my love life. "I don't know. I don't know anything right now. Anything except that I want to find Jonah."

"How do you plan on doing that?"

Determination roiled inside me with a fierceness I knew wouldn't wane. "I'm going to do a stakeout and figure out exactly what's going down at 5th and Vine this evening."

"If you get to leave the hospital in time."

I glanced at the clock hanging in front of me, and saw that it was five o'clock. "I will. If I have to forge my doctor's signature on the discharge papers, I will."

***

The unfortunate fact was that 5th and Vine just happened to be located in the heart of the city, near Fountain Square, which was always hustling and bustling.

The fortunate part was that I'd been released from the hospital just in time to go home, shower away the hospital grime that covered me, and change into a black outfit that would help me blend in.

The unfortunate part was that I'd seen Jonah's crib while I'd been home, and cried.

The fortunate part was that someone had cleaned up the broken lamp and the plaster that chipped from the wall when the door flung open. A piece of crime-scene tape still swayed in the wind on the porch—a simple but effective reminder of what had happened. It propelled me to action. If someone thought I was going to be bullied, they were wrong.

Jamie and I parked in a nearby garage, wandered down

the city sidewalk, and found a bench against a nearby restaurant. We camped out there. Though it had to look over-the-top cheesy, the only disguise we had been able to think of that wouldn't be too obvious was none other than a . . . newspaper.

Chase knew about this meeting site, and I feared he might show up and see me. I had a feeling he'd probably send patrol around the area to look for any signs of trouble. The lead was so vague that it was almost not a lead at all. But when it was all you had, it was all you had.

It was dark outside and cold—very cold. That didn't stop the nightlife from springing up all around us. Groups of people moved like schools of fish, headed from one bar to another. A musician played guitar and sang for change near the fountain. A horse and carriage rode past, the people inside laughing a little too hard.

"What are we looking for?" Jamie whispered while staring at the crossword section.

I refused to let my teeth chatter, even though they wanted to. "I have no idea. My best guess? Maybe it's some kind of drug deal that's going down."

I reviewed Bo's possible connection with this. There were two possibilities in my mind. Either Gage was tracking down a story lead and had come across Bo, or Bo had gone to Gage with a story idea.

Whatever that idea was had possibly gotten Bo killed—if someone had set up his murder to look like a suicide.

I remembered the facts Violet had shared with me. After beating cancer, Bo's personality changed. He'd become more reclusive and secretive; he'd begun to hang around some unsavory characters; and he'd come into some money.

What had he gotten mixed up in? Why had it killed him?

Drugs or weapons were the only things I kept coming back to. What if he'd gotten involved in some illegal dealings of that sort? It would have brought in some money. If it had been drugs, that would explain the changes in his personality.

The one thing Violet had remembered about her brother was that whatever was going down happened Thursday night at 5th and Vine. At least, according to his calendar.

"How long are we going to wait? I'm freezing," Jamie's newspaper practically vibrated as she shivered.

My heart thudded. I couldn't give up. Jonah's life depended on me finding some answers.

But what would I do if someone did show up? I wasn't exactly equipped to take anyone down myself. Maybe I'd hit my head a little too hard.

I straightened as someone caught my eye across the street. "Jamie, do you see that?"

Jamie peered around the newspaper. "Do I see what?"

"There's a woman over there. Alone. Does she look like Katie?"

"Katie?" She stared in the distance.

Was that Katie? It was so dark outside, and she was far away. I just couldn't tell. "I don't know, Holly. It could be. It might not be."

"Let's move closer."

We put the newspaper down and tried to look casual as we crossed the street toward the square. The woman remained near a bench on the edge of the area. She glanced at her watch.

I squinted again, going back and forth as to whether or not it was Katie. I just couldn't tell. Same size. Same hair. But . . .

"Should we approach her?" Jamie asked.

My heart rate spiked, but the choice was clear. "This is no time to be a wallflower. This is a time to be bold. Let's do it."

We started toward her. My mind raced with what I would say. *I'm sorry about Jonah. Why did you leave him? Do you have any idea who would have taken him?*

I cleared my throat, about to make my move, when a guy appeared.

The woman's face lit, and she threw her arms around the man. "Gregory!"

"Nina! I'm sorry I'm late. You ready for dinner?"

It wasn't Katie. This woman's profile was wrong, her forehead too wide, and her lips too full.

It looked like our evening here was all for nothing.

As sirens sounded in the distance, I wondered if this miscalculation had caused us to miss what we were really looking for.

***

Morbid curiosity led me in the direction of the sirens. Jamie and I had picked up my car. However, a police car had blocked the exit to the parking garage, and a cop there was dealing with some drunken twenty-somethings. By the time we were able to get out and navigate the streets, at least thirty minutes had passed.

Then we ran into a crew that was repaving some of the downtown streets. Whatever had happened would most likely be over by the time Jamie and I arrived. Still, I wanted to see.

I thought the sound of the emergency vehicles had come from a section of the city called Over the Rhine. The neighborhood had once been one of the worst in Cincinnati, but people had worked to restore it in recent years. Ralph's office—where I worked—wasn't far from that area.

When I saw an ambulance blocking the road ahead, I

slowed. As we came closer, I spotted two police cars also, as well as a fire truck. I probably shouldn't have done it, but I pulled over to the curb.

"What are you doing?" Jamie asked.

"I just want to make sure everything is all right. My brother's office is close to here. Sometimes people work late." Before Jamie could argue, I jumped out of the car and approached the scene.

Cops milled around. Tension filled the air. I didn't see anyone in handcuffs, but crime scene techs worked diligently, and numbered markers were on the ground near what I presumed were bullets.

My gaze fluttered around, but I didn't see any familiar faces. No coworkers. No Chase. No Ralph.

Then I came to Evan.

He spotted me at the same time I saw him. His expression looked grim, serious, and the normal sparkle was gone from his eyes. Was it because of our awkward conversation at the hospital?

He paced over to the police line and narrowed his eyes. "What are you doing here?"

I shrugged, not willing to give up too much information. "My office isn't too far away, and Jamie and I were out for the evening. When I heard sirens, I wanted to make sure everything was okay."

"I'm surprised they let you go from the hospital."

"I bounce back quickly. What's going on?"

His jaw tightened, and his radio crackled at his belt. "Homicide."

My heart pounded in my ears. Another one. There'd been too many lately. One was too many. Ever. "Who?"

"Can't say." He shrugged stiffly.

"How?" I continued.

"Gunshot."

"Suspect?"

"Long gone."

My gaze skittered around, stopping at a body in the distance, covered completely in a cloth. Was this even connected? Probably not. But it was all my mind could think about.

I looked up at the street sign.

15th and Vine.

Realization pounded with my heartbeat.

Violet had been wrong. It hadn't been 5th and Vine. There was a "1" missing from the address Bo had wrote on his calendar.

Whatever had gone down, it had gone down here tonight.

My gaze went back to the cloth-draped body. Two officials lifted it on a gurney and wheeled it toward a van. As they did so, the sheet slipped.

A face peered out.

It wasn't Katie.

No, it was the woman I'd seen walking into the drugstore. The one Evan had taken a picture of with Chase.

She'd been killed.

CHAPTER 21

I remained at the crime scene, but I paced away from the heart of the investigation in order to let everything sink in. Chase wasn't here, but another detective had shown up. Larson, if I remembered correctly. Several patrol officers lingered. Even Captain Abbott had come.

Murders of those encased in the drug and gang culture were relatively normal in this area. Normal seemed to be an insensitive way to put it. At the very least, most would say that those kinds of deaths weren't surprising here.

I didn't approve of the sentiment, but it was the truth.

This woman looked too ordinary and white-collar to be involved in either of those activities—though she could have been. What was her connection? Why had Chase met with her? Was she working with Katie and Heathcliff? Were they killing off anyone who got in their way? Or was Katie also a victim here?

"It just doesn't make sense, Jamie." I crossed my arms and leaned against the building behind me—a corner store and deli that had seen better days—no longer caring about the cold. "That was the woman who was following us that day. Evan showed me a picture of her meeting with Chase. I'm having trouble piecing it all together."

Jamie massaged her temples and opened her eyes. She'd been muttering prayers since she saw the dead body.

"I wish I could tell you. Somehow Gage and Katie are connected with all of this. The more I think about it, the more of a headache I get. I just can't wrap my mind around everything. Girl Genius's brain is starting to hurt."

"I have to figure out why these people are connected and figure out how to separate the good guys from the bad guys." I bit down, wishing that finding answers was as easy as making cookies.

"The problem is figuring out that connection. We're missing something."

I tapped my foot, disliking being in this state of confusion. "Exactly. The connections are coming slower than I would like. And time is ticking away. With every minute that passes, I wonder about Jonah and how he's doing." My voice cracked.

Jamie squeezed my arm. "What Chase said is true. If they'd wanted to hurt Jonah, that man would have done it right then and there. This guy wants Jonah alive for a reason."

I thought about the dead body in the Ohio. If that was Katie, then who were these guys trying to smoke out? Heathcliff, maybe? What if he really was Jonah's father?

"Let's assume Katie isn't dead." I inhaled before continuing. "To smoke her out, this guy would have to have a way to contact her and flaunt the facts in front of her. As far as we know, Katie is off the grid. Unless she's the one who left the note on my car. Maybe she's been hiding in plain sight."

I looked around. Was she here now? Or was she dead? Had that been her body in the Ohio?

Uncertainty plagued me. Gage was dead. Bo was dead. Katie could be dead. That was a lot of dead.

My list of suspects was short. Maybe Heathcliff. If not him, then who? Whom was I missing?

"I need answers, Jamie. I'll do whatever is needed to find them." First thing tomorrow, I was going to finish calling the rest of the babysitters on GregsList. I was going to track down Katie's old friends from church youth group. I would talk to Heathcliff myself.

Whatever it took.

"I'm sure you will," Jamie said. "You're the most polite investigator I know, but you've proven that please and thank you can lead to answers."

"I need to find Jonah—even if that means abandoning my manners."

***

Chase called first thing in the morning. As his voice rolled over the line, I remembered the blonde on the gurney. I recalled the picture Evan had shown me of her speaking with Chase. I pictured her dead, lifeless face.

And I felt more confused than ever.

Not only that, but my body ached from my encounter with the fake social worker. My shoulder had limited range of motion; I had a bump on the back of my head; and I'd probably need to see a chiropractor sometime soon. In the meantime, maybe I'd find some of my leftover prescription painkillers from my last hospital visit. They should get me through in the meantime.

Probably the most dominant emotion I was feeling, though, was loss. Loss of Jonah. Guilt that he'd been taken when I was supposed to be his protector. Worry that he wasn't being taken care of.

In an instant, I remembered that social worker coming to the door. I remembered the flash of fear when he'd shoved his way inside. I remembered the pain right before I blacked out.

The memories froze me a moment.

"Holly?"

I came back to the present and pushed myself up in bed, holding the phone to my ear. I'd been awake for a while, but I couldn't make myself get up. This wasn't normal for me. I was an early riser. A breakfast lover. A start-my-day-in-the-Word-of-God believer.

But I was off my game this morning.

"You were pretty beaten-up yesterday," Chase continued.

"I'm still sore, but I'll manage," I finally told him. Sore was really an understatement. Every muscle ached.

"I'm sorry, Holly." Compassion softened his voice. "Is there anything I can do for you?"

"Just find out what happened to Jonah."

"Of course."

I waited, wondering if he would tell me about the woman from last night. I'd said I trusted him. And trusting him meant waiting on his timing, in this case. If he could tell me about the blonde woman, he would.

That didn't stop me from holding my breath and waiting. When he offered no information, I asked, "Anything new on the search for Jonah?"

"I talked to the detective on this case this morning. They have a couple of leads, but nothing solid yet. We're collaborating to figure out who killed Jonah's father, as well. I promise you we're working around the clock."

"I know you are." I had no doubt he was doing just that. He'd probably worked all night. If I saw him now, he'd probably have circles under his eyes and his shirt would be wrinkled. He probably hadn't eaten but instead had downed six cups of coffee.

He was dedicated, and that made him good at his job.

"Sorry I've been so busy lately. I wanted to stop by last night, but I couldn't."

Little did he know I'd been busy last night also. He wouldn't approve.

"I was working a homicide downtown," he continued.

My heart pounded. But he hadn't been there. Was he lying to me?

I cleared my throat as I quickly weighed my options. "I see."

I wasn't going to address this now. I couldn't handle but so many tragedies at a time.

"Anyway, I wanted to let you know that body in the Ohio has been identified."

I held my breath. "And?"

"It's not Katie."

I released my breath. I still felt a sense of mourning for the woman who had died. For her family who would soon learn the news. For whatever had happened to her.

But at least I had an answer.

We hung up a few minutes later. My shoulder ached, each movement causing crippling pain to shoot through me. I walked into the bathroom and opened my medicine cabinet, looking for my prescription. I moved aside some Tylenol, some allergy medicine, and two bottles of vitamins.

No old pain medicine, though. What had I done with it?

I wondered if my mom had thrown it away. That would be my luck.

I downed some extra-strength Tylenol instead and rubbed my eyes.

I looked in the mirror and frowned. Circles lined my eyes; my hair was frizzy; and my skin looked dull. At the moment, I didn't even care. The only thing that concerned me was that precious baby boy who needed a guardian.

At that thought, I padded down the hallway and into Jonah's room.

He'd only been here for a few days, but I still thought of this room as his.

I picked up one of the blankets and pulled it to my nose. It still smelled like him. Just the scent of baby lotion brought tears to my eyes.

Dear Lord, please protect him.

An ache reverberated in my chest, topped with an unseen weight that pressed on my shoulders. You can't stand here all day and cry, I chided myself.

I dragged myself downstairs. Maybe I would bake. Baking always made me feel better. But as I wandered over to the kitchen counter, the first thing I saw was a note my mom had left.

> Alex wants us all over for dinner tonight. I already texted Chase about it. 6:30. Make a cake, please.

I inwardly groaned. The last thing I wanted to do was have a family dinner after everything that had happened. But if Alex was calling for a last-minute meeting, something must be up. She knew about Jonah, and it wasn't like her to be insensitive in the midst of tragedy.

The next thing I spotted was my old fifth-grade project my mom had found.

I picked it up and flipped to the first page.

Kids by twenty-five. That didn't happen. I wouldn't have any kids by thirty either. I'd be lucky to have them by thirty-five.

I remembered Samantha's words about Gage.

He's not the marrying type. You know how some guys are just like that? They'll lead a woman on for years but have no intentions of settling down.

I remembered what Evan said about Chase.

He's the type that likes to conquer. He likes the thrill of the hunt. He likes winning, and then moving on.

Were they right? Was I living in some kind of fantasy world thinking that Chase was going to change and marry me? What if he never got over his issues?

As icing on the cake, Truman's words came back to me about marriage and law enforcement.

I'm sure you've heard about the divorce rate among cops. It's high. Among homicide detectives? It's even higher.

Three different people. The same basic message. Was God trying to tell me something?

My phone rang again. I halfway expected it to be Chase. Instead, a woman's voice came on the line.

"You've got to help me."

I froze. "Who is this?"

"It's Katie Edwards. Listen closely."

CHAPTER 22

"Katie!" I muttered, dropping into the kitchen chair. "You're alive."

"How's Jonah?"

My heart leapt into my throat as the truth hit me. She didn't know. I had to break the news. "Katie, someone came by yesterday—"

She gasped, and I knew that I didn't have to finish. She intrinsically knew what I was going to say. "They took him, didn't they? I knew it. I could feel it in my gut."

"I'm sorry, Katie. I did my best. I fought with everything I had. I'm so, so sorry." My voice cracked, and a sob tried to escape.

"You've got to find him, Holly."

I did. Maybe she could offer information that would help me. I had so many questions for her. "Where are you?"

"I can't tell you. I can't come out of hiding. They'll kill me."

Kill her? Like they'd killed Gage? And she'd said "they." How many people were involved with this?

"Who's 'they'?" I finally asked.

"I can't say. It's complicated."

"Tell the police. They'll protect you."

"I can't do that. Like I said, it's complicated."

I needed to keep her talking until I got some answers. She'd put me in this situation. The least she could do was help. "Why'd you leave Jonah with me?"

"He's safer without me . . . or so I thought. I should have known they'd find him."

She'd mentioned the elusive "they" again. I needed to know who. "Who? Who found him?"

"I've got to go. My time is up. I'm afraid my call is being traced."

Panic surged in me. I couldn't lose her now. "By whom?"

"I've gotta go. Find Jonah. Please."

Guilt thudded inside my chest. "I'm doing my best. But I have no idea who snatched him. Is there anything you know that will help me find him?" I rushed, hoping she wouldn't hang up.

"It's complicated, Holly."

That was the third time she'd said that. And what was that emotion in her voice? I couldn't read it, and I was usually good at reading people. "Did you kill Gage, Katie?"

"No, I was set up."

"His blood was found on Jonah's car seat carrier. Your footprint was near his body. You fingerprint was on the gun . . ."

"I was set up. Please help me."

"Katie, you need to give me more to go on here."

"You won't believe me."

"Why?"

She gasped. "Holly, I've got to go. Please, find Jonah. Please."

The line went dead.

***

I sat in a stunned silence, still grasping the phone in my hands.

Who could have set Katie up in Gage's death? Heathcliff was the only person who came to mind. But if he had done it, why?

Was Gage going to write his article, exposing Heathcliff, even if it meant incriminating his girlfriend and baby mama in the process? It was a possibility.

Another theory raced into my mind. What if Katie was working with Heathcliff and trying to throw me off her trail by calling me now? The uncertainties tugged at my mental well-being. If I could just find one solid lead . . .

That reminded me that I needed to get started with this investigation. Now that someone had snatched Jonah, I had nothing to hold me back and every reason to move forward. I'd deal with my aches and pains later.

Where did I start?

I glanced around the kitchen. With tea, I decided. I wanted some tea.

After letting the water boil in the kettle, I fixed some oolong with a touch of cream and stevia. I turned on some Frank Sinatra—because he always made everything better. Then I sat down with some homemade scones I'd baked this past weekend.

I took a bite of my scone. It crumbled around my lips, but since there was no one home, I didn't really care. My mom was out showing more houses this morning.

I took a sip of tea and came back to my original question: Where did I start with this?

Chase had warned me to stay away from Heathcliff. It wasn't completely out of the realm of possibility that I'd speak with him, but I needed to figure out if there were any other places I could start first.

I'd still like to talk to Katie's babysitter. She was someone who'd most likely seen Katie five days a week. She might have a pulse about what was going on in her life. But I had to figure out who she was first.

I grabbed a tablet from the hutch beside me, jumped on GregsList, and I began scanning through the ads there since Samantha said this was where Katie had found her.

A lot of the ads were still scrambled, just as they'd been when Jamie and I looked earlier. This site really needed to work on their design a bit. That ad for bulk orders of juice boxes was still there, just waiting for a VBS organizer or preschool director to seize the opportunity.

I started at the top of the list of childcare providers and began making phone calls. Five calls in, and I'd had no luck. *Sixth time's a charm?*

Six, seven, and eight were dead ends also. But on the ninth call I found my first real lead.

"I'm calling about someone named Katie Edwards," I started, just as I'd started the past eight conversations.

The soft-spoken woman on the other end hesitated. "Are you a friend? I've been so worried about her. She was supposed to bring Jonah in this week, but I haven't heard from her. She sent me a text saying she was going out of town, but that just seems so unlike her."

"I am a friend, and I'm worried about Katie also. I was wondering if I might stop and ask you a few questions. I'm trying to find her."

"Of course. I'm only watching one little girl today for a while. Could you come by at two, after she's gone home?"

"Yes, that's fine. Thank you."

She rattled off the address, and I hung up. Finally, maybe I had a lead.

I hoped I did, at least.

CHAPTER 23

"I used my connections at the newspaper to find out two things for you," Jamie announced when she came over a few minutes later. She was fresh from jogging and still wearing her cute new workout clothes, which was fine with me. I was just glad she was here and that I had someone to rehash all of this with.

I sat down with her at the kitchen table. "What did you learn?"

"First of all, I'm glad you're here. I was afraid you might do something crazy like going into work or something."

I shook my head. It was Friday, and I'd already missed the earlier part of the week. I knew I wasn't in the right frame of mind to jump back into office work.

"Ralph already knows that I won't be able to concentrate until Jonah is found. He said to take as much time as I needed." That was the one plus to working for my brother. The job wasn't as demanding as social work had been.

"It's a good thing you put in so much overtime for him on a normal basis. I guess he has no reason to complain."

"That's what I keep telling myself. Now, please, go on."

"Second, I learned some things about the blonde woman who died last night. Her name was Morgan Bayfield, and she worked at the local jail."

I'd just started picking at a taco croissant ring that was left over from the meal train at church. Jamie now had my full attention, though. "Worked at the jail? Doing what?"

Jamie gulped down some more vinegar water before sucking in a deep breath. "A nurse. She was thirty. Raised in this area. Single with no kids. I couldn't find any connections between her and Katie or Gage—but that doesn't mean they're not there."

I chewed on that for a minute. "Heathcliff has a record. Maybe the two of them met while he was in jail."

"It's a possibility. As far as I can tell, Morgan had no prior history—she probably couldn't get a job at the jail if she did. In fact, everyone thought she was upstanding. Her mom is sick—needs a kidney transplant, apparently, and most of Morgan's time was devoted to caring for her."

"Then why was she involved in all of this? *How* was she involved, for that matter?" Jamie was right—she didn't seem like the type to get mixed up in something illegal.

"I have no idea." Jamie chugged more water. "Something really weird is going on."

"You can say that again." I crossed my arms, feeling like we were on the verge of discovering answers. We had to plan our next moves carefully. "She was definitely the person who was following us, and she had met with Chase. Why?"

"You could ask him."

I frowned and pulled off a flakey layer of croissant. "I have a feeling he'd say he can't tell me."

She spread her hands across the table, a look that clearly said she meant business. "We'll talk about that later. Because I have more. I talked to a reporter at the *Ledger* also. He was a friend of Gage's."

I sat up straighter. "Okay . . ."

"He said Gage was working on a story and was acting secretive. When this guy asked Gage about it, he got really defensive. Said it was a private matter."

"So he has no idea what it was on?" I knew it was connected with Bo. I just didn't know how exactly.

Jamie shook her head. "No idea."

I bit down, trying to put the pieces together and figure out the next step. That led me to only one logical conclusion. "I say we go talk to Heathcliff next. He seems like a good link."

"I'm up for anything. But the things I'm learning are putting me on edge. We could be digging into some ugly stuff."

"We've dug into some ugly stuff before."

"That's true. We've survived. I'm worried sometimes that we're pressing our luck." She made a face.

"There's no such thing as luck. We've got angels watching over us."

"You preach it, girl."

I stood. "Now, let's go track down this Heathcliff guy and see what we can find out."

***

Heathcliff Caswell lived in an apartment in a rough area near downtown. His complex was a huge brick building with litter clinging against the sides and patchy grass where flowerbeds were meant to thrive.

After we had looked up the address, Jamie convinced me not to wear a dress. Instead I'd thrown on some leggings and a tunic, along with some ballet flats—but only because she'd told me high heels were too hard to run away in. She had a point. She still wore her shiny spandex exercise outfit, so she was ready to jet if the need arose.

When I spotted the people loitering outside the building, I was glad I'd listened to her. It was never a good sign when groups of people gathered outside during the middle of the day and seemed to have nothing better to do rather than watch people come and go. That usually led to trouble and showed people who were territorial and, therefore, often dangerous.

I wouldn't be here—except I hoped to find answers about Jonah. Maybe even evidence that he'd been here.

Jamie and I pushed past the crowd, ignoring the wolf whistles and catcalls, and knocked on Heathcliff's door. I fully didn't expect him to answer. To my surprise, he did.

Heathcliff looked as I'd envisioned him from his pictures. He was tall and lanky and wore his jeans about four inches too low. He had scrawny facial hair. Dark, sporadic strands that contrasted with his pale skin almost made him look sickly. A diamond earring and a black trucker hat completed his look.

He blinked when he saw Jamie and me on the other side of the door. It was almost like he was expecting someone. But not us.

His eyes narrowed as he assessed us. "Can I help you?"

"We need to talk to you about Katie Edwards." I glanced behind him, desperate for a glance of Jonah. But I didn't see any signs that he was currently here or that he'd ever been here. No baby stuff lay around nor did the scent of dirty diapers linger in the air.

"What about Katie?" Heathcliff's voice was full of undue attitude.

I had a feeling it wasn't just reserved for us, but that this was the way he always spoke.

"We're looking for her," Jamie said. "Worried about her. Worried about Jonah."

"You think I know something? You think Katie talks to

me?" He pointed to himself and jerked his chin inward. "I don't know nothing."

"We think she might be in trouble," I continued, trying to somehow reach him.

His gaze volleyed from both of us. "You the police?"

"Just friends who are worried. The police don't really dress like this." I ran my hand down the length of my sheep-printed leggings.

He studied us both. "I don't remember Katie ever talking about you two. I think I'd remember Little Bo Peep and her Diana Ross sidekick."

"Did you talk to her a lot?" I tried to turn the questioning around on him and take the attention off of us. Information was key here—and I was not Little Bo Peep, although I could suddenly see why he and Katie got along so well. They both loved giving people unflattering nicknames.

Heathcliff's gaze burned into me. "No, not a lot. But enough. I knew most of her friends. You work with her or something?"

I shrugged, trying to remain levelheaded. "I knew her in high school. We went to church together."

Though I'd known Katie when I was younger, our connection only went as far as the church. She'd never brought her boyfriends with her, nor had we socialized outside of youth events at the church. Because of that, I'd never seen Heathcliff before, and I had to assume he'd never seen me either.

He nodded—if raising his chin could be considered a nod—as if that explanation made sense. "So you lost your peep and don't know where to find her?"

"Very funny." Actually, it was quite clever.

"What do you want to know?" He looked outside the door as some of the crowd gathered near his building got louder. It almost sounded like a fistfight was going to break out. "You need to come in."

I stepped inside but remained close to the door, just in case I needed to make a getaway. This would afford me the opportunity to get a better look in his apartment, which smelled like trash that hadn't been taken out for weeks.

As Heathcliff sauntered across the room, I saw a gun tucked into his waistband. My throat suddenly felt like sandpaper. Our lives were in his hands right now. We had to proceed carefully.

He plopped down on the couch and picked up a beer. Five empty cans rested on the end table, and I couldn't help but wonder how many he'd gone through just today.

My eyes fell on something else. Another gun rested on the kitchen counter on the other side of the room.

I cringed as a second surge of anxiety rose in me. "When did you last talk to Katie?"

"Saturday evening. She asked me to meet her at Club 21."

"What did you fight about there?" Jamie asked.

He gave her a sharp glance. "How'd you know we fought?"

"We've been following Katie's trail since Saturday evening," I said. "The bartender there told me. Told me you got kicked out."

He hoisted up one shoulder, and his eyes smoldered. "It's like I told the cops yesterday, I was trying to get her to leave that Gage jerk. The two of us were meant to be together. She knew it. She didn't think I'd be good with her little brat, though."

My insides churned when I heard him talking about Jonah like that. But I had to stay focused. "Is that the only reason you wanted her to leave Gage? Just so you could date her? Or was there more to it?"

"She'd never be happy with Gage. I just wanted her to see it. He wasn't going to settle down for her. He's the kind of guy that likes to string girls along."

He was the second person who'd said that about good old Gage.

"What did Katie say when you told her that?" I asked.

He puckered out his lips in an exaggerated frown. "She got all emotional. And then mad at me. Told me to leave her alone. Said Gage was an honorable man."

"Had they been having problems lately?"

He took another swig of beer before crushing the can in his hands and tossing it behind him. "You could say that. I mean, she didn't tell me any details. It was just my impression. Apparently, he was buried deep in some story he was writing. She didn't tell me that either. I overheard her on the phone outside the bar that night."

"What was she saying?" My blood spiked with anticipation.

"Said for the baby's sake he needed to let it go."

"Let what go?"

He shrugged. "No idea. She didn't spell it out. But she seemed real worried. Whatever it was, it wasn't worth risking anyone's life over."

"You posted something on one of your social media accounts that evening about Katie," I said. "You said: *Some women just string you along in an effort to get their way. They ain't worth it. Now or ever. Good riddance.* What did that mean?"

"You really do your research, don't you, Peep?" He shrugged. "Katie just wanted a gun. She didn't care about me. It was all about what I could do for her, and that evening proved it."

Was he angry enough about that to try and kill her? Had Gage interceded and been killed? "You know Gage is dead now, right?"

I watched his reaction.

He grimaced, almost snarled. But then his shoulders slumped. "Yeah, I heard. I didn't have nothing to do with it. In fact, I have an alibi for that evening. The police already checked it out. I'm into a lot of bad things in my life, but I ain't ever killed no one."

I shifted my weight from one foot to another before changing the course of the conversation. "Heathcliff, did you ever wonder if Jonah was yours?"

His eyes locked on mine. "At first, I did. I paid for her to have a paternity test. Turns out the baby was Gage's. That was part of the reason she wouldn't leave him. Said she wanted to do better than her own mom. She wanted her baby to know his dad. She wanted more for Jonah than she'd had growing up."

Jamie crossed her arms, looking as uncomfortable as I felt as we stood in the middle of his dirty, stinky, weapon-laden apartment. "But you have no idea what kind of article Gage was working on? Or if he was involved in something else dangerous?"

He shook his head. "No, I have no idea."

"How about Morgan Bayfield? Do you know her?" I asked.

No sign of recognition flashed across his face. "No, never heard of her."

"Thanks for your time," I finally said.

"I hope my Katie girl is okay. I really do love her. If someone hurt her, I just might have to hurt them."

CHAPTER 24

At two o'clock, Jamie and I showed up at Sarah Sullivan's house, just like I'd said we would. As we stood on her porch waiting for her to answer the doorbell, I glanced around. This place struck me as the home of someone who was struggling to make ends meet. The red bricks out front were cracked. The cement covering the porch below me was dingy. A tiny plastic slide was the only flowerbed decoration.

Sarah answered the door on the first knock, and I could see the lines of worry around her eyes. The woman was probably in her fifties with faded blonde hair that stretched halfway down her back. She was slim, even though the baggy clothes she wore weren't flattering to her frame and made her look a bit deflated.

"Holly?" She touched her throat, her voice sounding strained and painful.

I nodded. "This is my friend, Jamie."

"Come on in." She pushed the storm door open with a loud squeak.

We stepped into her house. In the front, in what was probably intended to be the formal living room, was a crib, some colorful foam flooring, and a tub of toys.

The carpet looked matted and old but clean. Wallpaper from the eighties wrapped the walls in peach-colored roses. But the scent of apples—from a candle burning on the ledge—made everything seem a little more welcoming.

She led us into the kitchen, where she offered us some juice. Both Jamie and I politely refused and sat across from her at the kitchen table instead. She smoothed an old placemat with her long fingers. Above the table there were some photos of Europe that looked like they'd been cut out of a magazine.

"I want to go there one day," Sarah said, following my gaze. "But it doesn't look like it will be happening any time soon."

I actually had some black and white placemats that someone had given me once that had scenes from Europe on them—the Eifel Tower, the Leaning Tower of Pisa, Irish castles, Stonehenge. When all of this was over, maybe I'd bring them by for her, along with a prepaid credit card to help her out. It was one of my greatest pleasures in life to help bless other people.

But, right now, I had another mission.

"You haven't heard from Katie all week?" I started.

She shook her head and snagged a stray Goldfish cracker from the table, popping it into her mouth. "Not other than the text I got on Sunday saying she had something come up and had to go out of town. Something just didn't feel right about it, though. It's not like Katie to just take off."

"The police didn't contact you?" I asked.

Sarah let out a soft sigh, and her eyes scanned the table, as if looking for any other discarded food. "No, they haven't."

Certainly they would have if they'd linked Sarah with Katie. It didn't appear the police had done that yet.

"How long had you babysat for Katie?" Jamie asked.

"Only three weeks. I know it wasn't that long, but it was long enough to bond with Jonah."

"You mentioned a text from Katie," I said. "What exactly did the text say?"

"Just that she was going out of town and she'd be gone a while. She was sorry for the late notice and would be in touch when she got back." Sarah shook her head. "I'm doing my best to make ends meet. When people take off without telling me, that means I don't get paid. If I don't get paid, I can't make my bills. So, I'm feeling a mixture of worry for Katie and annoyed that my checking account is ready to overdraft."

"I'm sorry, Sarah. That sounds difficult." I shifted, trying to remain sensitive yet focused. "Just a couple more questions. I promise. Did Katie seem to be having any problems lately?"

Her head shot up. "Problems? Not really. Why? Do you think she's in danger?"

"Katie is missing, and so is Jonah. We're looking for anyone with information."

She let out a gasp. "Missing? You think there's foul play involved?"

I decided not to skirt around the truth. "In Jonah's disappearance, yes. We're not sure about Katie."

"Oh, dear." A single tear trickled down her cheek. "Poor Jonah."

"We're doing everything we can to locate him."

Wrinkles appeared at the side of her eyes. "How did you say you were connected with her?"

"I'm a social worker, and I'm working with the police to find some answers." It wasn't the total truth, but there were strands of honesty in my words. "Besides that, I knew Katie back when we were teenagers, and I'm worried about her. Is there anything you can think of that might give us a clue as to what happened?"

Sarah stared off in the distance before shaking her

head, nearly looking resigned. “Not really. I mean, I watched Jonah last week, just like normal.”

I turned over my thoughts, hoping to find more information in the mundane details. Maybe a clue would be revealed there. “Did Katie pay you or did Gage?”

“Gage did. But he never picked up Jonah. I guess he worked longer hours than Katie.”

“Did Katie seem upset lately? Did she mention anything was bothering her?”

“She seemed like any normal working mother. She was tired. But she loved Jonah. Her face lit up whenever she saw him.”

I was happy to hear that. I’d dealt with too many parents who were apathetic when it came to their children. Usually drugs or depression triggered it, however. “Did you watch him on Saturday night? We understand that Katie went out that evening.”

“As a matter of fact, I did. It was unusual. I don’t normally work weekends. But Katie said it was important.”

Going clubbing was important? I wasn’t sure how to interpret that.

“Go on,” I said.

“She looked especially stressed when she dropped him off.”

I remembered what Heathcliff had said about Katie wanting to meet him about getting a gun. Did she feel threatened? Like her life was in danger?

“What time did she arrive back?” I asked.

“It was around midnight, I suppose. A little late for my tastes. I told her Jonah could spend the night here, but she insisted on picking him up. He was sleeping like a little baby doll when she arrived.”

"But she didn't say anything that gave you any clues about her evening?" I asked.

"Just that she had some matters she was attending to. She thanked me profusely before leaving."

Well, this conversation hadn't gotten us very far. Just like many of the rest of them we'd had, we only seemed to run into more questions. Just what was going on here? What had Gage and Katie found themselves mixed up in? How did Heathcliff fit in? He could just be an accessory—someone who'd provided a weapon to people who weren't on the up and up. People who were desperate to protect themselves.

Or Heathcliff could be lying and could have pulled Katie, and therefore Gage, into something shady and dangerous.

Jamie and I stood. I couldn't think of anything else to ask Sarah.

When we reached the door, Sarah let out an "Oh!" and we turned.

"There is one other thing. On last Thursday after Katie picked up Jonah, she went out to her car. A man met her there, and they began talking in low tones."

Now this could be interesting. "Did she seem scared?"

Sarah shook her head. "No, not scared. But, by all appearances, it was a pretty serious discussion."

"What did this man look like?" Jamie asked.

"He was a tall African American with lighter colored skin. He looked like he'd been jogging—he was wearing exercise shorts and had ear buds around his neck. And he had a tattoo."

"What kind of tattoo?" I asked.

"It was on his neck, and it looked like a lightning bolt."

CHAPTER 25

When we got back to Jamie's van, better known as the Ghettomobile—an old, rundown, ugly but paid-for vehicle—I noticed it seemed a little lower to the ground than usual.

"Oh no, girl," Jamie muttered, her jaw going slack. "Tell me I'm not seeing what I'm seeing."

I stayed silent—there was no need for me to reiterate the fact that her tires had been slashed.

She began circling her van.

"Jesus, help the person who did this." She closed her eyes and began praying. "Because I want to kill them right now. Jesus, help me too. Visions of murder aren't holy."

She rubbed the cross necklace at her throat.

"I'm so sorry, Jamie." I paced the sidewalk, looking for a sign of who'd done this. Instead, I saw a piece of paper on the windshield.

Another note.

Was this one from Katie also?

I plucked it off and opened it. It was written like the second note we'd found: black marker on white paper. But the handwriting was different from the note that had been left with Jonah—scrawled letters instead of block style.

This time, the message left was clear: Back off before you end up dead too.

The color drained from my face. Someone knew we were searching for answers. We must be getting close. But what did that mean?

"Let me call the police," I told Jamie. "And a tow truck. I'm so sorry this happened."

After I hung up and as we stood on the brisk sidewalk with our arms folded across our chests to keep warm, Jamie finally told me what was really bothering her.

Like I didn't already know.

"It can't be one of my guys," she finally said. "They're not connected with this."

She'd started referring to the three triathletes as her guys? That probably wasn't a good sign when it came to objectivity.

"They all have lightning tattoos, right? Isn't that what you said?" I'd seen it in the front-page news article myself, but I wanted to hear her say it.

She frowned. "But they can't be involved in this. It just doesn't make sense."

"We've seen stranger coincidences."

She shook her head again. "Other people have to have tattoos like that. Certainly."

"Right. They could. But it can't hurt to look into this, right? I mean, the *Ledger* did run an article on them also. Maybe Gage was connected to these athletes through that."

We both knew we were stretching it. The likelihood was that this was one of "her guys." The tattoo wasn't that common.

"Why is it that every time I meet a guy who seems perfect, it turns out he's a fraud?" She lowered her head into her hands. "I should just kiss any chance of a relationship goodbye. Single Jamie is here to stay."

I'd always assumed Girl Genius was okay being single. I

guess deep down inside, most people wanted to be loved, even the tough, most God-fearing of souls.

"Don't jump to conclusions." I squeezed her arm. "Maybe he's innocent here. Maybe the connection isn't what we think. We should go talk to them. Or, better yet, we should talk to Chase about them, just in case one of them is hiding a dangerous side."

Her head shot up, and her eyes went wide. "Not yet. Listen, Holly, all three of these guys are out of town—two doing a race and one at a wedding. Wesley and Anthony will be back tomorrow. Please don't tell Chase yet. I don't want to ruin their reputations—not until I give them a chance to explain first, and I have every confidence there's a logical, noncriminal explanation for this."

Unease sloshed inside me.

"What if we don't tell and they're involved? What if they have Jonah?" My heart pounded in my ears as I asked the question.

"They don't, Holly. Trust me. Please." Her eyes pleaded with me.

I still hesitated.

At that moment, Jamie's face lit with excitement. "They were gone when Jonah was snatched."

"What do you mean?"

"They went to Indy early to prepare for the race. They left Wednesday morning."

I nodded as I processed that, just as the police and a tow truck pulled up. They had alibies. Jamie trusted them. I trusted Jamie.

That settled it. "Okay then. I'll wait."

***

Chase had called at five to see if I needed to be picked up for the dinner tonight. I'd told him no, and he'd told me that he wouldn't be able to stay incredibly long due to his workload.

I again remembered Officer Truman's words about how many police officers' marriages ended in divorce because of long hours. Chase's workload only seemed to be getting larger lately, and there was no end in sight.

That thought made my heart heavy.

I hadn't had time to make that cake I'd been asked to bring, so I swung by my favorite bakery and bought one instead. I was also still wearing my dress-down outfit—leggings and a tunic, so I didn't even feel like myself.

I was late arriving—another unusual occurrence since serial late-ists—my made-up word—drove me crazy. Everyone else had already settled in by the time I pulled up to my sister's massive house on the outskirts of town.

Balancing the cake-laden box on my hip, I pulled open the door, not bothering to knock. Everyone was talking jollily when I walked in. "I'm here!"

Chase rose to meet me and took the cake from my hands. I instantly saw suspicion in his gaze.

"Store-bought cake and leggings?" He kissed my cheek.

I shrugged, my energy draining out of me. "Long day."

He let out a little *uh-huh*, which I knew meant he knew there was more to the story. Because there was. But I couldn't tell him. I'd promised Jamie.

My heart lurched again as I thought about eating with my family. It almost seemed like a celebration. We couldn't celebrate—not with Jonah missing.

Chase helped me out of my coat. "You doing okay?"

I nodded. "As well as can be expected."

He placed my coat with the other outerwear on the couch in the formal living room. Then he took my hand, and we joined the rest of the family in the great room at the back of the house.

Why was I feeling so many doubts about our relationship? Everything about being with Chase right now should feel perfect. Normal. Like we were on the right track.

Yet something didn't settle right in my gut.

I hated being a basket case, and I was beginning to feel like one.

"Glad to see you made it, Holly." My sister's gaze traveled up and down my outfit. "No dress?"

I really had trademarked my look, hadn't I? I hadn't realized it until this very moment. People expected me to look like a fifties housewife—minus the unmovable hair. I preferred mine long and flowy.

"It is cold outside," I explained.

Alex got everyone drinks, and I went to sit by my brother, as Chase and William, Alex's husband, began chatting.

"How are you doing?" Ralph asked, pushing his glasses higher.

I shrugged. "I miss Jonah. I can hardly sleep as I think about something happening to him."

"Chase was just telling us he's incredibly hopeful that Jonah is doing okay. He said if that man had wanted to harm him, he would have done it already."

"That's what I'm hoping also." I really had to change the subject before tears started flowing. "How are things at work? Am I messing you up too much by not being there?"

He shook his head. "We're managing. Do you think you'll come back on Monday? Or do you need more time?"

I thought about it a moment. Did I? I didn't feel like I

was in any hurry to return. Which was unlike me. I'd always loved working. But . . . working for Ralph hadn't been everything I'd expected, I supposed.

And what about Jonah? If he wasn't located by Monday, could I really resume life as normal? Could I simply move on? I wasn't sure.

"I'll do my best," I finally told him.

He gave me a look that indicated he'd read more into my pause than I'd intended. I didn't want to go there now. And I didn't have to because my mom stood and tapped a spoon against her glass.

"Can I have your attention, please?"

We all turned to her. Chase slipped down beside me and took my hand in his.

"There's something I want to share with all of you," my mom started. "As you all know, I've been cleaning out the attic. I found some old papers of your father's while I was doing so."

She paused and composed herself. I could see she was on the brink of tears.

Where was she going with this? Had she discovered something horrible?

Optimistic, Holly. Think positive!

"Some of your father's papers seemed strange to me, so I started doing some digging," she continued. "The short story is this: I've discovered that your father was adopted."

I gasped. "What?"

Ralph stiffened beside me. "Are you sure?"

Alex shook her head. "How can that be?"

"I didn't want to believe it either," Mom said. "But I couldn't find his birth certificate. I couldn't even find any photos from when he was younger. So I called around. Asked around. Talked to his family some. I also had Officer Truman help me."

She blushed ever-so-slightly. "Sure enough, your father was adopted at three years old."

"Adopted?" I repeated. "Who's his birth family?"

She shrugged. "I don't know. It was a closed adoption."

"So, we could have more cousins and aunts and uncles out there," Ralph said.

He was probably mentally calculating the effect this could have on his next election. It was a politician thing. They had to think about everything—everything. Just one wrong word or negative news story, and their career could end.

"Anyway, that's all I know," Mom said. "I have decided to look into it a little more, though. I wanted to share that news with you, and, as I learn more, if you want to know I'd be happy to share."

Well, that had been unexpected. It would take a while to let that sink in.

It looked like my mom had been the one who'd wanted to pull this dinner together.

"Actually, while you're here and we're making announcements, I have one also," Alex said.

She stood and William came to stand beside her. He put his hand around her waist, and I braced myself for their announcement. Chase squeezed my hand, as if he could sense my anxiety.

"I just wanted to share that William and I are . . . having a baby!" Alex said.

My heart thudded. Then soared. Then thudded again.

A baby. I was going to be an aunt. I was going to love being an aunt, and I was so happy for Alex.

But, deep inside, I wanted to be the one making that announcement—after I was married, of course.

Everyone stood, and hugs and congratulations went

around.

Then we ate lasagna and salad and garlic bread. The conversation was lighthearted and joyful. Emptiness spun inside me, though. Unfulfilled longings threw a pity party with my psyche. Indecision pulled at me.

I loved Chase, but did I have a future with him? And if I didn't have a future with him, then why were we together? Our decisions in life should have a purpose. In my estimation, dating was for marriage. If marriage wasn't the end goal, then the relationship needed to cease. The parties involved needed to move on.

My throat burned.

I wanted to be with Chase. I wanted our future to be together. I dreamed about a happy-ever-after with him at my side.

But what if that never happened?

"What are you thinking?" Chase whispered as we sat on the couch drinking coffee after dinner.

I glanced around, my mind reeling. My heart reeling. I wanted life to be simple and clear-cut. Life-changing decisions made it feel complicated.

This wasn't the place to hash it out, though.

"Nothing," I whispered.

"You look like you're in another world."

My cheeks burned. He knew me well enough to know something was wrong. He looked genuinely concerned—concerned enough that I questioned every thought that had crossed my mind in the last five minutes. In the last week, if I were to be honest.

Chase understood me. He loved me. He took care of me.

But did our end goals line up? Would they ever? Or was

he just stringing me along? Maybe not even purposefully. Maybe he was simply being true to himself. Maybe he thought it wouldn't be fair to me to pretend he was ready for something that he wasn't ready for.

But I loved him.

"Holly?" His breath brushed my cheek as he whispered into my ear.

I reached over and squeezed his hand, unsure what else to say. Should I call him outside? Ask to talk to him? To really talk and share my fears and insecurities and concerns?

I should, I decided.

Chase's phone chose that moment to ring—yes, I knew the thought was irrational. But that was how it felt at the moment.

He stepped away and put it to his ear. I have to admit that I lingered close, curious as to what the phone call was about. Especially when his back went rigid.

When the call ended, he turned toward me. His expression looked stormy. "They think they found Jonah."

CHAPTER 26

"I'm going with you," I announced, my thoughts catapulting into a million directions. I followed behind him as he rushed to the front door.

Chase halted mid-step and turned toward me. "You can't, Holly. The best thing you can do is stay here."

"But if it's Jonah, he'll need someone to hold him, to take care of him. Someone he knows." *Me. He needed me.*

Chase bit down and studied me. "Fine. Come with me. But you can't insert yourself in the situation without permission. Understand?"

I nodded a little too eagerly. "Understood."

We climbed into his police-issued sedan, and, before I even got my seatbelt on, Chase charged down the road. He was as anxious for answers as I was.

Could this be Jonah? I prayed that it was. I prayed that he was okay. I prayed for resolution.

My earlier discussion with Chase was now forgotten. Nothing else mattered but Jonah. I so desperately wanted to hold him in my arms again. To kiss his forehead. To see him drool as he smiled.

Please let him be okay.

It took fifteen minutes before we pulled up to a house on the north side of town. Police cars already surrounded the place, as well as an ambulance and a fire truck.

Three different vans were parked out front with news station emblems decorating the sides. Reporters with cameras and notepads waited on the street for an inside scoop.

Jonah's abduction had obviously moved from a buried news story to the headline of the day. A kidnapped baby with a missing mom? There was a good chance this would move beyond local news even. Maybe it already had. I largely avoided newspapers whenever I could because the majority of stories there induced worry and paranoia.

We pulled to a stop, and my thoughts tumbled ahead of me, causing nausea to churn in my stomach. What if this was the home of one of the triathletes? What if me keeping quiet about the triathletes had put Jonah in danger?

The thought caused a small cry to lodge in my throat.

I should tell Chase.

But I'd promised Jamie.

My emotions warred inside me, as they'd done so often lately.

But the triathletes had an alibi. They weren't even here when Jonah was snatched. Withholding that information should not affect this case.

"You can't go beyond the police line," Chase told me.

I nodded and followed him out of the car. He strode under the yellow tape, as if he belonged. Because he did. He knew how to own a crime scene. He lived for this stuff, and he was good at it.

I stood by the yellow police tape and shoved those thoughts aside.

I glanced around. For the first time, I didn't see Evan at the crime scene. Mclean, the officer who'd come to my house after the potential break-in, stood guard at the scene. I even spotted Captain Abbot in the distance.

The captain had come out? That was surprising. The case had obviously been kicked up to high-profile status.

Another car pulled up to the scene, and I spotted Bethany Ellis inside. I rushed to meet her, wondering if her presence meant that Jonah was here.

"They called you?" My stomach squeezed as I said the words.

She nodded as she climbed out of the car and tugged her plaid scarf closer. "I heard they might have found Jonah. Do you know if they did?"

"No idea. I just got here. I came with Chase—Detective Dexter, I mean."

Her expression remained stoic. "Let me see what I can find out."

She showed her ID, and then an officer lifted the police tape and she ducked under. I paced, desperately wanting to be on the other side of this investigation. I hated being on the sidelines.

Lord, am I doing the wrong thing with my life? Is that why I've felt dissatisfied lately?

By the time Chase emerged and walked over to me I couldn't feel my fingers or nose. The darkness outside had only deepened as the night wore on, and I still hadn't seen Jonah yet.

Dear Jonah. Sweet Jonah. Are you here?

"Well?" I could hardly breathe as I asked the question.

He frowned. "He's not here, but it looks like he may have been. The house was empty when we arrived. A neighbor called and said he saw a baby here earlier today."

"I take it that was unusual?"

He nodded. "There are also diapers and bottles, which is unusual since this woman doesn't have any children. There's also evidence that someone has been stalking Katie. There are pictures of her and Gage. There's a stolen gun. We believe it may match the weapon that killed a woman downtown last night."

Morgan Bayfield, I realized.

"Who lives here?" I held my breath as I waited for his response.

His frown deepened. "It's the woman from the gym—the one who argued with Katie. It's too early to say for sure, but it looks like she may have been behind some of this craziness after all."

***

I still felt numb the next morning as I reflected on what I'd learned last night.

The real suspect may have been right in front of us the whole time. That thought bothered me more than I'd realized. I should have followed up. If I had, maybe Jonah would still be safe right now.

I'd stuck around the crime scene for longer than I should have last night. But I'd learned a few things from various people I talked to. I'd learned that the woman who lived at the house was named Ingrid Palmer. She had a history of being unstable and obsessive. Apparently, Katie had been her latest obsession, and it mostly stemmed from their confrontations at the gym.

The police hadn't found her yet—at least, that was the last I'd heard. But they believed she was working with someone and had snatched Jonah. Maybe she was longing for a child of her own. I didn't know—I hadn't been able to piece it all together.

Something about it didn't quite fit for me, and I wasn't

sure what. I mean, people went off their rockers and did crazy things for no apparent explanation all the time. But had Ingrid really killed Gage? Had Katie taken off and left Jonah with me, feeling he was safer in my care than in her own—at least while Ingrid was after her? Had Ingrid discovered Jonah's location and intricately plotted to abduct him?

Furthermore, why was Katie seen talking to one of the triathletes? How did that tie in with all of this?

Despite the new developments, I still wanted to talk to Wesley today. Maybe it was a waste of time. Maybe it wasn't. But until the police found Ingrid and she confessed, I was going to keep searching for answers.

My phone buzzed with an incoming text. I picked it up from my dresser and glanced at the screen. Chase had sent me a message.

Heathcliff's prints found on the gun from last night.

Heathcliff? So he *was* connected with this somehow. I shook my head, trying to wrap my mind around everything, yet failing. The web of deceit in this case was wide and intricate.

After I got dressed, I thumped downstairs. I heard two voices. My mom's and . . . someone else's. My curiosity spiked.

As I rounded the corner, I spotted my mom and Officer Truman sitting at the breakfast nook sharing coffee and pastries. Officer Truman wasn't dressed like he normally was—he didn't have on his police uniform. Instead he wore khakis and a gray sweater that matched his eyes.

The two of them were looking at something on the electronic tablet, and they laughed together.

"Oh, Holly. Good morning," my mom said. "I didn't have

a chance to talk to you last night and tell you that Larry was coming over for breakfast."

Larry? She was on a first-name basis with him?

I nodded toward *Larry*. "Good morning."

He stood and nodded back. "Good morning, Holly."

"Today must be your day off." I walked past and grabbed a coffee mug.

"Just this morning. I head in to start my shift after lunch."

As I filled my cup with steaming liquid, I peered at the table. "What are you two watching?"

He sat back down—a little too close to my mom. "Cat videos. I guess you can teach an old dog new tricks. I'm actually learning how to use this tablet. It's kind of handy."

Cat videos? Oh my.

And when had all of this transpired? How? Through searching for my father's biological family?

"I heard there was some excitement last night," Officer Truman—Larry—said, looking away from the tablet.

I nodded and filled my mom in.

"Have you heard any updates?" I asked, taking a sip of my coffee.

He shook his head. "I wish I had, but no."

"I do hope they find that precious boy." Mom shook her head, her skin paling as she spoke about Jonah. "He deserves a safe place, you know?"

That was right. Jonah did deserve a safe place. Children, in general, deserve safe places—emotionally and physically.

That was why I wasn't giving up on this until Jonah was found.

I glanced at my watch.

It was time to pick up Jamie and pay a visit to her friend

Wesley.

***

An hour later, Jamie and I pulled up to a lovely house located on the top of a hill with stunning views of the Ohio River. The home was Tudor style, massive, and well-kept.

"This is where Wesley lives?" I questioned, staring up at the house.

She nodded. "He has his own computer IT firm. It must pay pretty well."

"You've been here before, I take it?"

She may have blushed. "To do the article. And then they had a little party last weekend, and I stopped by for a few minutes."

"Nice."

We climbed the steps to his front door, and I wondered if he was even home. Although he'd just competed in a race yesterday, Jamie made it sound like he worked out at every opportunity.

I hoped he was here now, and I also hoped things didn't turn ugly. Especially if this was all about guns.

Sarah had said the man she'd seen Katie speaking with was a light-skinned African-American man. Wesley, according to Jamie, had darker skin and liked to shave his head.

That was the good news.

The bad news was two-fold: Anthony was the light-skinned one of the group and, if the three of these triathletes really were sworn blood brothers, they could all be in on it.

Wesley answered a few minutes after we rang the bell, and his eyes lit up when he saw Jamie.

This was the first time I'd seen him in person, and I

observed him carefully. He was handsome, with a bright smile and sculpted body. His plastic-rimmed glasses gave him a smart vibe—a bit of nerdy cute. Jamie had said that he'd been geeky in high school and considered himself a late bloomer.

In fact, all three of the triathletes had talked about being bullied and how they were using the changes in their lives to be a positive role model to others. I could see it. My initial impression was smart, athletic, and down–to-earth.

There was nothing not to like about him—unless he was a killer.

"What are you doing here? You come over to do another story on me?" Wesley preened in an overdramatic, goofy manner.

Jamie smiled, almost looking nervous. "I'll do another story on you anytime."

It was at that moment that I realized just how nice Jamie looked today. She'd worn her favorite jeans and a flattering sweater that showed off her shrinking waistline. However, her actions seemed subdued. Even her hair seemed to have lost a little of its spring.

I knew what she was thinking. Her heart had already been broken once by someone who'd pretended to like her. Another betrayal would desperately set her back in her pursuit of love.

Oh my. She had it bad. Jamie *never* looked nervous.

"I'm not sure there's much else you could write about me. I'm a pretty boring guy."

Jamie's smile faded. "Actually, I wished we were doing a story. Can we talk?"

Some of the lightheartedness faded from his gaze, replaced with a touch of worry and curiosity. "Of course. Come in."

"This is my friend, Holly."

I shook his hand before stepping inside.

"I've heard a lot about you," he said.

"Hopefully, it was all good."

"You know it. Said you were like two peas in a pod."

"That's how good friends usually are." As I said the words, I wondered about the truth in them. Even if Wesley knew something about one of his friends, would he admit to it? Was he in on it? Or was all of this for nothing?

I had no idea yet. I hoped we might learn something soon, though.

"How did the triathlon go?" Jamie asked as we lingered in the two-story foyer.

"Great. I landed one of my best times yet."

"Congrats." She shifted uneasily. "I hope we're not interrupting anything."

He grinned. "Just taxes. You're much more interesting."

More romantic words had never been spoken.

I marveled at the inside of the place. The woodwork was amazing and intricate. And the walls were made from shiplap. I was obsessed with shiplap after watching too many shows on HGTV.

My dad, who'd loved to work with wood, would have been impressed with the interior design. He'd fixed up our family home, even adding some secret passages, just for fun. It was one of the many qualities I'd loved about him.

"Nice place."

"I like it." He leaned against a dark wooden banister. "I restored the whole thing. It was unlivable when I bought it."

"Fascinating," I muttered. The place was undoubtedly gorgeous. I wondered if he ever did any work on the side.

The thought startled me because I'd instantly thought

of the little bungalow my mom had shown me. What would it be like to fix it up? To have a place of my own?

Wesley led us to a library that smelled like leather and lemon Pledge. Not a bad combination, in my estimation, at least. The room was located off the entryway. Right as I walked in, I spotted an open Bible on a desk in the corner.

I really hoped he didn't end up being one of the bad guys—on so many levels I wished that.

He pointed to the leather couch. "Have a seat."

We did. He sat across from us.

"Now, what brings you here? It's not a social visit, I assume. Not based on the looks on your faces. If you two didn't both have me so nervous, I'd offer you some coffee. I don't think I can make myself wait long enough to make it. I'm anxious to hear what you have to say."

"I wish it was a social visit," Jamie started, her face deadly serious. "I have a question about Anthony."

I wanted to pat her back as a reassurance, but I was afraid it would make her even more nervous.

"What about him?" Wesley shifted and rubbed his hands on his jeans.

"Did you ever see him talking to this woman?" She pulled up a picture of Katie on her phone and showed it to him.

Wesley studied the photo before shaking his head. "I can't say I have. What's this about?"

I didn't see any flashes of recognition or signs of deceit.

I was going to have to trust Jamie here on how much to tell him. It was her call, and I knew she'd make a good choice.

"He was one of the last people seen with a woman who's missing and a baby who's been kidnapped." Jamie's chest heaved a little too hard.

Any semblance of a smile left Wesley. "What?"

Jamie nodded. "It's true. We think Anthony was seen with this woman last Thursday. He met her at her car as she was leaving the sitter's house."

He rubbed a hand over his head. "Is this the baby who was abducted, the one who's been on the news?"

Jamie nodded.

"You think Anthony has something to do with it?"

"We don't know. We're just looking for answers," I said, jumping in before Jamie passed out from not breathing properly. "We were hoping you knew something."

He sat in stunned silence. "I wish I knew something. I've never seen this woman before. And Anthony . . . he's a good guy. He wouldn't get mixed up in something like this. I can assure you of that. Besides, he's so busy with working and training that he wouldn't have time to get into trouble."

"Do you know where he was on Sunday?" I asked, saving Jamie the agony.

"I do, as a matter of fact. We went to church together. Then afterward we took a ten-mile run along the river. I had a barbecue with his family that afternoon. Does that put your mind more at ease?"

Jamie's shoulders slumped with visible relief. "It does. Thank you."

A shadow crossed his face. "I think I can help you find some more answers, though. How about if I ask Anthony to stop by?"

"You'd do that for me?" Jamie's voice lilted like she was impressed.

He nodded. "Anything for you, Jamie."

***

I paced as I waited for Anthony to show up. This could potentially bring us the answers we needed. Or it could lead us to more questions. I wasn't sure if I could handle more questions. I was up to my eyeballs in them already.

Jamie looked equally as nervous, though Wesley appeared to be a nice distraction. They sat on the couch beside each other, talking about ways to make popcorn. Both looked totally entrenched in the meaningless conversation.

I remembered those early days of dating when everything seemed new and fresh and exciting. Chase and I used to talk for hours about inconsequential things like four-leaf clovers, and the best way to shuck corn, and how calculus should be outlawed in high schools and a course on taxes should replace it.

Had that faded from our lives? Even if it had, it wouldn't necessarily be a bad thing. Relationships had different phases, as did life.

I only wished I felt more certain about things lately.

Just then, the doorbell rang. All three of us stiffened. Finally, Wesley stood and strode out of the room while Jamie and I remained in the library. In the distance, I could hear the door open and the two men exchange a jovial greeting. The suspicious side of me had to wonder: Was Wesley prepping Anthony? Whispering in his ear? Gathering weapons?

Finally, they appeared at the library entrance. I quickly soaked in Anthony's features. He was a tall, thin, light-skinned African-American with curly hair that was cropped close. His smile didn't come as easily as Wesley's had.

Actually, it didn't come at all.

I braced myself for whatever would happen next.

Wesley's face looked tight, and Anthony's face instantly showed confusion when he spotted us.

"What's going on?" Anthony's gaze fell on Jamie. "Another article?"

Wesley shook his head. "I'm sorry I didn't speak the total truth. Jamie and her friend, Holly, have some questions they're hoping you can answer. I know you're a stand-up guy who would want to help."

His body looked tense, with tight shoulders, a hard jaw, and piercing eyes. He undoubtedly felt like he'd been backed into a corner. Anyone would.

"Okay . . . what's going on?" Anthony didn't sit, but instead stood beside Wesley.

Wesley nodded toward Jamie, who then looked at me.

"You take it, Holly," my friend said.

It sounded totally unlike my brazen friend. She *really* liked this guy.

"I need to ask you about your connection with Katie Edwards," I started.

As soon as I said her name, Anthony's head subtly jerked back. He blinked. Flinched ever so slightly.

I held my breath, waiting to see what he would say or do next.

"Who said I know a Katie Edwards?" he finally said, his expression stone cold.

"Well, based on your reaction, you did," I said.

His gaze darted from person to person. He was a man on the edge, I realized. He was ready to run. Fight or flight. Even more than that, I realized, he knew something. I wasn't leaving until I found out what.

"What about her?"

I got right to the point. "She's missing. So is her baby. Her boyfriend is dead."

He closed his eyes and hung his head, transforming in

an instant from on the edge to burdened. "I tried to warn her."

My heart pounded in my chest. We were close. So close. I could feel it. "Warn her about what?"

"That she was in over her head." He paced toward a seat beside the couch. "I need to sit down."

I swallowed hard. All the optimism in the world couldn't defeat the power of bad news. And bad news loomed like a storm in the distance right now.

"How did you know Katie?" I asked, trying to gather all the facts I could.

He shook his head, which was still lowered. "I didn't. Not really. I knew her boyfriend, though. I'd seen her picture on his phone and asked if he was married. My mom always told me I had the gift of gab." He let out a chuckle, but it quickly faded. "Anyway, he mentioned her name to me, and, with a little research, I was able to figure out where she lived. I thought if I could reach Katie, maybe she could get through to Gage."

"And how did you know Gage?" I continued.

He raised his head, but his face looked like it had aged a decade since he arrived. "He showed up at my house asking questions one day."

"About . . . ?" I was going to have to pull each detail from him, wasn't I? He was obviously nervous and hesitant to share. In fact, if Wesley hadn't been here, I wasn't sure he *would* be sharing.

"You really don't want to know. The less you know, the safer you are. You've got to believe me."

That kicked my curiosity up another notch.

But I wasn't buying it, not when so much was on the line. "I think we can handle the truth. We have no choice but to handle the truth. The life of a little six-month-old depends on it. Every minute that passes makes this more critical."

He hung his head and swung it back and forth. "I was afraid something like this was going to happen."

"Why don't you start at the beginning?" Wesley's gaze never left his friend.

Anthony raised his head but remained quiet. I thought he might refuse to speak. Finally, he drew in a deep breath.

"It all started when Gage showed up on my doorstep about three weeks ago. He was doing some research into a string of robberies in the area. My home was one of those that had been broken into."

"He was writing about the robberies?" Jamie clarified.

"That's right," Anthony said. "It was a little odd because the guy who broke into my house was caught. He'd been slapped with a fine but not given any jail time. Pretty light sentence, right? Especially since he stole around $5,000 worth of things from my place."

"I remember you mentioning that," Wesley said.

"Yeah, it was a headache. But that's not really what Gage wanted to talk to me about. It went deeper than that."

"What was it?" I asked, desperate to put together the pieces and tired of being fed a tiny morsel at a time.

"He was asking about some prescription drugs I'd been taking."

I let that settle in my mind. It hadn't been what I'd expected to hear. Not at all. "Prescription drugs? How'd Gage know you were taking prescription drugs?"

He shrugged. "I guess it was any easy assumption since my accident. Most people whose bodies have been through the kind of trauma mine has end up taking something to control the pain. Anyway, after the robbery, my drugs disappeared."

"Gage thought that was newsworthy, I guess?" I asked, trying to grasp what he was getting at. I was determined to follow this through to completion.

He dragged in another deep breath. "Not in itself. He got a lead that someone was stealing prescription drugs from people's homes and selling them at top dollar on the street."

Heathcliff. Was that what Heathcliff was doing? Was he behind the break-ins? We'd thought it was weapons, but what if it wasn't? What if it was both?

"The strange thing was this: While the burglar was still in jail—this was before he went before the judge and was let off too easy—my house was broken into again. Nothing was taken the second time—except my prescriptions."

"Interesting." I remembered my own medicine that was missing. I needed to look for those pill bottles again when I had the chance. I hadn't thought about them again until this conversation. "But I'm still not sure why knowing that information puts my life in danger."

"There's more to it." He swallowed hard. "In each of the cases where drugs were stolen, different people were behind the crimes. The burglaries themselves weren't connected, other than the missing drugs."

"So there's a ring of guys who are breaking in and making it look like they're stealing electronics when they're actually stealing drugs?" I clarified, feeling like I was missing something.

"On the surface that might be what it seemed like, but Gage had a different theory. He apparently thought someone else connected with the scenes was stealing the drugs."

"Who would do that? I mean, that would require the same people being at these crimes and being unseen by the officers there. They would almost have to be—" Before I finished my sentence, my voice caught.

I knew exactly what he was getting at. But I hoped I was

wrong, that I'd jumped to conclusions too hastily.

"First responders." Anthony frowned. "Gage thought they were pocketing the drugs as they did their investigations. He was trying to collect enough evidence to prove it."

CHAPTER 27

I gave myself a minute to let that sink in. This wasn't about weapons. It wasn't about street drugs. It was about *prescription* drugs all along.

The color drained from my face. When had I last seen my own prescription painkillers? Was it before the police had come to my house this week? "So what do you think happened?"

Anthony's gaze locked with mine. "I think one of the first responders picked up on what Gage was researching for his article, and I think he was killed to keep him silent. I think Katie was set up to look like the one who did it, and that the police manipulated the evidence."

My heart pounded in my ears.

It couldn't be.

First responders? I'd worked with them numerous times. They were all stand-up men and women . . . right? They'd only done justice by me—as far as I knew.

My next thought was of Chase. He wasn't involved in this, was he?

I had seen that picture of him meeting with Morgan Bayfield. He'd lied about being at the homicide that night.

No, Holly. Have faith. You know him better than that.

Even that thought didn't calm my stomach, which churned with anxiety.

Jamie's hand went to my back. She must have read my thoughts. The tables here had turned, and I was the one now nervous.

"So you went to warn Katie on Thursday?" I could hardly speak because my throat was so tight. "How did you know danger was closing in?"

"Ever since Gage talked to me, I felt like I was being watched. It made me suspicious. I started talking to people at the break-ins, and their stories confirmed Gage's theory. Someone has been stealing drugs, but it's been like a slight-of-hand trick. There's always been a bigger crime involved that helped to cover up the missing prescriptions."

"Did you confront the police officers or do anything to make them suspicious of you?"

He shook his head. "No, but I started getting threats. Weird stuff started happening. Then my neighbor's car was vandalized. Somehow the things that were stolen ended up in my shed. I thought they were going to arrest me on the spot."

Wesley nodded. "It's true. I was there for all of it. The weird thing was when the robbery supposedly went down, Anthony had an alibi. We were training together out of town."

Whoever was involved in this ring was using evidence tampering. They didn't deserve to have a badge. They were wielding their power to hurt others.

"Do you remember what any of the cops looked like?" I asked.

Anthony shook his head. "I'm nearly certain there were different cops who showed up each time. I couldn't tell you which one was involved."

"Do you remember anything about any of them?" I asked. I was close—so close. But narrowing down who was involved would only make this more complicated.

He sighed. "One was older with a square face. I thought he was too old to be on patrol. But his voice seemed kind."

I sucked in a deep breath. Officer Truman.

Was he involved this?

I prayed that wasn't the case.

Because I was beginning to lose faith in humanity . . . something an optimist should never have to say.

CHAPTER 28

"When was the last time you saw Katie?"

As soon as the question left my lips, Anthony stiffened again, and I knew there was more to the story. Digging for more answers had paid off.

His jaw flexed, and he rubbed it. Closed his eyes. Sighed. Opened his eyes again and stared in the distance. Finally, he said, "I talked to her again on Sunday."

Anticipation buzzed through me. This man was the link I'd been looking for. He'd been so close yet so far away this whole time. "When on Sunday?"

"That evening."

"She called you after she discovered Gage was dead . . ." I realized. After she dropped off Jonah. As she went on the run after everything that had gone down.

Anthony nodded. "She did. She told me what happened. She told me she was going to hide out, but she didn't know where yet. Said she'd made sure the baby was safe and had tried to cover her tracks."

"What did you tell her?" Jamie's eyes were riveted on Anthony.

"Between the four of us, I told her I had a place out in Brown County, Indiana, that she could use. I figured no one would find her there—for a while, at least."

"Did she go there?" The question came out quickly, as if

my mouth was trying to keep up with my thoughts.

He leaned closer and lowered his voice until it was raspy. “You can’t tell anyone this. Her life is on the line.”

“Because she was framed?” I filled in the blanks. All that evidence at the crime scene had most likely been set up by someone else. Someone experienced, who knew how to cover his or her tracks. Someone who had access to things if they forgot anything.

“Exactly,” Anthony said. “And if the cops who set her up get to her first, she’s as good as dead. They’ll kill her and make it look like an accident. Maybe a suicide.”

He had a point. It suddenly made sense why she ran. Why she left the note. I still wasn’t quite sure why she left Jonah with me—maybe because our connection was so disconnected—or why she addressed the note to “Ms. Holly,” unless she’d done that just to throw me off her trail. It was a possibility.

And speaking of setting someone up to look like a suicide . . . what about Bo, Violet’s brother? He’d supposedly taken his life. What if it was all staged also? What if he’d actually been killed and the police had swept it under the rug?

Things were starting to make sense, but I wasn’t liking the answers I got. That was the danger of searching for answers, I supposed. Sometimes you found them, and they made you sick to your stomach when you did.

“I can only assume that any evidence Gage found to prove his theory was taken after he was killed,” I mused aloud. The police had been there at the scene. Covering up after themselves would have been easy.

“Most likely.” Anthony nodded. “So we’ve got nothing. No proof. Only speculation. We take this information to the wrong person, we’re all sitting ducks. That’s why I didn’t want to tell anyone."

"Thank you for sharing this," I told him. "There's only one person I trust to help us. Do I have your permission to speak with him?"

Anthony didn't say anything for a moment. "Is he a cop?"

I nodded.

He rubbed his jaw. "I don't know."

"You can't let the bullies win," Jamie said. "Then everyone loses."

That was a line from the article. I remembered reading it.

He rolled his shoulders back at her pronouncement. "Are you sure he's trustworthy?"

I nodded again.

Finally Anthony bobbed his head up and then down. "Tell him about the drug ring. Tell him other cops are involved. But don't tell him you know where Katie is. Deal?"

"Deal."

***

Jamie and I were both quiet as we stepped into the cold outdoors. I pulled my coat closer as I walked toward my car. The conversation had left me chilled.

Truman? Really?

I still couldn't believe it.

I climbed into my Mustang and cranked the heat.

I couldn't bring myself to put the car into Drive. Not yet. I had too much on my mind.

"You really think you can trust Chase?" Jamie asked beside me.

"Yes, of course, I can trust him. Why?"

Her shoulder shrugged upward. "He did get that new truck recently."

"He said he got a good deal on it . . ." Even as I said the words, I realized how it sounded. "Jamie, you know him. He wouldn't be involved in something like this."

"Let me play devil's advocate for a moment. Then why was he photographed with the blonde woman? Morgan Bayfield?"

I didn't have the answers yet. "He had to have good reason."

She made a face before nodding. "If you think he's on the up and up, then I'll go with your decision."

"Thank you." A hint of doubt lingered in the back of my mind, though.

Trust, Holly. Trust.

Before I could second-guess myself, I picked up my phone and dialed Chase's number. He answered right away. His voice sounded short and hurried. That meant he was on the job, usually. "What's up?"

"Chase, there are some things I need to tell you," I started.

"Is this about Jonah?"

"Yes. Jonah and Katie."

He paused a moment. "I'm at a crime scene right now, but I can meet you in an hour. Does that work?"

"Yes, I'll see you then. My house."

"Are you safe?"

"I think so."

"Good. Stay that way until I meet you."

"See you then."

As he said the words, a small part of me really hoped I

didn't regret this.

Whoever was behind this had quite the scheme going on. Stealing drugs. Selling them. Setting up other people to look guilty. Abusing power to the full extent. I put the car into drive and took off, feeling like I was on autopilot.

"Your mom and Truman," Jamie said, probably reading my thoughts.

"I know." I dreaded telling my mom the news. Even if it wasn't true, she'd eventually learn about the allegations and would be crushed by them. "He just seems better than this."

"Looks can be deceiving. We've seen that before."

Silence stretched a moment as the roadside blurred past. My thoughts turned and raced and skittered.

Finally, I blurted, "Wesley seems nice."

My words seemed so inconsequential, but I needed time to process everything.

"He is."

I glanced at my best friend. "You really like him?"

"I do."

"I don't think you ruined your chances."

She frowned. "Who knows what they're saying about me now."

"That you have integrity."

"Or that I've got nerve."

"Nerve isn't a bad thing." I'd developed a lot more nerve after my misdiagnosis. When you think you have only a year to live, your perspective changes.

Apparently Bo's perspective had changed also, but not for the better. How did he tie into all of this? I wondered, my mind unable to escape the thought.

A theory took shape in my mind, but I wanted some confirmation. I needed more pieces of the puzzle to fit together.

I could feel we were close to the truth—so close that I could nearly taste it—like you could taste the salty ocean air before you even saw the water on the horizon.

"Where are we going?" Jamie asked. "You just missed the turn going back to your house."

"I think we have time for one more stop."

***

The one-hour time frame gave me enough time to swing by the hotel in downtown Cincinnati where Violet worked. Hotel Plaid. How could I forget a name like that? I just wanted to confirm a few things with Violet about what she'd seen and ask her a few more questions before I threw anyone under the bus.

Hotel Plaid was a trendy hotel located downtown. It wasn't large, but there were bright, vibrant colors on the wall; a busy restaurant located off the lobby; and it was mostly patronized by people in their twenties and thirties.

As soon as we walked in, I spotted Violet working the front desk. Her eyes widened when she saw me. She still looked as jittery as ever with her quick motions and high-pitched voice.

"How'd you find me?" She leaned in close and lowered her voice as we approached the desk.

I leaned toward her. "It's a long story. Violet, I just have a couple of questions for you. It's important."

She glanced behind me nervously, as if the bad guys had followed me inside. They could have, for all I knew. I mean, I'd watched my back as we'd driven here and hadn't seen anyone. But apparently I rarely saw the people who followed me.

"Not here," Violet whispered, her gaze still shifting back and forth. "Let's go to the lobby."

She rounded the desk and led Jamie and me over into a corner. She walked briskly, but she didn't look back once she started. Away from any listening ears, she leaned closer to us. "What's going on? Is this about Bo?"

"Possibly," I started. "Did your brother take prescription drugs?"

"For a while he did. After his cancer surgeries he was in a lot of pain. Demerol was his best friend. Why do you ask? What does that have to do with anything?"

I had to ask her more questions before I explained. "You said he came into some money?"

"That's right. I'm not sure where it came from."

"And that he was acting differently?" I continued.

Her eyebrows jammed together. "What's this about?"

I touched her arm, trying to convince her to trust me now, just like she'd done a couple of days ago. "I just need to know. Then I'll explain."

She finally nodded. "Yes, he was."

"Last question. I promise. Was he friends with any cops?"

Her gaze swept to the left then the right as she assessed different parts of her brain. Psychology 101. "Not really. I mean, not that I know of."

I released my breath. "Violet, I've uncovered some new information that's led me to believe Bo may have been involved in a prescription-drug ring."

She gasped and then her shoulders slumped. "Maybe. I guess that would make sense. Prescription drugs . . . even though they're not illegal, per se, they can still change people."

"Especially opioids." I'd worked with a few people who'd gotten caught up in prescription drugs after surgeries. It hadn't been pretty, and, the even sadder part was, it generally started innocently and eventually turned into a monster that they couldn't control.

Violet sniffled. "I don't know how he got mixed up in it. I mean, I understand that he could have been taking those drugs and maybe even become addicted to them. But . . . you think that's what got him killed?"

"That's my best guess," I told her. "I think someone staged it to look like a suicide."

She pinched the skin between her eyes. It was a lot for anyone to take in.

Finally, she raised her head, drew in a breath to compose herself, and nodded. "Thank you for finding some answers. If you hear any more, will you let me know?"

"Of course."

Now I had to get home in time to meet Chase.

As Jamie and I headed upstairs toward the parking garage entry, the skin on my neck rose. I paused and looked over my shoulder.

There were crowds of people behind us. It looked like a session had ended at the convention center, which was connected with this hotel.

I didn't see anyone who stood out.

So why did I feel like someone was watching me?

"What's going on?" Jamie asked.

I glanced over my shoulder again. "I've got a bad feeling."

"About what?"

"I'm not sure. I think we're getting too close to the truth, though."

"Now you're freaking me out."

The crowd continued to thicken. I thought I'd heard something about a homeschool convention that was taking place here and had brought in thousands of people.

I looked behind me one more time. This time, a face caught my eye.

It was the man with the crazy hands. The one who'd stood near Jamie and me in the coffee house that day.

And he was following us.

I didn't have to stare long to know that the look in his eyes was full of vengeance. This encounter wasn't meant to scare or warn us.

He was going to hurt us.

I took her arm and quickened my steps. "We've got to move."

"What do you mean?"

I pulled her along, not daring to slow for even a minute. "No time to explain. But there's a man following us. He'll kill us if he has the chance."

She started to look over her shoulder, but I stopped her.

"Don't," I urged her. "Just move. Please."

I scanned in front of us. All I saw were thick crowds, moving leisurely. Eventually Jamie and I could head down an escalator, and there would be various points of exit onto the streets of downtown.

Could we make it that far?

I'd guess the man had a gun. If he got close enough, he'd shove it into our backs. Force us to do what he wanted. Take us somewhere quiet and finish us off. My instincts had never felt as sharp as now.

Right now, the throng of people could be our friend. The masses could conceal us and protect us. But all of that could change in an instant. I didn't want to put other people's lives in danger.

"Do you have a plan?" Jamie whispered as the

multitudes jostled us.

"Stay away from the bad man."

She snorted. "Glad you've thought this through."

"I try."

Up ahead, the swarms of homeschoolers began thinning. That wasn't good. We'd stand out, be less concealed. But we were going to have to use that to our advantage somehow.

I glanced behind me again.

The man was getting closer. He was pushing his way past people now, upping his pace so he could reach us.

I had to think fast. Desperate times called for desperate measures, right?

Drawing in a breath, I shouted, "Fire!"

Panic erupted around us as people scrambled for safety. Families clung together. Businessmen began to jog. A few people stopped to look around.

Please, forgive me.

However, a man with a gun in a crowd was a danger to all of us. I just prayed no one got trampled in the process.

Jamie and I reached the escalator. I looked over my shoulder one more time.

I'd lost sight of the man, but I knew he was still on our tail.

"Holly, there's a cop out there. Maybe we can get to him."

I looked straight ahead and saw a uniformed officer standing near the exit. With a touch of confusion on his face, he watched everyone fleeing the building. He picked up his radio and talked to someone.

"We can't, Jamie. We don't know whom we can trust."

"What are you saying?

"Cops are in on this. We don't know which ones. But we can't risk it. What if he's one of the ones involved in this?"

Her face paled. "Then what are we going to do?"

I glanced around again. "I have an idea."

I only hoped it didn't get us killed.

CHAPTER 29

I grabbed Jamie's hand and pulled her to another hallway on the first floor. We ran against the crowds as they exited.

On this side of the convention center, word hadn't spread about the fire, so people were calmer. The crowd was still thick, though, which worked in our favor.

"What are you doing?" Jamie whispered.

"Trying to keep us alive."

I darted into the exhibit area where what appeared to be hundreds of booths were set up by vendors—everything from curriculum to toys to bookstores.

I found the first unmanned one I saw—it appeared to have some kind of science theme, based on the beakers and test tubes at the back—and I pulled Jamie behind it. We ducked under the table there, beneath the tablecloth.

And then we waited.

"This was your plan?" Jamie whispered.

"Did you have a better idea?"

Underneath the table it was dark. A black piece of fabric covered it, but slits at the corners allowed me to watch people as they walked past. Occasionally, fast walkers caused the edges to breeze open. I prayed that we'd stay concealed.

I didn't think anyone had seen us duck under here, but I couldn't be sure.

I could see the shoes on the other side—only shadows of them, really. Some people had probably taken their lunch hour to peruse the area in search of free items, new ideas, or gifts to take home.

Footsteps paused on the other side of the table. I drew in a deep breath. Was it the man? Had he seen us? Would he finish us right here?

I glanced at Jamie. Even though it was dark, I could see the fear in her eyes.

I prayed this decision didn't get us both killed.

I dared not move. I hardly wanted to breathe.

Finally, the feet moved. One step. Then two. Then back again.

It was the man who was chasing us. I felt certain of it.

Drawing in a deep breath, I moved the tablecloth ever so slightly and peered out.

I was right. It was the man. His hands still clenched and unclenched. But he wasn't looking down at us. No, he was surveying the rest of the convention hall, trying to figure out where we'd gone.

If we could remain low-key, maybe we had a chance.

Just then, Jamie fanned her face. Her eyes narrowed. She sucked in a breath.

Oh no! She had to sneeze.

I shook my head and mouthed, "Not now!"

It was too late. Her high-pitched sneeze cut through the air. From where I sat, it sounded loud enough to startle someone from the dead. I held my breath and watched to see what the man would do.

He turned.

I braced myself for a struggle.

But before he could look our way, something hit the table.

Voices sounded overhead.

The people who managed this booth were back, I realized.

The man seemed satisfied that the sneeze had come from one of them. He walked away.

That had been close. Too close.

***

Chase was waiting for me when we got back to the house. He sat in his truck, looking at something on his computer. I sent Jamie inside to distract my mom, and I hoisted myself into the passenger seat.

I told Chase everything I'd learned. He grunted with each new fact that I presented but said very little until I finished.

"I don't even want to know how you put all of this together. You never cease to amaze me. Truth is, I've suspected something has been going on for a while."

My breath caught. "You have?"

He nodded, his jaw flexing. "One of my neighbors approached me about some missing prescriptions. He mentioned a burglary at his house a couple of weeks ago. Someone else had reported to another detective that the same thing had happened. That got my attention, and I started looking into it. I've been trying to review police reports and pinpoint who was involved and how deeply this went."

"Is that why you met with Morgan Bayfield?" I slipped the question in, unable to resist any longer.

He shot me a quick look, his forehead lined with surprise. "Morgan Bayfield? How do you know about her?"

I wasn't sure I wanted to launch into Evan's sudden interest in me. "Long story."

He studied my face a moment—quietly, discerning. "Were you following me?"

"No, I wasn't. I've learned my lesson on that. I found out accidentally, I suppose."

"You weren't supposed to see me with her. No one was."

My spine stiffened. I didn't like the sound of that. "Why?"

He sighed. "While doing my off-the-books investigation, I came across her name. I'm working with another detective in narcotics, and a doctor at the jail came to him with some concerns about his nurse."

"Morgan was his nurse?"

Chase nodded. "I was able to connect this ring with Morgan. She was writing prescriptions for fake patients under the doctor's name and sending them electronically to the pharmacy. She went as far as to sell to certain inmates after they were released from jail."

"Why'd you meet with her?"

"I was trying to run her—and I was close. We were supposed to meet again at 15th and Vine on Thursday. She was going to hand over the names of everyone involved. But she was already dead when I arrived."

That explained why he'd said he worked the homicide that night. He had been there—unofficially. "You think someone else involved in this ring killed her?"

"I do, probably to keep her quiet. I could tell she had some qualms about doing what she was doing. My guess was that she saw this as an easy way to make some money. Her mom's treatments were expensive, and Morgan was desperate."

"Does that mean other cops know about this

investigation?"

"Just one. We can't come forward with information until we have all the evidence."

"Did you know Jonah was connected with this?"

"Not at first. I had no idea Gage or Katie might be involved with this. I didn't suspect anything until you told me about Bo and that he'd met with Gage concerning an article."

"How did that clue you in?"

"His death shook up Morgan, and she mentioned that she thought someone she knew had been killed, but his murder had been covered up."

"Why didn't you tell me?" Hurt stretched throughout my voice.

He glanced at me, and his eyes softened. "It was too risky, Holly. You know there are certain things I can't tell you. This was one of them. No one could know. It would have put you in danger."

This was no time for hurt feelings. I licked my lips, bracing myself for what I had to say next. "Chase, my source hinted that Officer Truman is involved."

Chase's face tightened. "I don't want to believe that's true. I don't know Truman very well, but he seems like a good cop. I can confirm that he was at many of the crime scenes where prescription drugs were stolen."

"He's fallen on some hard times. I know his son died and his wife left him. Maybe selling these prescription drugs seemed like an easy way to get more money."

He nodded, still looking somber. "It's a possibility."

"How does Ingrid from the gym tie in with this?" I asked.

He grimaced. "I'm not 100 percent sure, but I think we can safely assume she was set up. I think a lot of false clues have been planted to throw off us of the scent of what was really going on. One of the cops involved must have heard us talking about questioning her—it was in the briefing we had to do about Jonah, and there was no way I could keep it quiet. I didn't think anyone would take it this far. She must have seemed like a good scapegoat, and these guys utilized that fact to their full advantage."

"But she was seen with a baby."

"Her sister recently had a baby. She denied putting the photos of Katie in her house. She said someone put them there after she left."

Silence—thick and unpleasant—stretched.

"What are you going to do?" I finally asked.

"I'm going to go check out Truman's house."

"You're not going to report it first? You still don't have enough evidence?"

He shook his head. "Just the seed of doubt about his integrity could ruin his career. I won't do that to him until I know something for sure. He's on patrol right now, if I remember correctly."

"He wouldn't leave a baby there alone . . . right?" Panic quelled in me at the thought.

Chase grimaced. "We can only hope. He may have, however, left some kind of evidence that a baby has been there. That's what we'll look for."

I had doubts in my mind about that. After all, Truman would be smarter than that. If he'd snatched the baby, he would have taken Jonah somewhere else . . . right?

And what about the man who posed as a social worker? Who was he, and how did he tie into all of this? This operation was more than a one-man job.

I still had so many questions.

I cleared my throat, anticipating Chase's answer to my next question. "Can I go with you?"

His eyebrow quirked up. "Can I stop you?"

"Probably not."

"You can come, but only if you promise to play by my rules."

***

Truman lived in an old, brick ranch-style house that looked out of place next to the hodgepodge of other houses on his street. Most had battered wood siding and overgrown lawns. His house was neat but simple.

We crammed into Chase's truck, which wasn't ideal since I had to straddle the gearshift, but we figured my car would be too noticeable. Jamie had agreed to remain as lookout in the truck while Chase and I checked out the house.

I was actually stunned Chase hadn't put his foot down and insisted I stay home. Maybe he knew me well enough to know there was a good chance I'd show up anyway, and he figured he'd head off trouble by letting me tag along.

There were no cars outside Truman's house, so we could most likely safely assume he was still on patrol and that no one was home.

I really hoped he wasn't guilty. I liked Truman. Obviously, my mom liked Truman also. He seemed level-headed and kind.

However, I'd encountered enough criminals to know that those traits didn't determine innocence or guilt. The kindest of souls could be desperate enough to break the law.

After we climbed out of the truck, Chase took my hand. He looked left and then right before pulling me toward the back of the house, where a privacy fence better concealed us.

Once we were safely in the backyard, I breathed a little easier. At least we were out of sight. For a moment.

"What are we looking for?" My breath frosted in front of me in the gray winter air.

"I just want to peer inside. Without a warrant, that's the best I can do right now."

A small deck jutted from the backdoor, and three windows were close enough to allow for easy snooping. I headed that way while Chase, who was considerably taller, checked the other windows.

Whenever I closed my eyes, I imagined a gunshot cracking the air. The thought made my bones shudder. Whoever was behind this was dangerous, and I hoped we hadn't just walked into a trap.

The first window I came to displayed the kitchen on the other side. There was nothing there except some overripe bananas, some papers stacked on the counter, and a neat-looking fridge. Nothing out of the ordinary.

Next, I peered into the glass of the backdoor. Again, nothing stood out. A living room was on the other side, including an old couch with a blanket draped over it and some mismatched pillows.

The man could use some decorating help, but that was no crime. My mom would have been a great one to assist him. His loss.

My breaths came even easier. If Truman had anything to do with this—and I couldn't believe he did—then he'd left no evidence behind. I knew there would be more investigations after today, that this wouldn't be the judge and jury of his innocence. But at least it was a good start.

Just then, my phone beeped. It was Jamie.

"There's a patrol car coming your way," she whispered. "I can't tell who's driving it, and I'm down low in the seat right now so I won't be spotted."

My pulse spiked. I motioned to Chase, and he nodded, starting back toward me.

I just wanted to peek in that last window. I had time to do that . . . right?

Quickly, I peered inside.

What I saw stopped me in my tracks.

It was the green dinosaur Ralph had bought for Jonah. The rattle rested on the floor, like it had been dropped in a hurry.

CHAPTER 30

From down below on the grass, Chase motioned for me to follow him. "We need to hide. Now."

I nodded, unable to get the image of the dinosaur out of my mind as I skirted around a picnic table toward the steps.

Truman couldn't have done this.

Yet all the evidence was right there.

As soon as I reached the edge of the deck, Chase grabbed my hand and tugged me across the yard so quickly that my feet could hardly keep up. He pulled me behind a shed at the corner of the yard and drew me closer as we waited. The cold chilled my skin and made me shiver.

Or maybe it was the situation.

I couldn't be sure.

"There's baby stuff in there," I whispered. "Stuff that was Jonah's."

"Are you sure that's what you saw?" Chase stood in front of me and leaned one arm against the shed, shielding me from everything around us. His expression looked stormy.

"It was definitely the rattle Ralph bought for Jonah." My voice cracked with each word.

Chase stared off in the distance, and his jaw flexed. "I'm going to have to take this to Captain Abbott."

"What will happen then?"

"We'll get a warrant to search his place. When we're able to bag the evidence, we'll be able to question him. Hopefully, with a little pressure, he'll tell us where Jonah is now."

"My impression is that he doesn't have family in the area."

"He could have convinced a friend to take care of the baby for him. Maybe made up a cover story that the baby is his nephew or something."

That could be true but another fact remained. "He's working with someone, Chase. Who was the man posing as a Children's Services worker?"

"I have no idea. It could be someone connected with Children's Services. You said the man used specific names of people who worked there, right?"

I nodded. "He seemed knowledgeable. Some of that information he could have gotten online, I suppose."

"Who knows how deeply this runs." Chase grimaced, his thoughts obviously intense.

I glanced around. An old brick wall, painted white and looking ripe for snakes, lined the backside. Vines covered the ground, wrapping around an old tire. Peeling red paint pricked my skin.

I waited, unable to see beyond the shed. Unwilling to risk being spotted. Incapable of stopping my thoughts from racing ahead.

Where was Jonah now? He obviously wasn't in the house. Where would Truman have taken him?

Could this be the reason Truman was never nearby when anything bad was going down? Was it because he'd planned it that way? Had he intentionally turned a blind eye and let everything happen?

Maybe he'd also planned to get close to my mom, to earn our trust so we wouldn't suspect him.

My phone beeped again, this time with an incoming text from Jamie. I read it and then looked up at Chase. "She said she's nearly certain it is Truman in the patrol car."

"This is within his patrol area. He could just be driving by to check things out and keep an eye on his house. Officers do that sometimes."

"Or he could have another purpose."

We waited, the minutes ticking by. I wondered if I wasn't with Chase if he'd be hiding out. I figured he wouldn't be. But we didn't want to tip our hand, to show Officer Truman that we were on to him.

My phone buzzed again with a text from Jamie.

He's gone.

"I need to get down to the station," Chase said. "Now."

***

Chase took Jamie and me to the station with him, only because he didn't have time to drop us off at home. That was fine by me.

We sat in a waiting area. In the distance, I could see Chase in a glass-enclosed office talking to Captain Abbott. His hands flew in the air as if he tried to drive home a point. Abbott, as usual, remained expressionless. I tried to get a read on the situation but couldn't.

Finally Chase stormed out, an unhappy expression on his face. I half-expected him to tell me that the captain had refused to pursue this, had refused to believe the truth if it meant putting the department's reputation on the line.

He thundered over to us and stopped with his hands on

his hips. "The judge approved a search warrant, so we're sending someone to check out Truman's house. Until we have evidence in hand, we have to keep it quiet. We're checking into his financials also. The money trail usually reveals the truth about what's going on."

"I'm glad the captain listened to you."

Chase's shoulders remained tight and his expression stormy. "He was disbelieving. Skeptical. Concerned. But I showed him everything I'd been collecting and finally got his attention."

"At least he listened."

He nodded, scanning everything around him in the lobby. Like a good cop, his back was toward the wall so he could be on the lookout for trouble. "He doesn't like dirty cops anymore than I do. We still have more work to do, though. The department is just recovering from those riots. We don't need this right now. But if there's corruption, we can't cover it up."

"Of course not."

He shifted, his shoulders still tight and stiff. "Can you guys call someone for a ride home? I'm going to be here for a while, running the investigation from this end. I need to figure out the connection between Truman and Bayfield. I'm also going to review the linked crimes and interview homeowners. People who learned about this ring ended up dead, so we can't tip anyone off."

I shivered at his words.

"When you get home, stay there. Please. And lock the doors."

I wasn't good at staying home with the doors locked. Besides, locked doors hadn't stopped the bad guys before. If someone was determined enough . . .

"Okay?" Chase said.

Finally I nodded. "Okay."

"I'll keep you updated as much as I'm able." He kissed my cheek before walking away.

Stay inside with the doors locked. I'd promised Chase. I could do that. Besides, how long could it take for Chase to nail down the details on this and arrest Truman? By tomorrow morning, I'd be free. Jonah would be found. And the bad guys would be in jail.

John, Jamie's nineteen-year-old brother, promised to come and pick us up, but his shift at the grocery store wasn't over for another forty minutes. I would have called my mom, but then I might have to break the news about Truman. Jamie's mom was busy, so John had seemed like a good option. He'd been in trouble with the law in the past, however, so it took some prodding to get him to do us the favor—prodding that included a free meal at Skyline Chili on the way home.

In the meantime, Jamie and I couldn't discuss the case. There were too many officers around. We couldn't risk it, so we passed time talking about our favorite baby names.

Finally, John arrived. He refused to come inside, but instead he called Jamie's cell and told us to come out. We sat in the back of his sedan, and he turned up his music a little too loud for my taste. I could feel the bass reverberating in my chest. But that was fine. I wasn't in the mood to talk, and we couldn't risk her brother overhearing anything.

My mind turned over everything that had happened. Who was Truman working with? He just didn't seem like the type to do something like this. But I'd seen the rattle with my own eyes. Chase said Truman was linked to the crime scenes where prescription drugs had been stolen.

John dropped us off at my house after we went through the drive-through at Skyline Chili. The savory scent of Cincinnati-style chili filled the vehicle and made me realize how hungry I was. It didn't matter. I could eat later. Right now, we had to see this through to completion.

As we started toward my front door, Jamie and I had our first real opportunity to talk privately.

"We have bad luck," Jamie muttered.

"Bad luck with what? Being followed?" Speaking of which . . . I looked over my shoulder but didn't see anyone.

"Well, that. But also with trusting people. Dating people with ulterior motives. It's hard being a single gal."

I frowned. "You're talking about my mom and Truman?"

"She seems smitten. You almost need to do background checks on any potential boyfriends."

I bit down. "It wouldn't have shown this."

Just then, a cop car pulled up to the curb outside my house.

I sucked in a deep breath when I saw who was in the driver's seat.

It was Officer Truman.

CHAPTER 31

"Everything okay, ladies?" Officer Truman rolled down his window, concern etched into his wrinkles.

I forced myself to nod and try to look casual. "We're just worried about Jonah. With every minute that passes, he could be farther away."

He frowned, the lines on his face deepening even more. "I know the police are working on it. They'll find him soon. They're competent."

Those didn't sound like the words of someone who'd snatched Jonah. Then again, maybe Truman was a great actor.

"I just hope the cops are truly putting all of their manpower into this," I said. I knew I should play it cool, but I couldn't help but weigh my responses in order to see his reaction. "The life of an innocent baby could be on the line. And all for something senseless."

He raised his eyebrows and surprise flashed through his gaze. "Senseless? Do you know why he was taken?"

"I just meant he was probably taken to wield power over someone else. Maybe because of greed. That's senseless." Why was I continuing this conversation? If I kept going, I might dig myself into a hole. I should do what Chase suggested and go inside and lock the doors until he called with an update.

"I see." Officer Truman nodded. But his gaze told me he

didn't quite buy it.

I stepped closer, curiosity burning inside me and some kind of instinct taking over—an instinct to find answers. Jamie tried to tug me back, but I didn't budge.

"Do you have a different theory?" I asked.

He shrugged and ran a hand over his face. Was he plotting ways to get out of this conversation? To turn the tables? To redirect my suspicions? "No theories. It's better not to draw conclusions but to follow the evidence instead."

"I agree."

"Something will come up soon. Just hold tight, Holly. I know you really cared about that little boy. I could see it in your gaze. You can't fake that kind of affection."

Jamie tugged me again, but I still didn't move. Why did Truman have to seem so kind? His words had squeezed at my heart with their fatherly undertones.

At that moment, sirens wailed in the distance. The air crackled with the unknown. Truman bristled.

"Something must be going on," he muttered. "Surprised I didn't hear about it over the scanner."

Four police cars squealed to a stop around us. Officers jumped out, guns drawn and aimed at Truman.

When Jamie pulled me back this time, I didn't fight it. But my heart plummeted with disappointment and ache.

"We need to see your hands," Mclean yelled.

A wrinkle formed between Truman's eyes. "See my hands?"

"That's right. Hands in the air. Now!"

Truman's wrinkles deepened, but he did as Mclean ordered.

Chase pulled up in his sedan and parked haphazardly on the street. He strode toward Truman with handcuffs, jerked the door open, and pulled him from the car. "Larry Truman, you're under arrest."

Truman's eyes widened with alarm. He glanced at Jamie and me as if desperate to ascertain answers. Then he looked back at Chase. "For what . . . ?"

Did he look so confused because he didn't think he'd be caught? It had seemed sincere, though. My emotions clashed inside me.

"For the kidnapping of Jonah Edwards, for stealing prescription medications, for selling drugs, and for a long list of other crimes." Chase jerked him from the car and handcuffed him. "You give cops a bad name."

"I don't understand."

I had to look away. I couldn't imagine the desperation that had led Truman to go to such great lengths to do something like this. He'd fooled me. He'd fooled my mom. He'd fooled the other cops who worked with him.

But if all of this meant that Jonah would be safe soon, this was what had to happen. I had to remind myself of that. Truman had been at the crime scenes where drugs were stolen. Jonah's rattle had been in his house. Chase must have found other evidence also in order to get an arrest warrant.

Chase approached me as Truman was led away into a squad car.

"The two of you are to thank for this," he started. "You know I don't approve of your tactics a lot of times, but you are able to find answers. People will talk to you who won't talk to authorities. There's a lot to be said for that."

I may have actually blushed under his compliment. But delight felt distant right now. Until Jonah was found, nothing would seem bright or joyful. "Thank you."

"We're hoping he'll break under the questioning and

tell us whom he's working with and where Jonah is."

"Did you find more evidence?" I asked, wondering what exactly had transpired in the last hour.

Chase nodded. "Larry has unexplained cash in his checking account—ten thousand dollars worth. And there were baby items in his house. He denied knowing anything about the money or the rattle. The truth will prevail, though."

I nodded. "I hope so."

"In the meantime, you should both stay here. I'll assign an officer to remain outside the door, just in case any more trouble arises. We believe he's working with others—maybe some dealers. Maybe someone from social services. We don't know yet."

"Thank you."

"I'll keep you updated on what happens. When we find Jonah, we'll call you. You should give Doris at Children's Services a heads up. Until Katie is located, you'll take care of Jonah, as far as I'm concerned."

"I'll give her a call and let her know what's going on."

I hoped—prayed—that I would have little Sweet Pea back in my arms soon.

That was the only thing that would make all of this worth it.

***

Anxiety still buzzed through me for some reason as I picked up the phone to call Doris. I'd checked the windows and doors. Turned on the alarm. And remembered Chase's words: *People who learned about this ended up dead.*

I couldn't get the look on Officer Truman's face out of my mind. He'd looked so . . . stunned. Perhaps he'd thought he would never be caught. But was he ignorant enough to leave evidence in his house and in his bank account?

I didn't know. I didn't know him well enough to know. But I hated the thought of breaking the news to my mom.

Jamie sat across from me at the kitchen table, tapping away on my laptop computer. Thankfully Mom was doing a closing on a house right now and would be occupied for a while.

I pushed those thoughts aside and called Doris. She answered right away. "Holly, are there any updates?"

Maybe beneath her chilly exterior she did have a heart. She sounded genuinely concerned. "The police arrested someone who's supposedly linked with the man who took Jonah. They're hoping to have some answers soon. Chase wanted me to let you know that. When Jonah's found, I'd like to take care of him again until his mom is located."

"Of course. That would be best for Jonah. He'll have to be checked out, naturally."

"I wouldn't expect anything less."

"Bethany will want to be your caseworker again, I'm assuming, so I'll put the two of you in touch."

Her words made me pause. "She'll want to be?"

"She requested that she work the case," Doris said.

"Is that right?" I hardly knew Bethany. Why would she request that?

"I'll keep you updated," I finally told Doris before hanging up.

Before I could talk to Jamie, she called me over to the computer.

"Check this out, Holly." She pointed to the screen. "These random ads that kept popping up in the wrong places on GregsList? Something was bugging me about them. Out of curiosity the other day, I responded to one. I thought maybe there could be a story in there somewhere. Anyway, I just got a response. The seller claims to live near 15th and Vine."

"That's where . . . where Morgan Bayfield was killed."

She nodded, satisfaction in her gaze. "Exactly. I read these ads again. *Five hundred cases of juice boxes. Bought in bulk. I've got loads of it for sale. Come get yours for cheap, Friend.*"

"I remember that one."

"Or this one: *You'll hit the jackpot with this little monkey. She's like TNT but you'll love having her around.*"

"They're weird, but what about them?"

"Little monkey, TNT, juice, friend. Those are the street names for prescription drugs. Opioids, to be exact."

I gasped as the truth rolled over me. "Jamie, you're brilliant. You're right. These guys were selling their drugs through GregsList. I'll pass this on to Chase. Maybe he can track down the sender through their IP address. In the meantime, I need to look up something also . . ."

I found Bethany Ellis's social media profile and scrolled through her pictures until one in particular stopped me. It was a photo of her beside a man with dark hair.

The fake Children's Services worker. Jim.

He appeared to be her boyfriend. His real name was Jim Andrews.

Could Bethany be the other link to this? She went into people's homes in her role as social worker. She would know—with a little snooping—if they used prescription drugs. Had she passed that information on to the drug ring in order to get some extra cash?

Again, another person I'd trusted who ended up being dirty.

I was really going to have to watch whom I trusted.

I clicked on Jim's profile. It appeared he was currently out of work. That would fit the profile of someone who might be involved in this. How all of it had come together, I wasn't sure. Somewhere down the road, these people had made connections with Bo, with Officer Truman, with Morgan Bayfield.

What had started as something to earn more money had obviously turned into something deadly.

"I can't believe all of this," Jamie muttered. "Some people are the lowest of the low."

"Some people are just desperate."

"Agreed." I tapped my finger.

My phone rang. It was Chase, and his voice sounded urgent.

"Don't let anyone into the house," he said. "Not even police officers."

"What's going on?"

"I found evidence to indicate that Mclean is also involved in this."

Mclean? He was the officer stationed right outside the door.

Before I could ask any more questions, a gun clicked behind me.

I didn't have to turn to know who it was.

CHAPTER 32

"How'd you get inside?" I stood and raised my hands in the air, dropping my cell phone in the process. I hoped Chase could still hear what was going on.

"I picked the lock out back. I've seen you type in the alarm code enough that it was easy to bypass." Each word came out as a bark. "I don't have much time to dispose of you two."

My stomach roiled at his words. He'd kill us if it meant getting away with his crimes.

I turned around slowly until Mclean's face came into view. His scowl was deep and brooding. He gripped the gun in his hands, but it was the vengeance in his eyes that scared me the most.

"It's a good thing I came inside when I did," he muttered. "Although, I must say, I have some time. The police are going to be tied up with Truman for quite a while."

"How could you do this? Your job is to uphold the law, not to use it to your advantage."

He snorted. "Do you know how much cops get paid? Hardly anything. Hardly enough to live on."

Repulsion caused bile to rise in my throat. "That's no excuse for you to do what you're doing."

"All those drugs we confiscate from crime scenes—they just sit in evidence. Taking that was too obvious, especially since there were other options. There's a huge market out there for prescription drugs."

"How did all of this start? Were you the mastermind behind it all?" I kept him talking, hoping to buy time. I knew Chase was on his way. I just needed to stay alive until he arrived.

"You could say that."

He had an ego, and he wanted to take all the credit he could for this. I had to use that to my advantage. I backed toward the wall, trying to put distance between his gun and myself.

"You got Bo involved, didn't you? Or did you pull Morgan in first?"

"It's amazing how you can manipulate people to do what you want," he continued with that evil glare in his eyes. "I met Morgan through a dating site. At first, it seemed like we could be a good match. Then I heard she worked at the jail as a nurse. I knew I had to use that to my advantage. When I learned her mom was dying, I knew exactly how to give her the motivation she needed."

He was even more despicable than I thought. "That's reprehensible."

He shrugged, no evidence of a conscience in sight. "Maybe. But it worked. Once she was in, she was in deep and couldn't get out."

"Until you killed her."

"Her conscious was getting to her, and I was afraid she was going to spill everything. Especially after that baby was left with you. She was beside herself."

I took another step back. How close was Chase? He should be here any time now . . . right? "Is that why she kept driving past my place? She was worried about Jonah?"

Mclean frowned again. "Yeah, she was on the verge of a breakdown. I knew it was just a matter of time before she blabbed everything."

Did he know that Morgan had met with Chase? If so, why hadn't he tried to eliminate Chase as well? He must not have known. That was the only explanation.

"What about Bo? How did he get involved?"

"He found us through a friend. Starting buying. Then we found out he worked for GregsList, and we knew we had to get him to help us out."

GregsList? Violet had said he worked in advertising. I never thought about that connection, but it made sense. He must have made sure those loaded fake advertisements were posted. People looking for drugs would have picked up on the code words.

"I guess Bo had a change of heart as well?" I continued.

"He wanted more medication. Went crazy nearly. There was nothing else we could do. He started talking to that reporter, and he was going to come forward with his story. He said he wanted to make things right." Mclean straightened.

He wanted us to know just how brilliant he was. His ego hopefully would lead to his demise.

"Enough talking," he growled. "My friend Bill is going to help us out here."

Crazy Hands stepped from the kitchen, and he had an even crazier look in his eyes than before. He would kill us.

I licked my lips as my heart pounded in my ears. "Why not just let us go? Why make things worse?"

"We have enough money now that we can run," Mclean continued. "But we've got to get rid of anyone who might stand in our way first. That includes you two. You just kept digging and digging."

"But you set up Truman. He's in jail. He took the fall for you. You can get away scot-free now."

That arrogant glint returned to his gaze. "It was easy to set up his house as a crime scene. I made sure to break into other homes where he'd worked the crime scenes. You'd be amazed at how many people have prescription opioids. That way, Truman's records would indicate he was on the scene and not me."

"You're clever."

He smiled for the first time. "Yes, I am. Now move. We've got to get you out of here before your boyfriend comes back."

Jamie and I glanced at each other. How were we going to get out of this?

My mind scrambled through the possibilities.

Please don't let my mom return home. Please. There's no need to add more casualties to this.

"Where's Jonah?" I asked as Mclean shoved me toward the back door.

"He's safe. For now." He grabbed my arm and squeezed my bicep so hard that I nearly squealed. "Move."

"Where are you taking us?"

"Somewhere you won't be found. Don't worry—we'll leave evidence to prove you were involved in all of this. Since your mom was all school-girl giddy for Truman, it should be pretty easy."

He really thought he had all his bases covered, didn't he? What if he was right? His plan seemed far-fetched to me, though. If we left this house, I knew we'd die. I couldn't let that happen. However, I didn't see how Jamie and I could take down both of these men. They were armed and we weren't.

He'd underestimated us.

As soon as we reached the backdoor, I made a quick decision. I threw all of my weight back into Mclean. Using my feet, I leveraged myself against the door. The action caused Mclean to tumble backward and drop his gun.

Crazy Hands tried to grab Jamie, but she reached for his face. He yelped with pain as her thumbs pressed into his eye sockets.

As soon as Mclean realized what was happening, he put me in a chokehold and dragged me toward the door.

I couldn't breathe. I clawed at his arm, but he didn't budge.

I'd made him mad.

I was quickly losing consciousness. I had to break his hold on me.

My gaze searched the room. Nothing. There was nothing I could reach.

I needed to use the element of surprise again.

Using some self-defense moves Chase had taught me, I twisted my body, using it as leverage.

Mclean flew over my back and onto his side.

Before I could catch my breath, he was on his feet and had grabbed me again.

His fist slammed into my jaw. I literally saw stars. Struggled to remain lucid.

Just as all the fight left me, the backdoor flew open.

Chase. Chase was here.

Thank You, Jesus.

CHAPTER 33

"Are you sure you're okay?" Chase still lingered over me with that concerned look in his eyes as I lay on the couch.

My body ached like I'd just been sucked up in a tornado and then spit back out. In a way, it had been. But we were all alive, and that was the important thing. "I'm just glad you came when you did."

Jamie looked like she was in reporter mode. She hadn't been hurt—thank goodness—and now her instinct for a good story was kicking in. She was lingering at the scene, watching everything that happened. The paramedics had already cleared her. I wasn't quite as lucky.

"How'd you know Mclean was involved?" I asked, holding some ice against my jaw.

"Truman said Mclean was a little too curious about some of the scenes Truman had worked. I started looking into his background. My gut told me he was involved, and I knew I couldn't chance having him here guarding your house if he could be guilty."

"Good call."

He kissed my forehead. "I was really worried."

"You're always really worried about me."

"You should still be checked out." He examined my jaw. "You hit your head pretty hard."

"I don't want to go back to the hospital."

"Head wounds are nothing to mess with."

"I'll go with you," Jamie called.

"You don't have to. I'll be fine. Both of you just do whatever you have to do to find Jonah."

Chase helped me to my feet as paramedics surrounded me, waiting to check my vitals. No, make that as *Evan* evaluated me. He *had* to be the one who was here with his larger-than-life personality. Like things weren't complicated enough.

"I can take it from here," Evan said. "She's in good hands."

Chase scowled at Evan.

"I'll be fine," I said again.

He kissed my forehead. "I'll send a police cruiser behind you, just in case. We still don't know how deep this runs."

"How do you know the officer is clean?"

"Captain Abbott set this up himself. He pulled someone from a different precinct, just to be safe."

Chase sent Evan one more scowl before releasing me to his care.

Dread filled me. I'd just gone through all of that drama. The last thing I wanted was to have any uncomfortable conversations with Evan about why I should dump Chase for him. I didn't need that right now.

"That was a close call back there," Evan said once we were in the back of the ambulance.

I rubbed my jaw, trying not to replay the whole confrontation in my mind. I was ready to put this behind me. All of it. "Yeah, it was. I really don't think I need to go to the hospital again, though. My medical bills are already hard enough to pay without all these extra expenses."

"You know how it is. We'd rather be safe than sorry." He smiled down at me. "We can't have you getting hurt."

"It's too late for that." I shifted on the gurney, wishing my body didn't ache so much. "Where's everyone else? Aren't there usually a few EMTs back here?"

"The other two guys stayed behind to keep an eye on your friend Jamie and to make sure Mclean was okay. Even though he was a bad guy, we still have to make sure he's not hurt in our care. Honestly, guys like that . . . I couldn't care less about. I'm glad I wasn't the one left behind with him."

He reached behind him. "Let me give you an IV. We can run some pain meds through that."

Pain meds? Like the ones people got addicted to and did horrible things to get more of? No, thank you. Not unless I was desperate, which I wasn't at this point.

I shooed him away. "I'll be okay."

He raised the needle, his eyes wide and convincing. "You're going to be hurting later."

I lifted my hand to stop him. "I'll deal with it."

He shrugged and put the equipment down. "Have it your way, then. Don't say I didn't offer."

"I promise not to hold it against you." I flashed what I hoped was an affable smile.

"Thank you." He grinned before turning around to fiddle with something behind him. "That was pretty crazy back there, wasn't it?"

"You can say that again." I watched carefully, trying to figure out what he was doing. His shoulder blocked sight of his hands, though. I assumed he was organizing some of the medicine compartments.

"Hopefully they'll find the baby soon. I know he wants to be reunited with his mom."

"Moms and babies belong together," I agreed. "It's just a shame someone had to use a baby as part of their greed."

"They do." When he turned back around, he held a needle in his hands and a strange expression on his face.

Fear exploded in me, and I scooted back. My gaze shot from the syringe to Evan. A new, cold expression captured his face.

"What's that for?"

"To keep you quiet."

My throat went dry as reality hit me. Evan was in on this. Evan. "What do you mean?"

I glanced around. There was no way out. I was trapped back here.

"It's just a matter of time before everyone figures out what's going on. If I have you as a hostage, it will buy me some time to escape. I certainly have enough money for it now."

"Evan . . ." How could I convince him this was a bad idea? I couldn't, could I? His mind was made up.

"You're so cute, Holly. You don't really think you're going to talk me out of this, do you?"

I tried to scoot back, but there was nowhere to go. "You need to think this through. You don't need me to run. It will be a lot easier if you do that by yourself."

"I don't think so."

"What about the driver? Is he in on this also?"

Evan smirked. "No, I'm going to ask him to stop by my house. Then I'm going to knock him out and take off with you myself. Easy, huh?"

This whole thing was just one never-ending nightmare, wasn't it? I had to think fast.

Subtly, I reached into my purse—I had it with me this time. My fingers closed over some pepper spray I kept there.

As Evan continued to smirk, I flipped the cap off. "You really surprised me, Evan."

"Oh, yeah?"

"We could have had something together."

"I tried to convince you to come over to my side."

"I guess I should have listened."

I jerked my hand up and jammed on the button up top. Pepper spray covered his face. It was stained with a blue dye so police would be sure not to miss him.

Evan hollered with pain and blindly reached for me.

I withdrew into the corner. My hands connected with a plastic-sided box. I threw it at him.

He cried out in pain.

The driver threw on brakes. I scrambled toward the backdoor. After a few failed attempts, I pulled it open and practically fell onto the ground outside.

The police officer pulled me behind him and turned his gun on Evan.

Evan. Not me.

It was over, I realized. It was finally over.

CHAPTER 34

The next day was a blur of being questioned by the police, of unending media coverage, and of ducking the paparazzi-like reporters outside my home.

The good news was that Katie had been found. Jonah had been located. And today they'd be reunited.

Doris had arranged it so the meeting would take place at a home owned by one of Ralph's friends and colleagues. It was out of the way, and the media shouldn't catch wind of our location.

I'd been pacing since I got there. The door opened, and my spine went ramrod straight. I held my breath, waiting to see if Jonah would appear.

Instead, Chase popped his head in. We met halfway, and he pulled me into his arms. We'd hardly had a chance to talk since all of this craziness started. I was anxious to find out how he was doing.

"Not here yet?" he asked.

I shook my head. "No, they should be any time now."

"Let's sit down a minute."

I nodded, and we sat across from each other on a massive leather couch.

"So . . ." I started, anxious for details. I knew Evan, Mclean, Jim, and Crazy Hands had been arrested. Bethany Ellis, as well as Larry Truman, had been cleared of any charges. That had all come out in the news stories.

"We tracked down Jonah. Mclean had asked his girlfriend to take care of him."

My heart spiked. I already knew Jonah was okay, but every time I heard it, I felt reassured again.

Thank You, Jesus.

"Mclean's girlfriend didn't get suspicious?"

"He said it was a big case they were working on and everything had to be hush-hush," Chase said. "He paid for her to stay in a house down in Lexington, insisting that she was working as part of the police investigation."

"She trusted him, so she had no reason to question his story, I suppose."

"Most likely."

"But he's okay?" I'd already heard that answer before also, but I wanted to hear it again.

Chase nodded. "He's doing fine. Mclean and his partners knew that they had to eliminate Katie if they wanted their operations to continue. She knew too much. They hoped if they had the baby, they could smoke her out."

They were heartless. Truly heartless. All of this for some cash in their pockets? It was greed, pure and simple. "But it didn't work?"

"She was staying somewhere without any phone or Internet, so she wasn't aware of what was happening. She'd tried to get a couple of updates, but the media was pretty quiet about it. She felt Jonah was safer without her."

"Who left the note on my car then?"

"Most likely someone else who saw you were snooping and wanted you to back off. One of Evan and Mclean's minions."

Crazy Hands, if I had to guess. "What about this drug

ring? How did all of that work?"

"We're still putting together all of the details. But it looks like Evan started it. He was always a bit of a troublemaker throughout his youth, but he seemed to have turned his life around. We think he started this on his own and then pulled in other people, tempting them with the money. In fact, Evan and Jim went to high school together."

"And Bo?"

"When Bo caught onto what they were doing, they pulled him in to be a front man. That would eliminate the risk of them being caught. He posted the ads on GregsList for them, which ended up bringing in more customers. More than they could handle almost. The need to get more drugs grew. They lured Morgan Bayfield in."

"They had their whole system down to a science," I muttered.

Chase nodded. "You could say that."

"Did you suspect Evan all along?" I remembered the hostility between them that day at Katie's house, after Gage's dead body had been discovered.

He sucked in a breath. "No, I didn't suspect him. I would have never sent you with him in the ambulance if I had. Honestly, he told me he was interested in you and that I was the wrong guy for you."

"He had a lot of nerve."

Chase frowned. "Tell me about it. I tried not to let him get to me because I knew that's what he was looking for. But every time I saw him talking to you . . . I remembered those conversations."

"I wonder why Jim didn't kill me that day he took Jonah. They killed everyone else who knew too much."

"My guess is that it was because of Evan. I think he

honestly did like you. He hoped maybe he could turn you over to their side."

I leaned back to process all of that. People's hearts could be turned so easily. Was mine included in that? What had I compromised my values to obtain? "Their whole scheme sounds intricate."

"It was. And lucrative. They were bringing in some big bucks. That's the way opium works. Once you become hooked on it, you just want more and more. Physically, your body starts to crave it, and it's very hard to break the cycle."

"Truman was obviously set up."

"He's been cleared and will return to the job."

Satisfaction filled me. "Good. I'm glad, because he seemed like a nice guy."

"I think he'll be fine."

Just then, I heard the rumble of a car pulling over gravel. I rushed to the door and saw Doris coming with Jonah. I met her outside, desperate to see Jonah for myself.

As soon as his smiling face came into view in the car seat, my heart fluttered out of control. He really was fine.

At the first chance inside, I took him from his seat and held him to me. "How are you, Little Man?"

He smiled in response, and my bones turned to jelly.

"I've missed you so much," I cooed.

Before I had the chance to baby talk with him for too long, another car pulled up. My breath caught. I knew who this was. It was Katie. Captain Abbot himself had brought her.

I braced myself for Katie's entrance. As soon as she stepped inside, she ran toward her baby. Tears streamed from her eyes.

It was a beautiful sight.

I gave them a few minutes to reunite. I really wanted to

ask Katie some questions, though. I really wanted to see Jonah again, for that matter.

Finally, Katie looked at me.

"Thank you for taking care of my baby," she said, mascara trailing down her cheeks.

"You're welcome. I'm just sorry about everything that happened . . ." I shifted as Chase put a steadying hand on my shoulder. "Can I ask you something?"

"Of course."

"Why me?"

Katie let out a long sigh and sat down with Jonah in her lap. "I know I always gave you a hard time in high school. But the truth was, I knew you were a good person. I was almost jealous of that, feeling like I couldn't measure up. I couldn't leave my baby with someone close to me because that would be too obvious. So I thought of you. I knew he'd be in good care."

"You addressed the note to Ms. Holly?"

She shrugged. "Just to throw you off. I didn't know if you'd come look for me or not, but I had heard that you liked to volunteer. I figured using that name would make you think it was one of the kids you worked with."

"You were correct." I leaned toward Jonah and my heart pounded so loudly in my ears that everything else faded for a moment. I didn't want to say goodbye to him, but I knew my stay here was limited. Katie deserved to have time alone with her son.

"Thank you again, Holly. You were a real lifesaver."

"You're welcome." I rubbed Jonah's hand, fighting back the tears. "Good bye, little guy. I'm going to miss you."

"Feel free to come over and visit some."

I nodded. "And if you ever need a sitter . . ."

"I'll know who to call." She hugged me again. "Thank you."

***

Four days later, Chase and I were able to talk. To really talk.

And I was dreading it.

He came over, and we sat on the back patio. The weather had warmed up, just for the day. The sunshine seemed promising and hopeful.

Too bad my spirits didn't match.

"What are you thinking, Holly?" Chase asked.

My heart felt heavy and burdened. I didn't want to have this conversation, but I knew I had to. "I feel conflicted, Chase."

"Tell me why."

I licked my lips, not wanting to speak, but knowing I needed to say it. "I love you, Chase. I really do. But I guess there's a part of me that wants to change you, and I know that's deeply unhealthy."

His eyes darkened. "What do you mean 'change me'?"

"I mean, I want you to be the settling-down type. I want to get married and have a family. It's my heart's desire. It always has been. But I'm not sure that's what you want."

"We've had this talk before," he said quietly, compassionately.

"I know. And if I keep bringing it up, I'll only be nagging, and that's not who I am. Besides, you told me you wanted me to be safe. I'm not sure my heart is safe around you."

"I see." His gaze looked tumultuous. "So what's this mean?"

My gut roiled. "I don't know."

"I want you to be happy, Holly."

"I want you to be happy, Chase."

"It doesn't sound like I can make you happy right now, though." He looked down, swallowed hard, and leaned back.

My heart lurched into my throat. "Chase—"

"I wish I could promise you the world. It's what I want more than anything. I want to give you everything you want and more. But there are some things I know I'd be setting myself up for failure for. Marriage, right now, is one of them. I need to be in the right place before I make a lifelong commitment. I hate to think about having children with my issues being unresolved. And the last thing I want is to raise kids in a household like the one where I grew up."

There was so much I wanted to say and make him realize about the burdens we carried with us in life. But none of it seemed useful. He had to come to those conclusions on his own. We'd already rehashed them before.

Until he made up his mind, all of my arguments were useless.

When I got married one day, I wanted the man of my dreams to desire me. To desire marriage. To desire family.

I didn't want to push anyone into something he wasn't ready for. The strains of that could last long into our marriage.

All of this was made even harder because . . . I loved Chase. I did. And I was pretty sure he loved me. I only wished our goals lined up.

"Where do we go from here?" he asked.

"Maybe we should take some time," I finally said. "Because I don't know if I can date you indefinitely. Temptation wise . . . it would remain very difficult." I felt my cheeks heat at the admittance.

Fire burned in his eyes. "I know."

There was no doubt about it that we were attracted to each other. That we cared about each other. That we had chemistry.

"So we take a break?" Chase's voice cracked as he said each word. He started to reach for me but dropped his hands to the side.

"Maybe we should until we're both on the same page."

His gaze burned into mine. "I understand. I love you, Holly."

My throat ached. "I love you too, Chase."

He wiped a final tear from my eyes, planted a soft kiss on my forehead, and walked through the backyard to his truck.

Just as he disappeared, Jamie appeared around the corner.

"Are you okay?" Jamie asked.

I shrugged. "I always talk about having faith in God and in His timing. Now I get to live like I believe it. What good is it to talk about trusting God when there's no action behind it?"

"That's some wisdom there, Girlfriend."

A tear escaped down my cheek. "But it's going to be hard."

She hooked her arm around my neck. "No one said this life would be easy."

I smiled at her and wiped away my tear. "But at least I have a friend like you to get me through the hard times, right?"

"Always."

"I'm going to make some other changes too, Jamie."

"They don't include a new best friend?"

"Never."

"Then what?"

"I'm thinking about putting a contract on that house we looked at with my mom," I started.

"Really? That's a big step."

I nodded. "I know. But my mom is ready to move on. She and Officer Truman—Larry—have practically been inseparable the past few days. I think it's time."

"It sounds like you've thought this through."

"I might also go back and get my master's degree in counseling."

Her eyebrows shot up. "Really?"

"Really. I need to make some changes in my career. I love working for my brother, but how long will this last? And I can't really see myself doing this long-term. My heart just isn't that into it."

"Counseling? I know you've counseled me on many occasions."

"I just want to work hands-on with people again."

"It sounds like change is in the air."

I nodded. "It is. But with change comes growth, right?"

"Right on, Girlfriend. Right on."

###

Coming Next:

AWARD-WINNING AUTHOR
CHRISTY BARRITT
A stranger may
not be who she claims...
RANDOM
ACTS
OF FRAUD
A HOLLY ANNA PALADIN MYSTERY
BK 5

If you enjoyed this book, you may also enjoy these books in the Holly Anna Paladin series:

***Random Acts of Murder* (Book 1)**
When Holly Anna Paladin is given a year to live, she embraces her final days doing what she loves most—random acts of kindness. But one of her extreme good deeds goes horribly wrong, implicating her in a string of murders. Holly is suddenly thrust into a different kind of fight for her life. Could it also be random that the detective assigned to the case is her old high school crush and present-day nemesis? Will Holly find the killer before he ruins what is left of her life? Or will she spend her final days alone and behind bars?

***Random Acts of Deceit* (Book 2)**
"Break up with Chase Dexter, or I'll kill him." Holly Anna Paladin never expected such a gut-wrenching ultimatum. With home invasions, hidden cameras, and bomb threats, Holly must make some serious choices. Whatever she decides, the consequences will either break her heart or break her soul. She tries to match wits with the Shadow Man, but the more she fights, the deeper she's drawn into the perilous situation. With her sister's wedding problems and the riots in the city, Holly has nearly reached her breaking point. She must stop this mystery man before someone she loves dies. But the deceit is threatening to pull her under . . . six feet under.

***Random Acts of Murder* (Book 3)**
When Holly Anna Paladin's boyfriend, police detective Chase

Dexter, says he's leaving for two weeks and can't give any details, she wants to trust him. But when she discovers Chase may be involved in some unwise and dangerous pursuits, she's compelled to intervene. Holly gets a run for her money as she's swept into the world of horseracing. The stakes turn deadly when a dead body surfaces and suspicion is cast on Chase. At every turn, more trouble emerges, making Holly question what she holds true about her relationship and her future. Just when she thinks she's on the homestretch, a dark horse arises. Holly might lose everything in a nail-biting fight to the finish.

***Random Acts of Scrooge* (Book 3.5)**
Christmas is supposed to be the most wonderful time of the year, but a real-life Scrooge is threatening to ruin the season's good will. Holly Anna Paladin can't wait to celebrate Christmas with family and friends. She loves everything about the season—celebrating the birth of Jesus, singing carols, and baking Christmas treats, just to name a few. But when a local family needs help, how can she say no? Holly's community has come together to help raise funds to save the home of Greg and Babette Sullivan, but a Bah-Humburgler has snatched the canisters of cash. Holly and her boyfriend, police detective Chase Dexter, team up to catch the Christmas crook. Will they succeed in collecting enough cash to cover the Sullivans' overdue bills? Or will someone succeed in ruining Christmas for all those involved?

Other Books by Christy Barritt:

Squeaky Clean Mysteries

***Hazardous Duty* (Book 1)**
On her way to completing a degree in forensic science, Gabby St. Claire drops out of school and starts her own crime-scene cleaning business. When a routine cleaning job uncovers a murder weapon the police overlooked, she realizes that the wrong person is in jail. But the owner of the weapon is a powerful foe . . . and willing to do anything to keep Gabby quiet. With the help of her new neighbor, Riley Thomas, a man whose life and faith fascinate her, Gabby seeks to find the killer before another murder occurs.

***Suspicious Minds* (Book 2)**
In this smart and suspenseful sequel to *Hazardous Duty*, crime-scene cleaner Gabby St. Claire finds herself stuck doing mold remediation to pay the bills. Her first day on the job, she uncovers a surprise in the crawlspace of a dilapidated home: Elvis, dead as a doornail and still wearing his blue-suede shoes. How could she possibly keep her nose out of a case like this?

***It Came Upon a Midnight Crime* (Book 2.5, a Novella)**
Someone is intent on destroying the true meaning of Christmas—at least, destroying anything that hints of it. All around crime-scene cleaner Gabby St. Claire's hometown, anything pointing to Jesus as "the reason for the season" is being sabotaged. The crimes become more twisted as dismembered body parts are found at the vandalisms. Someone

is determined to destroy Christmas . . . but Gabby is just as determined to find the Grinch and let peace on earth and goodwill prevail.

***Organized Grime* (Book 3)**

Gabby St. Claire knows her best friend, Sierra, isn't guilty of killing three people in what appears to be an eco-terrorist attack. But Sierra has disappeared, her only contact a frantic phone call to Gabby proclaiming she's being hunted. Gabby is determined to prove her friend is innocent and to keep Sierra alive. While trying to track down the real perpetrator, Gabby notices a disturbing trend at the crime scenes she's cleaning, one that ties random crimes together—and points to Sierra as the guilty party. Just what has her friend gotten herself involved in?

***Dirty Deeds* (Book 4)**

"Promise me one thing. No snooping. Just for one week." Gabby St. Claire knows that her fiancé's request is a simple one she should be able to honor. After all, Riley's law school reunion and attorneys' conference at a posh resort is a chance for them to get away from the mysteries Gabby often finds herself involved in as a crime-scene cleaner. Then an old friend of Riley's goes missing. Gabby suspects one of Riley's buddies might be behind the disappearance. When the missing woman's mom asks Gabby for help, how can she say no?

***The Scum of All Fears* (Book 5)**

Gabby St. Claire is back to crime-scene cleaning and needs help after a weekend killing spree fills her work docket. A serial killer her fiancé put behind bars has escaped. His last words to Riley were: *I'll get out, and I'll get even*. Pictures of Gabby are found in the man's prison cell, messages are left for Gabby at crime scenes, someone keeps slipping in and out of her apartment, and her temporary assistant disappears. The search for answers becomes darker when Gabby realizes she's dealing with a criminal who is truly the scum of the earth. He will do anything to make Gabby's and Riley's lives a living nightmare.

To Love, Honor, and Perish **(Book 6)**
Just when Gabby St. Claire's life is on the right track, the unthinkable happens. Her fiancé, Riley Thomas, is shot and in life-threatening condition only a week before their wedding. Gabby is determined to figure out who pulled the trigger, even if investigating puts her own life at risk. As she digs deeper into the case, she discovers secrets better left alone. Doubts arise in her mind, and the one man with answers lies on death's doorstep. Then an old foe returns and tests everything Gabby is made of—physically, mentally, and spiritually. Will all she's worked for be destroyed?

Mucky Streak **(Book 7)**
Gabby St. Claire feels her life is smeared with the stain of tragedy. She takes a short-term gig as a private investigator—a cold case that's eluded detectives for ten years. The mass murder of a wealthy family seems impossible to solve, but Gabby brings more clues to light. Add to the mix a flirtatious client, travels to an exciting new city, and some quirky—albeit temporary—new sidekicks, and things get complicated. With every new development, Gabby prays that her "mucky streak" will end and the future will become clear. Yet every answer she uncovers leads her closer to danger—both for her life and for her heart.

Foul Play **(Book 8)**

Gabby St. Claire is crying "foul play" in every sense of the phrase. When the crime-scene cleaner agrees to go undercover at a local community theater, she discovers more than backstage bickering, atrocious acting, and rotten writing. The female lead is dead, and an old classmate who has staked everything on the musical production's success is about to go under. In her dual role of investigator and star of the show, Gabby finds the stakes rising faster than the opening-night curtain. She must face her past and make monumental decisions, not just about the play but also concerning her future relationships and career. Will Gabby find the killer before the curtain goes down—not only on the play, but also on life as she knows it?

Broom and Gloom **(Book 9)**

Gabby St. Claire is determined to get back in the saddle again. While in Oklahoma for a forensic conference, she meets her soon-to-be stepbrother, Trace Ryan, an up-and-coming country singer. A woman he was dating has disappeared, and he suspects a crazy fan may be behind it. Gabby agrees to investigate, as she tries to juggle her conference, navigate being alone in a new place, and locate a woman who may not want to be found. She discovers that sometimes taking life by the horns means staring danger in the face, no matter the consequences.

Dust and Obey **(Book 10)**

When Gabby St. Claire's ex-fiancé, Riley Thomas, asks for her help in investigating a possible murder at a couples retreat, she knows she should say no. She knows she should run far, far away from the danger of both being around Riley and the crime. But her nosy instincts and determination take precedence over her logic. Gabby and Riley must work together to find the killer. In the process, they have to confront demons from their past and deal with their present relationship.

***Thrill Squeaker* (Book 11)**
An abandoned theme park. An unsolved murder. A decision that will change Gabby's life forever. Restoring an old amusement park and turning it into a destination resort seems like a fun idea for former crime-scene cleaner Gabby St. Claire. The side job gives her the chance to spend time with her friends, something she's missed since beginning a new career. The job turns out to be more than Gabby bargained for when she finds a dead body on her first day. Add to the mix legends of Bigfoot, creepy clowns, and ghostlike remnants of happier times at the park, and her stay begins to feel like a rollercoaster ride. Someone doesn't want the decrepit Mythical Falls to open again, but just how far is this person willing to go to ensure this venture fails? As the stakes rise and danger creeps closer, will Gabby be able to restore things in her own life that time has destroyed—including broken relationships? Or is her future closer to the fate of the doomed Mythical Falls?

***Cunning Attractions* (Book 12)**
Coming soon

***While You Were Sweeping*, a Riley Thomas Novella**
Riley Thomas is trying to come to terms with life after a traumatic brain injury turned his world upside down. Away from everything familiar—including his crime-scene-cleaning former fiancée and his career as a social-rights attorney—he's determined to prove himself and regain his old life. But when he claims he witnessed his neighbor shoot and kill someone,

everyone thinks he's crazy. When all evidence of the crime disappears, even Riley has to wonder if he's losing his mind.

Note: *While You Were Sweeping* is a spin-off mystery written in conjunction with the Squeaky Clean series featuring crime-scene cleaner Gabby St. Claire.

The Sierra Files

Pounced **(Book 1)**
Animal-rights activist Sierra Nakamura never expected to stumble upon the dead body of a coworker while filming a project nor get involved in the investigation. But when someone threatens to kill her cats unless she hands over the "information," she becomes more bristly than an angry feline. Making matters worse is the fact that her cats—and the investigation—are driving a wedge between her and her boyfriend, Chad. With every answer she uncovers, old hurts rise to the surface and test her beliefs. Saving her cats might mean ruining everything else in her life. In the fight for survival, one thing is certain: either pounce or be pounced.

Hunted **(Book 2)**
Who knew a stray dog could cause so much trouble? Newlywed animal-rights activist Sierra Nakamura Davis must face her worst nightmare: breaking the news she eloped with Chad to her ultra-opinionated tiger mom. Her perfectionist parents have planned a vow-renewal ceremony at Sierra's lush childhood home, but a neighborhood dog ruins the rehearsal dinner when it shows up toting what appears to be a fresh human bone. While dealing with the dog, a nosy neighbor, and an old flame turning up at the wrong times, Sierra hunts for answers. Her journey of discovery leads to more than just who committed the crime.

Pranced **(Book 2.5, a Christmas novella)**
Sierra Nakamura Davis thinks spending Christmas with her husband's relatives will be a real Yuletide treat. But when the animal-rights activist learns his family has a reindeer farm, she

begins to feel more like the Grinch. Even worse, when Sierra arrives, she discovers the reindeer are missing. Sierra fears the animals might be suffering a worse fate than being used for entertainment purposes. Can Sierra set aside her dogmatic opinions to help get the reindeer home in time for the holidays? Or will secrets tear the family apart and ruin Sierra's dream of the perfect Christmas?

***Rattled* (Book 3)**

"What do you mean a thirteen-foot lavender albino ball python is missing?" Tough-as-nails Sierra Nakamura Davis isn't one to get flustered. But trying to balance being a wife and a new mom with her crusade to help animals is proving harder than she imagined. Add a missing python, a high maintenance intern, and a dead body to the mix, and Sierra becomes the definition of rattled. Can she balance it all—and solve a possible murder—without losing her mind?

The Carolina Moon series:

***Home Before Dark* (Book 1)**

Nothing good ever happens after dark. Country singer Daleigh McDermott's father often repeated those words. Now, her father is dead. As she's about to flee back to Nashville, she finds his hidden journal with hints that his death was no accident. Mechanic Ryan Shields is the only one who seems to believe Daleigh. Her father trusted the man, but her attraction to Ryan scares her. She knows her life and career are back in Nashville and her time in the sleepy North Carolina town is only temporary. As Daleigh and Ryan work to unravel the mystery, it becomes obvious that someone wants them dead. They must rely on each other—and on God—if they hope to make it home before the darkness swallows them.

***Gone By Dark* (Book 2)**

Charity White can't forget what happened ten years earlier when she and her best friend, Andrea, cut through the woods on their way home from school. A man abducted Andrea, who hasn't been seen since. Charity has tried to outrun the memories and guilt. What if they hadn't taken that shortcut? Why wasn't Charity kidnapped instead of Andrea? And why weren't the police able to track down the bad guy? When Charity receives a mysterious letter that promises answers, she returns to North Carolina in search of closure and the peace that has eluded her. With the help of her new neighbor, Police Officer Joshua Haven, Charity begins to track down mysterious clues. They soon discover that they must work together or both of them will be swallowed by the looming darkness.

Wait Until Dark (Book 3)

A woman grieving broken dreams. A man struggling to regain memories. A secret entrenched in folklore dating back two centuries. Antiquarian Felicity French has no clue the trouble she's inviting in when she rescues a man outside her grandma's old plantation house during a treacherous snowstorm. All she wants is to nurse her battered heart and wounded ego, as well as come to terms with her past. Now she's stuck inside with a stranger sporting an old bullet wound and forgotten hours. Coast Guardsman Brody Joyner can't remember why he was out in such perilous weather, how he injured his head, or how a strange key got into his pocket. He also has no idea why his pint-sized savior has such a huge chip on her shoulder. He has no choice but to make the best of things until the storm passes. Brody and Felicity's rocky start goes from tense to worse when danger closes in. Who else wants the mysterious key that somehow ended up in Brody's pocket? Why? The unlikely duo quickly becomes entrenched in an adventure of a lifetime, one that could have ties to local folklore and Felicity's ancestors. But sometimes the past leads to darkness . . . darkness that doesn't wait for anyone.

Other Books by Christy Barritt:

Cape Thomas Series:

***Dubiosity* (Book 1)**
Savannah Harris vowed to leave behind her old life as an investigative reporter. But when two migrant workers go missing, her curiosity spikes. As more eerie incidents begin afflicting the area, each works to draw Savannah out of her seclusion and raise the stakes—for her and the surrounding community. Even as Savannah's new boarder, Clive Miller, makes her feel things she thought long forgotten, she suspects he's hiding something too, and he's not the only one. As secrets emerge and danger closes in, Savannah must choose between faith and uncertainty. One wrong decision might spell the end . . . not just for her but for everyone around her. Will she unravel the mystery in time, or will doubt get the best of her?

***Disillusioned* (Book 2)**
Nikki Wright is desperate to help her brother, Bobby, who hasn't been the same since escaping from a detainment camp run by terrorists in Colombia. Rumor has it that he betrayed his navy brothers and conspired with those who held him hostage, and both the press and the military are hounding him for answers. All Nikki wants is to shield her brother so he has time to recover and heal. But soon they realize the paparazzi are the least of their worries. When a group of men try to abduct Nikki and her brother, Bobby insists that Kade Wheaton, another former SEAL, can keep them out of harm's way. But can Nikki trust Kade? After all, the man who broke her heart eight years ago is anything but safe... Hiding out in a farmhouse on the Chesapeake Bay, Nikki finds her loyalties—and the remnants of

her long-held faith—tested as she and Kade put aside their differences to keep Bobby's increasingly erratic behavior under wraps. But when Bobby disappears, Nikki will have to trust Kade completely if she wants to uncover the truth about a rumored conspiracy. Nikki's life—and the fate of the nation—depends on it.

The Good Girl

Tara Lancaster can sing "Amazing Grace" in three harmonies, two languages, and interpret it for the hearing impaired. She can list the Bible canon backward, forward, and alphabetized. The only time she ever missed church was when she had pneumonia and her mom made her stay home. Then her life shatters and her reputation is left in ruins. She flees halfway across the country to dog-sit, but the quiet anonymity she needs isn't waiting at her sister's house. Instead, she finds a knife with a threatening message, a fame-hungry friend, a too-hunky neighbor, and evidence of . . . a ghost? Following all the rules has gotten her nowhere. And nothing she learned in Sunday School can tell her where to go from there.

***Death of the Couch Potato's Wife* (Suburban Sleuth Mysteries)**

You haven't seen desperate until you've met Laura Berry, a career-oriented city slicker turned suburbanite housewife. Well-trained in the big-city commandment, "mind your own business," Laura is persuaded by her spunky seventy-year-old neighbor, Babe, to check on another neighbor who hasn't been seen in days. She finds Candace Flynn, wife of the infamous "Couch King," dead, and at last has a reason to get up in the morning. Someone is determined to stop her from digging deeper into the death of her neighbor, but Laura is just as determined to figure out who is behind the death-by-poisoned-pork-rinds.

Imperfect

Since the death of her fiancé two years ago, novelist Morgan Blake's life has been in a holding pattern. She has a major case of writer's block, and a book signing in the mountain town of Perfect sounds as perfect as its name. Her trip takes a wrong turn when she's involved in a hit-and-run: She hit a man, and he ran from the scene. Before fleeing, he mouthed the word "Help." First she must find him. In Perfect, she finds a small town that offers all she ever wanted. But is something sinister going on behind its cheery exterior? Was she invited as a guest of honor simply to do a book signing? Or was she lured to town for another purpose—a deadly purpose?

The Gabby St. Claire Diaries (a tween mystery series)

The Curtain Call Caper **(Book 1)**

Is a ghost haunting the Oceanside Middle School auditorium? What else could explain the disasters surrounding the play—everything from missing scripts to a falling spotlight and damaged props? Seventh-grader Gabby St. Claire has dreamed about being part of her school's musical, but a series of unfortunate events threatens to shut down the production. While trying to uncover the culprit and save her fifteen minutes of fame, she also has to manage impossible teachers, cliques, her dysfunctional family, and a secret she can't tell even her best friend. Will Gabby figure out who or what is sabotaging the show . . . or will it be curtains for her and the rest of the cast?

The Disappearing Dog Dilemma **(Book 2)**

Why are dogs disappearing around town? When two friends ask seventh-grader Gabby St. Claire for her help in finding their missing canines, Gabby decides to unleash her sleuthing skills to sniff out whoever is behind the act. But time management and relationships get tricky as worrisome weather, a part-time job, and a new crush interfere with Gabby's investigation. Will her determination crack the case? Or will shadowy villains, a penchant for overcommitting, and even her own heart put her in the doghouse?

The Bungled Bike Burglaries **(Book 3)**

Stolen bikes and a long-forgotten time capsule leave one amateur sleuth baffled and busy. Seventh-grader Gabby St. Claire is determined to bring a bike burglar to justice—and not just because mean girl Donabell Bullock is strong-arming her. But each new clue brings its own set of trouble. As if that's not enough, Gabby finds evidence of a decades-old murder within the contents of the time capsule, but no one seems to take her seriously. As her investigation heats up, will Gabby's knack for being in the wrong place at the wrong time with the wrong people crack the case? Or will it prove hazardous to her health?

About the Author:

USA Today has called Christy Barritt's books "scary, funny, passionate, and quirky."

Christy writes both mystery and romantic suspense novels that are clean with underlying messages of faith. Her books have won the Daphne du Maurier Award for Excellence in Suspense and Mystery, have been twice nominated for the Romantic Times Reviewers' Choice Award, and have finaled for both a Carol Award and Foreword Magazine's Book of the Year.

She is married to her Prince Charming, a man who thinks she's hilarious—but only when she's not trying to be. Christy is a self-proclaimed klutz, an avid music lover who's known for spontaneously bursting into song, and a road trip aficionado.

When she's not working or spending time with her family, she enjoys singing, playing the guitar, and exploring small, unsuspecting towns where people have no idea how accident-prone she is.

Find Christy online at:
www.christybarritt.com
www.facebook.com/christybarritt
www.twitter.com/cbarritt

Sign up for Christy's newsletter to get information on all of her latest releases here: **www.christybarritt.com/newsletter-sign-up/**

If you enjoyed this book, please consider leaving a review.